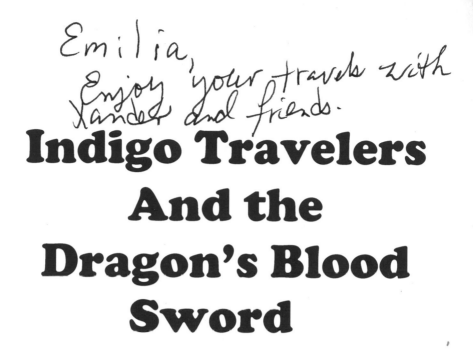

Emilia,
Enjoy your travels with
Xander and friends.

# Indigo Travelers
# And the
# Dragon's Blood
# Sword

Book I

Love,
Merri Halma

by

Merri Halma

Retelling of *Jamie and the Magic Digger* published 2007 by PublishAmerica. Copyright purchased by Merri Halma 2012.

Published 2013 under the title *Indigo Traveler*.

Extensively revised.

Cover Art by Cynthia Martinez

Third Edition

LCCN 2015906688

ISBN-13: 9780692425572
ISBN-10: 0692425578

*Dedicated to my husband, Kevin, for encouraging me, listening to me complain and being one of my sounding boards. Kevin is the one who suggested I put a griffin in my story many years ago.*

*And to my son, James, for being my original inspiration and another of my sounding boards.*

# Acknowledgements

I want to thank everyone who assisted me with making Indigo Traveler the best book it could be. Those who have assisted as they could: Jennifer Cavaness-Williams; Tina O'Rourke, owner of Socialwrites; and Mariah W. Armes.

I especially want to thank Carolyn Fritschle and Carolyn Gold for the many hours they put in working with me, discussing each portion of Indigo Traveler as we went through it to improve this second edition. They have such a beautiful insight into storytelling and gave me a new insight into my world that I had not seen before.

I also want to thank Mike Hanson of the UPS Store, number 3067, in Nampa, Idaho, for all his help with the logo, and his suggestions for the formatting. Mike is a wonderful graphic artist.

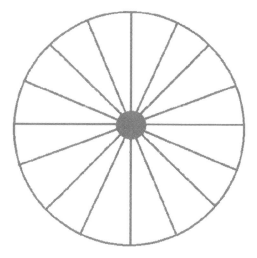

All paths lead to Albagoth
All are equal
Albagoth leads all within.
**Teachings of Albagoth**

# The Creation of Curá and Other Worlds

Albagoth looked around the vast galaxies that he had made. He envisioned the many worlds in each one busy with life that could experience love and sorrow, learning to love one another, and themselves, as well as learning how to settle problems. Being a spirit, Albagoth could be in all places at once. He created humans for planet Earth in the galaxy he named The Milky Way. He put animals of all kinds, including crows of noble heritage, in each world.

On the planet Curá, he put several life forms; tall and muscular humanoids with one eye in the center of their foreheads, and plant life. He created both griffins and gryphons for Curá. Both had the heads of eagles, the bodies of lions, and strong wings. The only difference was their forelegs. Gryphons had the feathered chests and sinewy legs of eagles, with clawed feet, while griffins had lion's paws they could change into talons.

The gryphons lived away on a mountain overlooking the desert, where they could view many kingdoms and other mountains with precious metals and jewels deep inside. The griffins lived in valley, sharing a village with the minotaurs, who had bulls' heads, human torsos and hands, and the strong bodies and hoofed legs of bulls.

He stepped back and observed them all. He installed a consciousness into all life forms on Curá, even the sands, plants and trees, and made the Reflection Pond, where those who peered into it would see an older version of themselves. This older version would guide them, answering all questions they needed to help them with their journey.

As time went on, the Creator noticed the humanoids were making war on the humans, jealous of the humans. The dragons looked favorably on the humans, and they chose to be their guardians. The humanoids called their country Arimaspia.

The humans, with darker skin than the Arimaspians, named their country Kent, and the plant beings called themselves Criatias and their village a Garden.

As Albagoth watched, he noticed how intelligent the crows were. They would group together to discuss the politics of each inhabitant and long to ensure that each being was respected and treated fairly. This gave him the idea of forming a special realm for them: The Crow Court Realm. He brought the crows to their new Realm and trained them to observe the world of Curá. He gave them invisibility, except when they needed to reveal themselves.

In Crow Court Realm, a building was erected for educating the young crows to be judges. Another building was erected, called the Library of Records, where anyone from any world could come to learn more about who he or she was, and ask questions that pertained to their life and life's mission.

Above all, Albagoth, who embodied both the male and female energies, knew that Curá would be a world where travelers from all over the various galaxies would come to learn about themselves. He saw how several humans in the Milky Way Galaxy on the world known as Earth often felt lost. Thus, he set aside children who would have certain gifts, like telepathy and insight, and gave them an aura of deep purple, also known as Indigo. These children would often feel special, yet odd. Others, too, would feel lost. Some of the travelers would not meet the Crow Judge,

Centuries passed after Albagoth created the Crow Court, training many crows and assigning them to their individual roles and to certain worlds. Connor, a large, black Crow Judge, was assigned to Curá, a world that contained several countries. Peace prevailed in Curá for over one hundred years, and as time passed, Connor became more a legend to the people than anything real or of consequence, although he had observed each person, animal and plant life form. It came as a great surprise to any who did encounter him. The usual response was a startled stutter, "You-you-you're real!"

# Chapter 1

Crow Judge Connor flew over his lands as was his role, like a policeman assigned to patrol a specific community. He knew all the people by name and was usually pleased with what he saw. When he stopped in to observe the Arimaspian kingdom, he became upset by what their king was planning.

The Arimaspians were a tall race, with one eye in the center of their foreheads. Their king, Titus, had veered from his parents' training. He ruled with a bullwhip, stern and angry. He wanted riches and would stop at nothing to get his way. He had no pity for the poor in his kingdom, demanding they turn over most of their harvest that there was barely enough to feed their young.

Titus lusted after more land and more riches, desiring to mine the caves that were rumored to have gold, silver, and many priceless jewels. He also turned an eye to the Kingdom of Kent, a human kingdom that had riches beyond all description - and he felt their king wasted it by not mining its wealth. He wanted it more than anything. He wanted it enough to start a war, even though there hadn't been one in centuries.

King Titus had his firstborn son, Kontar, and hadn't planned on any other children. But his wife did give him one more child, a girl named Jaden, so named because he was jaded by her appearance. She disgraced the throne, he said, because she was born with two eyes. "She's so ugly and hideous to me. I can't bear to look at her," he told his wizard, Seabon, when she was two days old.

Wizard Seabon, half Arimaspian and half human, came from a long line of wizards and healers dating back to the time when Dragon Grandor oversaw the Kent Kingdom. Seabon felt loyal to King Titus, yet more loyal to ensure peace that would continue within all countries of Curá. Wizard Seabon knew the newborn princess, Jaden, was one of the signs of change, and he trembled at the visions of what she would see with her second eye. Seabon respected the Crow Judge and feared his judgments.

"Sire, you must get rid of her. She will be your downfall," the wizard counseled King Titus. "But don't do it yet. The Crow Judge will frown on you for turning out your helpless child."

King Titus snapped his whip, "The Crow Judge this! The Crow Judge that! The Crow Judge won't like the war I'm planning either! He has no riches and no pride. He's jealous of what I have!"

Connor frowned at the Arimaspian king's words. He flew on, wondering what to do. He knew he must talk to his brothers on the Crow Court, but he couldn't act yet as no war had been started. The plans were just being laid.

\*\*\*

The skies of the world of Curá varied from kingdom to kingdom. Under a vast desert called Senilona, the skies changed in response to travelers' emotions. Within Senilona Desert was the Reflection Pond. Anybody who looked into it would see themselves as older and wiser, answering questions of the soul. It was here that Connor sought answers.

He could see heat waves like ripples in the air and a warm breeze swirled across the sand, bringing the smell of water. He felt very thirsty and wanted to cool off his body, wash the dust from his feathers and rest. He knew he could get the guidance he needed, as well as a drink and a bath, at the Reflection Pond. The sky clouded the minute he landed. He paused for a moment to watch the clouds knot up across it, their bellies lit up from the lightning within.

Connor, as was his habit, asked Albagoth what he was feeling to cause the sky to darken, even though intuitively he knew the answer and did not want to admit it.

He peered into the pool of water, seeing his older self; he paid no mind, wanting to drink first. As he bobbed his head, he heard the croaking sound of a crow clearing his throat. He paused and looked at the reflection with one eye.

"Many travelers who do not know the mystical abilities of this pond drink and bathe first. You know," his reflection said. "You have a heavy heart. Albagoth won't answer you until you consult with your brother and sister Crow Judges."

"I know, but the war has not started yet. I must not do anything until I know for sure."

"You know the war will be starting within the week. You must act. King Titus will not abide by the ruling. Go to your brothers, and get the judgment. Know this: The war will not end until the one Indigo Traveler comes. Geoffrey is a young griffin who values his own life. Prince Tayson of the Kent Kingdom will choose him to be his protector, even though Geoffrey will not fight for a cause that cannot be won. Take him to the Indigo boy in the world called Nampa. He, too, feels lost. Geoffrey and the boy are the secret that Titus will overlook. However, the Indigo boy will have something Titus will want, he is to be on guard against the king."

"What about Titus's offspring? Surely they play a role in this."

"Children are not pawns, Connor," his older Crow reflection continued to counsel. "Yet they are heirs to the throne and need to be taught to respect their ancestors, who adhered to the spiritual laws handed down from the Creator and the contract the dragon, Grandor, made between Kent Kingdom and the Arimaspian kingdom centuries ago. Consider a way to get the message through to King Titus without removing the children."

"Yes," Connor paused to think, visualizing what would happen when he got to the Crow Court Realm, imagining what he would say. "I will do that after I finish my rounds." His reflection smiled back, nodding in approval, and then vanished.

# Chapter 2

Connor flew on, remembering how special this world was. Albagoth had endowed all who dwelt in it with soul and breath. The stones and plants had souls; even the Criatia plants, with all their spiky bodies and limbs, knew they did. But travelers from other worlds did not realize it.

He stopped in the Criatia garden to observe them. The elder plants were surrounding Cranny, one of the young offshoots, reminding him not to go near the travelers who came through the land.

"Remember, some of the travelers have plants on their world that look like us, with many needles, and arms which have water. These travelers have not seen plants like us who can walk, talk, and think. They are taught to look for food and water inside those plants. We are not food. Do not go near them, otherwise, they may want to open you up."

"They don't want to eat me, because I tell them I'm not water or food and they're shocked to hear me speak, they run away," Cranny replied. The elder plants exchanged worried looks, while the other offshoots suppressed giggles.

Connor also laughed, happy that this young one was thinking for himself.

"Cranny, you need to listen to us. One day, you may meet a traveler who isn't afraid of you, but who is just as curious about you as you are of him. Stay away, because he may be the one to open you up for your insides!"

"No, he won't. He will listen to me, talk with me and answer questions that I have about his world. I want to hear stories about other places, because I can't travel outside of here," Cranny said, showing his baby seed teeth.

"Cranium, you are hopeless!" the elder plant teacher exclaimed, his limbs drooping. The other adults shook their spiky heads and turned, pulling their long roots up and swerving away from him. Cranny smiled, pleased with himself.

Connor flew down and whispered into the ear of young Cranny, "You will find that one traveler, young Criatia, and he will not hunger after you. When you do, lead him to the Reflection Pond."

Cranny looked around, his smile vanishing, "Who said that?" He couldn't see the Crow Judge.

"I didn't say anything," the offshoot next him said.

Connor took flight, leaving the Senilona Desert and venturing to the griffin village. The village buzzed with griffins and minotaurs going about their daily chores. He stopped and perched on a tree branch, observing two young griffins, Geoffrey and Sebastian, and their minotaur friend, Donnair. Geoffrey had white feathers on his eagle head and white fur on his lion body. Even his wings were all white. His four paws were usually lion, too; though when he needed, he could change his front paws into eagle talons to grip objects. Sebastian looked different, with a tan lion body and black and white feathers on his eagle head. His paws were lion, but he could also change them to talons when need be.

"I've heard there might be a war, said Donnair. "That the Arimaspian king is restless for more land and is threatening King Tonyar of Kent," Donnair, the minotaur, adjusted the sheaves of scrolls he was writing on. His lyre lay beside him, as he was a poet and musician.

"If there is war, it won't be King Tonyar going, but his son, Prince Tayson," Geoffrey corrected.

"If there is war, we will be called to serve as protectors of the king's knights," Sebastian added. Geoffrey shook his head.

"What do you mean 'no', Geoffrey?" Sebastian asked.

"I mean, I won't be assigned. My sire and dame are leaders in this village. I won't be allowed to go, because I'm next in line. And my Grandsire is healer of our village. I'm being trained in the specialty." The albino griffin lifted his head up and looked down his beak at his friend.

"Your Grandsire has always stepped forward to aid King Tonyar's kingdom when called on. You will go or suffer the judgment of the Crow Court." Sebastian admonished.

"No, I won't. I'm above their judgment. Besides, the Crow Court isn't real. It's just something our sires tell us so we will listen to their rules. If the Crow Judge is real, then why can't we see him?"

"He only reveals himself when he needs to be seen, Geoff. He appears when he renders a judgment, and it is instantaneous."

"How do you know all this?" Geoffrey asked, narrowing his eyes.

"In my visions, I have seen him and the other crows on the court. Albagoth has shown me secrets that only the Crows on the court know. I'm being prepared for something. I'm not sure what. I follow the promptings of my soul," Sebastian replied. "For all we know, the Crow Judge is observing us right now."

Connor's heart felt a jolt, sensing Sebastian could see him. He met the young griffin's eyes. Sebastian smiled, winked his right golden eye, and then lowered his eyes back to his friends.

"There is no avoiding it, for me," Donnair whined. "I'm a wimp. I will be captured by the enemy, placed in a labyrinth and forced to eat the other prisoners." He shuddered with distaste.

"There is no such thing as labyrinths!" Geoffrey laughed. "That's another old story handed down from other worlds. You have an amazing imagination, Donnair. Continue your writings. You will be the company's scribe and tell stories of our adventures. And you, Sebastian, will likely go to work with a Crow Judge of another world." He laughed again.

A horn blew from a distance. "There is the horn. We better go back to the shade to finish our class for the day." Geoffrey sighed. The two griffins stood up, stretching their legs out, arching their backs and extending their wings, flapping briefly to get the blood flowing. Donnair stood and stretched, shook his bull head, put his lyre over his left shoulder and his scrolls under his arm. They walked off, keeping their private thought to themselves.

Connor thought for a minute, smiling as he watched them walk back to their classroom under the shade of a tree. "Those are three close friends and very smart animals." Connor spoke out loud to no one. "The human half softens Donnair's bull side, providing him a love for words and a keen insight the others haven't noticed. And Sebastian's strength is his ability to hear Albagoth speak through meditation. He would be a good companion for a Crow Judge, if the Creator approved a griffin to travel and be trained in such a way. Though, he couldn't sit on the court...." He paused, seeing other birds and insects overhead listening to him, and sensing they were puzzled why he was talking out loud and still there. "Yes," he said aloud to himself, "I need to move on."

***

The richness of the day was fading when Connor flew into the Kingdom of Kent. He saw Prince Tayson out in the exercise yard training with his knights. Prince Tayson, eighteen years of age, with blond, wavy hair, chiseled features, thin lips, and sea green eyes, smiled. Two of his men battled each other with training swords, each putting their all into the clangs and slashes of the blades, lifting their shields to block each other's attacks in turn. Neither missed a step, until they heard a messenger come up on horseback. The one on defense looked away to see who it was, and the offensive knight managed to hit him just right to make him stumble and fall. Prince Tayson laughed.

"Remember to never let yourself be distracted be what is going on behind you. Keep your concentration on the enemy," He said. "Take a break while I confer with the messenger." The men smiled as they took off their hot helmets, talking excitedly about the training.

The messenger handed Tayson a formal declaration of war from King Titus.

*To King Tonyar,*

*Since you will not give me your land freely—land that is owed me from the time our grandfathers' grandfathers were young, I hereby declare war on your land and people. Be prepared to defend yourself. My men are much bigger and stronger than you puny humans; we will take this land by force within three weeks.*

Connor read it before Tayson could even open it. Startled, he closed his onyx eyes, centered himself, and called to the leader of the Crow Judges in the Crow Court Realm, *I am coming back with alarming news.* The answer was instantaneous; they would be awaiting his arrival.

\*\*\*

The Superior Crow Court Judge and the other Crow Judges under him gathered around a mystical screen, reviewing all King Titus's transgressions to prepare for the hearing that would take place. As part of the preparations, Albagoth revealed King Titus's heart and soul, reminding them he would be present in their presiding.

\*\*\*

Connor left the astrosphere of Curá for the Crow Court Realm. It was a lovely land, with clear skies and vast buildings; libraries, schools, and streets of gold and silver. The trees were tall, had vast numbers of branches with rich green colors, healthy in all ways. Connor landed in the center of town to await the other members.

The population was mostly crows: tall, noble birds that strolled with purpose and honor. A few humans and other beings were allowed to come, but not many. Connor had been hatched in this world, being of the lineage of the first crows chosen to be judges of the court; taught to observe unseen; taught to guide certain travelers who would be coming through the world he would be assigned.

The Superior Crow Court Judge of the Crow Court joined him in the center of the town. He wore a ring of keys around his neck that he had to keep safe. When he wasn't wearing them, the keys stayed locked in a drawer. The other members gathered around them.

"Well, Connor, we've been expecting King Titus to rebel and start a war. However, it's happening sooner than we anticipated. Come, let's hear the evidence and decide what do. The other members are already in the judgment hall and the Creator will be listening to the proceedings, since he has news of the boy in the world called Nampa."

The Creator's presence felt like a warm dome over them, as if he sat among the members of the court at the same time as he was above them. The Superior Crow Judge stepped into the ring and began to speak.

"We have played the scenes Connor has shown us. We've seen King Titus's heart and soul. He knows the way he is tied to King Tonyar of Kent, yet refuses to abide by the dragon's terms. King Titus has the blood of the dragon in his veins, as does King Tonyar. The dragon's blood terms must be kept." The Superior Crow Judge, the graying feathers on his head looking like a British barrister's wig, spoke as he paced in the middle of the group.

"Yes, but what will convince him not to follow through with this war?" Connor spoke up.

"Remove his firstborn child, the boy he adores. Second to gold, treasures and land, King Titus adores him. Give him to the gryphons. They will raise him to respect all species: men and Arimaspians alike," the Superior Court Crow answered.

"Have you visited the gryphons, yet?" the Superior asked, looking towards Connor.

Connor avoided the look of his fellows on the court, choosing instead to look down the lane at a group of young crows playing catch with a pebble. "No, I didn't get over to see them. I went to their cousins, the griffins instead. I wanted to see what the young griffin, Geoffrey, was doing."

"You had time to supervise the gryphons, too. This war will call on the griffins to be at the side of the humans either as protectors and healers, or trained in other aspects of the war. It is central to remember, Connor, Geoffrey doesn't have the heart for battle. He will give us great pain, what with him being the promised one. Be ready to render a quick judgment of him once he has left the side of the one he is to protect," warned the next senior judge.

"Yes, my older self let me know this already. But where do I take him?"

The other crows looked at each other as if Connor should've known this. Albagoth spoke from above and all around them. "Connor, you will drop him at the opening of the vortex to the Milky Way galaxy to the world called Nampa. He will land at the home of the young Indigo traveler named Xander Veh. Be a guide and a teacher to this traveler, but do not neglect your duties as a judge of your assigned world."

There was silence for a while as they all considered what the Creator had said. Connor remembered hearing his reflection share something like this, but remembered hearing Xander and Geoffrey were to come back to Curá.

"Why do the Indigo Traveler and Geoffrey need to come back to my world?"

"The young traveler is looking for reasons why he was created as he was. I will explain more as needed. This young traveler must find the blade imbued with the dragon's blood and the other two blades. One is poisoned, and the other is tainted with acid. The three blades must become one in the fires of the alchemist blacksmith in the village of the Kingdom of Kent."

The others let out an exclamation. Connor felt a burst of electricity run through him, and his neck feathers rose up on end. "How can he fight with three blades?"

"It isn't your place to question the Creator!" an elder Crow Judge admonished him.

"But I cannot just blindly follow a decree without understanding why it must be that way," Connor defended himself.

"It is all right to question me," Albagoth answered. "Connor, when the time comes you will understand. The three blades will be explained by Manitor, the dragon who watches over the Kingdom of Kent now."

All the Crow Judges felt Albagoth bid them adieu as he receded back to his place in another part of the galaxy.

The crows all spread their wings and started beating them, all cawing at once. Connor was stunned that they had lapsed into their old language; he didn't know what to do. He stepped out of the circle, trying to get his center back.

An idea popped into his head, but he was distracted as the pebble the young crows were tossing fell at his talons. He cocked his head to one side, considering it, as one of the young crows came up half flying and half running. The young crow stopped right in front of him.

"Excuse me, your Honor, but may I have that pebble back?" the young bird asked.

"Yes, you may. What is your name?"

"Tanner, your honor." Tanner's friends called him to hurry since they had to go back to their class soon.

"Nice to meet to meet you, Tanner. Are you training to be a judge?" Connor asked, picking up the pebble with his right talon.

"Yes, I am. There's a rumor that one Crow Judge will be sent to another place in the Milky Way galaxy," Tanner replied, catching the pebble in his talon. "Thanks, your honor." He put it up to his beak and took off in flight.

Connor felt a surge of excitement run through his body, wondering what this could mean.

The Superior Crow Judge held a hammer in his right talon. He brought it down, the sound echoing through the small area, silencing the loud cawing. "We must talk in modern language since the young judges do not remember the old tongue." He looked around, "Where is Connor?"

"Yes, your honor?" Connor said as he stepped back into the circle.

"You have your orders. The Creator has spoken. Go now to your land. Sentence King Titus, revealing yourself if you have to; take the leaders of the gryphons with you so they can take Kontar. All will be well."

Connor left, heading straight to the gryphon's mountain, and apprised the leader, Valor, of the verdict on King Titus. The noble gryphon, twelve hands tall, bowed his black and white eagle head, extended his eagle leg out and acknowledged the Crow Judge's role. He called to his second and third charge to follow him. They flew off to the Arimaspian kingdom.

Prince Kontar, a boy of six years, was excited to go with the gryphons for a visit. King Titus objected and ordered his men to fight them off. In the end, Connor appeared to the Arimaspian men, frightening them by growing taller than any of them.

"Your king is making war on the humans. It is against Curá's laws. The Crow Court has ruled that Titus must forfeit his firstborn son. The boy is in the gryphons care for now."

King Titus paced back and forth, jaws set and fists clenching and unclenching, muttering of the injustices of the gryphons taking his only heir. He did not count his deformed daughter as an heir. He stopped by a window, lifted his right fist in the air and shook it, "Why couldn't you have taken my wife's ill mistake? The child born with two eyes? No Arimaspian boy will ever see her as marriage material! I don't even want to claim her! You call yourself a just judge, Crow! I dare you to show yourself to me!"

Months went by. Connor observed nothing going right. Half of King Titus's men marched into the lands owned by King Tonyar while another group searched the mountains and foothills for treasure. King Titus mourned for his lost son and blamed his remaining heir, calling her every name in the book. He did not want her under his roof or trained.

Connor flew down to the princess' playroom. Jaden looked up. Her center blue eye twinkled and the second eye, which was vertical on the left side of her face, looking like a lopsided cut that had healed, opened fully. She smiled joyfully.

"Hello, Crow Judge,". I'm Jaden. Are you here to punish my Papa?" Jaden's second eye enabled her to see what others could not. She saw hidden truths, and heard thoughts and feelings most people around her tried to hide; truths these people would not admit to anyone. It also allowed her to see Connor.

"No, I am here to tell you not to worry. You are safe. You'll be sent away any day."

"My Papa's heart is no good. I see the words in his mind. He calls me ugly. He doesn't want me. Who will care for me?" Jaden didn't look hurt, though Connor could sense her young heart was breaking, and she was trying not to cry.

"I will send someone to care for you. He will love the person you really are."

Jaden smiled. Hearing footsteps coming down the hall, Connor made certain he was invisible.

The king stalked down the hallway, snapping his whip as he passed at anyone he felt was not working hard enough, barking orders as he did so. He even barked to empty rooms. His wizard walked beside him, doing his best to avoid the snake-like leather strap.

Titus heard his daughter talking to someone in her playroom as they entered it. "Who was in here with you?" he demanded.

"No one, Papa," she babbled. "Just me and my dollies."

"I heard you talking to someone! I demand to know who! If it was that darn Crow Judge who has punished me for my free will to find treasure and claim back land that is supposed to be *mine*, then I will turn you out this minute!"

"Sire, calm down," Wizard Seabon advised, raising a hand to stop his tirade. "She's just a girl playing childish games."

"I will tar and feather that Crow Judge if I ever see him. I demand he uncloak himself!"

"Father, he is already feathered and as black as tar, you just can't see him because he's invisible to us," Jaden said in her sweetest voice.

"Jaden has a special gift to see what we cannot," the wizard explained,

"Yes, yes, and she will be my downfall! You've told me enough already. Guards! Come, toss this ugly fool out of my kingdom! Take her to the desert to starve or be eaten by those walking, talking plant creatures!"

"Sire, please reconsider. She will find her way back. You must remember, she is but a child and in need of your protection."

"She needs *my* protection? Look wizard, I need to be protected from *her!* She speaks with my enemy! That Crow Judge took my only heir from me! I will not be left with this one who does not deserve to be on the throne!"

The guards came in and grabbed the princess by both arms. She screamed for her mom, but the king would not allow the queen in, though she was outside pleading.

"Sire, if I may, you are not making a wise decision. You risk more judgment from the Crow Court. Do not do this!"

"One more word from you, wizard, and I will throw you out with her!" Connor managed to move just as King Titus pulled out the whip he kept around his waist. The wizard, much smaller than Titus because he was part human, put out his hand and muttered a spell, throwing the king back.

Titus roared. "How dare you!" He gripped the handle tight as he pulled back his arm, the whip slashing through the air, and then snapped it abruptly.

Connor flew up, grabbed the end of the whip and yanked it out the king's hand, then flew out the open window and dropped it. It seemed to fall endlessly down the inhumanly tall castle.

"What happened?" King Titus roared. "Did you cause that?" Wizard Seabon shrugged his shoulders. He sensed it was the Crow Judge but he kept his mouth closed.

\*\*\*

Connor flew on to Prince Tayson's field office where his troops were planning strategies to meet the Arimaspian army head-on. Geoffrey was assigned to the prince as a protector, Sebastian was a healer apprentice, and Donnair was assigned company scribe.

Geoffrey paced the path between his tent and the prince's tent, very unhappy with the way things were going. Each day he put himself in harm's way to make sure nothing happened to the prince. When all was quiet and he was alone, all Geoffrey could think of was how he could escape to solitude, how he could get out alive from this battle. He felt sure this was a lost cause. *War has no place in the scheme of life,* Geoffrey thought. He hated having to dive bomb the enemy while carrying the prince on his back, and all the prince could do was criticize him for not getting close enough to the Arimaspian soldiers. He wanted peace and he wanted to live long enough to travel to other places beyond this world; *if* there really was a way to travel there.

*Grandsire taught me to be true to myself and follow my gut,* Geoffrey remembered. *Well, my gut says to flee this place.* He also felt a voice telling him to talk to the Prince. Every time he thought of fighting, he felt a sense of panic rise from his gut and grab him around the chest, cutting off his breath, choking him, and paralyzing him so he couldn't move. The Arimaspian soldiers were scary—they towered over him and Prince Tayson.

As he walked back to his tent, Geoffrey observed how quiet it was. His gut spoke loudly to him that he didn't belong. He decided to abide by that. He saw a vision of himself flying away from here and finding a place where no one could find him. He was tired of being cooped up here and knew he would be killed if he stayed. He decided this was the way it had to be. After all, the Crow Judge wasn't real. The griffin spread his mighty wings and started flapping as he ran down the path. Two knights on patrol saw him and ran towards him, yelling at him not to leave, but he jumped into the air just as they were about to collide. Connor took flight right behind him.

The night air was cool to Geoffrey, and he felt free and was happy that humans didn't have wings to fly after him. A white light appeared next to him and suddenly there was a large black crow in the middle of it.

"Greetings, Geoffrey. I am Connor, the Crow Judge of this world."

Geoffrey's heart sank, "Y-y-you-re *it*! You're real!"

"Yes, I am very real. You have transgressed the law by leaving Prince Tayson's side. You are sentenced to be exiled until the time is right for your return." A wormhole opened. "You will be a statue only able to move when you are alone with your new charge."

Connor went to the opening of the wormhole, dropped Geoffrey through it, turned and headed back to the tree he called home. Landing on a branch, he let out a sigh; he preened his feathers, then tucked his beak under his left wing to sleep. In his dream, he saw Albagoth standing next to him, smiling. The Creator said he was being given the opportunity to go to the land through the Milky Way to show himself to the boy from the world called Nampa, to guide the Indigo Traveler and Geoffrey back to Curá.

***

As Geoffrey fell through the wormhole, he felt a heaviness creep over his body, starting at his hindquarters and creeping over the rest of him; at the same time, he felt himself shrinking. He cried out, screaming for help as his wings grew heavy, as if he'd become entangled in the tree branches back home. He tumbled head over tail and he struggled to get control. He reached out with his mind as well as his voice, pleading with anyone to come help him slow his descent. Geoffrey had never believed that much in Albagoth, but he saw his young life flash before his eyes. He saw his mistake, and knew he should've put his own life on the line to protect Prince Tayson.

He soared past stars, falling ever so fast toward a world that appeared full of large bodies of water and sparse land. He closed his eyes as he entered the atmosphere, feeling a searing heat like he was passing through a fire, yet it didn't harm him.

A small voice spoke to his mind. "I heard you call for help. I am here and alone, too."

Geoffrey landed on a hard surface. It was dark out, but he sensed a bright light from somewhere flash on. He didn't know it was a motion controlled light from the patio of a nearby house. He trembled. Then he sensed an animal come sniff him, and lick him, before the animal picked him up and carried him off.

# Chapter 3

Clarence, a white cat with orange ears, slept outside on top of an old dog house, the moonlight reflected off his white fur, making it appear midnight blue, and his orange tinges appear brown. His ears perked when he heard something land in the yard in the dead of the night. Curious, he climbed down to see what it was. He found a griffin encased in stone.

Being psychically in-tuned, Clarence knew the creature still lived inside. He picked it up with his mouth and took it to the house. He went to his young master's room. Eying where he wanted to land, he crouched, bounced lightly from one front paw to the other and sprung onto the bed, landing next to Xander's head. He laid the griffin statue next to him. Xander rolled over, his hand hitting the object. Clarence dragged his sandpaper tongue across Xander's face, pausing in mid lick to chew lightly on the small lobe as if it had a tough spot that needed to be worked out.

"Cut it out, Clarence!" the teen whined, still half-asleep. The moon shone through his curtains, giving the room an eerie color. He felt the object. "I heard someone screaming for help. He said he was falling and couldn't use his wings." Suddenly wide awake, Xander sat up. "Wings? I wonder what that was about."

Clarence peered at his young master.

"You brought me a gift in the middle of the night." The teen switched on the lamp that hung over the bed to see it better. "What's this?"

Clarence licked at a paw. "It's a griffin."

"Wait, did you just speak to me?" Xander was used to reading his cat's body and facial expressions or hearing his thoughts in his mind, not hearing his actual voice out loud. Some people see the animal's thoughts in pictures, Xander saw them in words and the emotions.

"Why aren't you meowing?"

Clarence shrugged. "Maybe because the griffin is magical and I've decided I can trust you with my secret. Maybe it's because I need to be able to talk with you so you can understand me. After all, this is a new day and strange things will begin to happen to you, young master."

Touching the statue, Xander felt a warmth radiate through the stone and sensed a heartbeat.

*My name is Geoffrey,* the statue said to the boy's mind. *Can you hear me?*

"Yes, I can," Xander said, startled. "The kids I go to school with think I'm strange. If they could see me talking to a statue.... What happened to you? I Did some evil villain trap you in this stone?"

*No. I was punished for not staying to fight in the war. I don't belong there. I probably don't belong here, either. Who are you?*

"I'm Alexander, but everyone calls me Xander." He heard shuffling footsteps down the hallway and switched off the lamp. *I better talk mind-to-mind so my parents don't hear me.* He glanced at the clock on the bedside table. *It's the middle of the night. I need to go back to sleep.*

"Son, what's going on in there?" his mom called from the doorway. "I can hear you from our bedroom."

Xander made snoring sounds, acting like he didn't hear her. His heartbeat quickened, and he hoped she wouldn't pursue talking him.

"I know you're awake, I can tell when you're faking."

He opened his eyes and yawned, "Mom? Is that you? Why'd you wake me up? It's three in the morning. The bus comes in three and half hours!"

"I'm sorry I woke you, kiddo; I thought I heard voices coming from your room."

Xander waited until he heard her footfalls recede. *I can't wait to see what you look like in the morning,* he thought to the griffin.

Geoffrey felt safe and reassured, but didn't quite understand why.

A sharp piercing ring sheared through the quiet of the room.

*What's that?*

The griffin's terrified thoughts woke Xander. "Relax, Geoffrey," he said sleepily. "It's just my alarm clock. He banged his hand hard on the source of the ringing noise and it shut off abruptly. "Morning always comes too early," he mumbled.

Sitting up, he saw Clarence waiting at the foot of his bed, smiling like he had just swallowed the canary. "We don't have a canary, Clarence," he muttered through a yawn.

"No, but you have a griffin in stone. You need to talk to him. I've tried to, but he's ignoring me."

"So now that you're talking to me, you can tell me what to do? Like feed you and clean your litter box?"

"No, your mom does that. That's her job; she's my staff. You are my pupil," Clarence's ice blue eyes twinkled as the sun rose up from its slumber.

Xander glanced down at the statue. In the morning sun, he could see it better. The griffin had fur and feathers, as well as four lion paws. Also, he wore armor over his chest, and front legs. The chest plate had a dragon on it, with words too small to read.

"Alexander," his Mom called from downstairs, "It's time to get up! I heard your alarm go off, young man. The bus will be here any minute!"

"I know, Mom! Be right down!"

Xander wasn't looking forward to this day. He had a test in almost every class and no time to study. After he thought this, he remembered his mom telling him to own up to the truth instead of making excuses. *Wait*, he thought, *let me rephrase that, I had plenty of time to study, but no interest in actually studying.*

He looked up at the ceiling of his room, at the stars and crescent moons, which glowed in the dark. His parents had pasted them up there when he was a baby because his mom said he came from the stars. She wanted to remind Xander of that as he grew up. He shook his head. "There really is no such thing as an Indigo Child," he mused half aloud. Clarence rubbed against his leg, meowing. In his mind, he translated it to words: *There is a special place for you. Indigo Children are very real. Do not run from who and what you are.*

Xander went into the bathroom and caught his reflection in the mirror. His jet-black hair stuck to the left side of his face and his skin looked so pale he could've been a ghost. He quickly washed his face, thankful it wasn't covered in pimples like some of the kids in his school. He put his head under the faucet to wet his hair and then raked his fingers through to get it to go down. His mom came to the doorway.

"Wouldn't it be better to take a full shower?" she asked. He straightened up and studied his appearance. Wet hair dripped water down his face, shoulders and back. His nose was narrow and his nostrils flared a bit. His cheeks had a touch of pink, and his green eyes twinkled like freshly polished jade in a museum display.

"Maybe, but I don't have time, Mom. Gotta run!" He ran back to his room and threw on the t-shirt from the day before, smelling it to make sure it didn't reek too bad, and found a pair of jeans with small rips around the knees. He threw on a pair of socks and stuffed his feet into athletic shoes. The smell of toaster waffles drifted up the stairs as he took the steps several at a time. His stomach rumbled. His mind showed him the statue his cat had dragged in. He turned and went back to his room, picked it up and stuffed in his jacket. "Don't worry, Butch won't find you," he whispered to it.

Xander glanced at the clock., "Did Dad already go to work?" he asked his mom. He grabbed a waffle off a plate and took a bite, then went to the cupboard and took down a glass, which he filled with cold milk from the pitcher on the counter.

"Yes, dear. He left an hour ago. He wanted to tell you to be sure to pass your exams today."

"Don't worry, Mom. I'll do my best."

"Your best is usually making sure you get a 'D' or 'C'. You can do better. You're a smart kid."

"Yeah, I know, but ...."

"Don't blame the kids at school, Xander. Take responsibility for your own life. One day . . . . "

"I know, I know, Mom." Xander rolled his eyes. "One day someone important will see my hard work and give me a really good job. Dad didn't finish school and he has a good job and you have several college degrees, but you aren't working in your fields. I can't see how a school that teaches us a bunch of garbage can get me a good job. We won't be using most of it in our adult life! The history is outdated and doesn't record what actually happened. It's all a bunch of lies!" he said spraying bits of waffle.

"Alexander Michael Veh!" his mom exclaimed.

"Yeah, I know, ignore the facts and just spit out the information the teachers want us to say. That's just so stupid! Mom, you're always talking about education reform. We need real education reform, not just lip service. First, they need to let us kids tell them what we want to learn."

"Not just that, don't talk with your mouth full! And watch your time. The bus will be . . . ."

"Rounding the corner any minute. Bye!" He slammed down the plastic glass and grabbed two more waffles as he ran towards the door. He saw his mom sitting at the dining room table, shaking her head, but with a smile on her face.

*I wish I could tune into my mom's thoughts all the time,* Xander mused to himself, *Sometimes I can get glimpses of her thoughts or know she's going to be here to get me, but other times....*

Xander felt someone jostle him as he stood at the side of the road waiting for the bus. He glanced over, but no one was there. Other kids drifted to the bus stop; all stayed in their own groups, not wanting to get close to him. Xander flashed back to when he was a first grader, when the other kids were a bit older than him and used to pick up rocks and throw them at him, yelling, "Stay away and don't follow us!" He couldn't help but follow because they were neighbors.

He looked at them now, seeing different energy fields around them, each with pictures that pertained to their secret lives and thoughts. One boy, usually the chief one that verbally and physically pushed him, was running a memory from the night before, afraid the cops would be on to him.

"What are you so afraid of?" Xander asked. "I won't bite you. I won't tell anyone about that car you broke into last night, either." The other kids sucked in their breath.

A girl, who was trying to hold the robber's hand, whispered to him, "You didn't?" The boy tried to laugh it off, but his face showed a sickening grimace.

"You know that Veh kid is looney!" He put a finger up to his temple and made a circling motion.

"Look, just leave us alone! No one likes you, so just turn around and go home!" one of them shouted.

Xander looked around, "I can't! I gotta go to school, just like you," he replied just as the bus pulled up and stopped. The teens filed onto it.

On the way to school, Xander held the griffin statue as if it would bring him comfort. No one sat with him. He stared out the window, watching the trees and cars go by. The other students were happy, joking and laughing as they shared about their weekend, the TV shows and movies they saw, or the video games they played. He looked at them: the popular girls with their fancy hairstyles and makeup, flirting with the boys, and boys putting the moves on them. *I'm so different. They all wear the same label jeans from mall shops and here I am in my thrift shop clothes. Cheerleaders are so phony. The boys who chase them are phony, too,* he thought.

*What's a cheerleader?*

*Who said that?* Xander asked in his mind, startled, not expecting anyone to hear his private thoughts or reply to them.

*I did, Geoffrey. The griffin inside the statue you're holding, remember?*

*Cheerleaders are girls that dress in matching outfits with the school colors and cheer for our school sports team to win at games. They all act the same, giggle the same and act like they don't have any original thoughts.*

*Sports?* the griffin asked. *What is sports?*

*You know, like football, basketball. Don't you have games where you are from? You divide into teams and battle to see who can get a ball from one side of a field to another to score touchdowns.*

Geoffrey thought for moment. He considered the games they played on breaks from their lessons with his grandsire. The minotaurs and griffins would pick sides. They would be mixed teams. The minotaurs would ride the griffins, simulating an intense battle. Each rider would have to knock off the rival member, without hurting them. On the ground the female and male minotaurs who weren't playing would often root for the team their friends were on.

*Could you send me a picture of what football is?* Geoffrey asked.

Xander sent him a memory of a football game he'd watched from TV, with the pretty girls jumping up, shaking their pompoms, and doing the splits once they landed.

Geoffrey compared it to the game they played on his world.

*Yes, we have something similar to that where I'm from. Only we don't use that funny oblong thing you throw. We use our brute strength.* Geoffrey sent Xander a memory of their game so they both understood each other.

They were quiet for a while. The kids around Xander talked, joked with each other and yelled, but he didn't hear them much. He was focused on his own thoughts and anxiety about school and meeting Butch, the bully. Still, he could feel the energy of the griffin within the rock, and sensed a faint heartbeat.

*Can you hear all of my thoughts?*

*Yeah. I can sense most of what you're feeling. But I don't understand where we are or where we're going.*

*We're going to school. We're on a school bus.*

*What's a bus? And what is a school?*

*A bus is a large vehicle that's yellow and looks like a caterpillar but has wheels. It transports children and teens to a large building where they're supposed to be educated in things that they need to know to be adults. I hate it because most of the subjects aren't even what we will need to know when we grow up.*

*You said that before to a female. You called her 'Mom,' I think. Don't you have any friends?*

*I don't think so. I'm too strange. Most kids want me to leave them alone.* Xander caught a girl with shoulder length blond hair, dressed in black t-shirt and track pants, looking at him. *Take that girl over there, she's cute, but she wouldn't ever admit to liking me, if she does.*

*I can't see her. My eyes are covered in stone. All I see is black, but I can sense and see through your eyes, a bit, if I try. She has blue eyes? Or are they green?*

*Yeah, sort of a blue-green color. Her name is Sarah.* Xander looked away so she wouldn't think he was staring at her.

*Where would you rather be if not on this bus?*

*I'd want to travel to the stars. I want to travel to the land of the Creator, if there is one, to see him or her and ask why I'm an Indigo Child. I want to know what's so special about being one. I hate it. I hate knowing what other people are thinking.*

All the seats on the bus were full, except for the seat next to Xander. He felt so hollow that if he knocked on his chest it would echo. There was barely any room for all the kids who got on at each stop. The kids would start to sit next to him, then grimace and move on. Finally, someone had to sit with him, a girl, dressed in short skirt, leggings, designer heels and a blouse from a high-end department store. The girl sat on the edge of her seat, trying not to touch Xander's backpack that was in the middle of the seat, or his shoulder, as if she was afraid he'd give her cooties.

Xander watched the girl as she struggled to get the attention of another girl and a boy across the way from them. They refused to notice her. They just rolled their eyes and shook their heads. The girl next to him was dressed similar to the one across the way. She appeared nervous, though, fidgeting with her short skirt and glancing around her.

*Why won't they talk to me or even notice me?* The girl's thoughts invaded Xander's mind. *Have I done something wrong or offended them in some way? I dressed just like China, like she told me to do. Am I wearing the wrong clothes? I spent all I had in my savings at Hollister buying everything she said she wears and now she's ignoring me!*

"You are her play toy," Xander answered out loud. "Be yourself."

The girl looked at him, frowning, "I didn't say anything to you. Why would you say something so awful?"

"I heard your thoughts. They don't like you. They're just using you like a dog playing with a new toy. When they get tired of you, they'll move on to someone new."

"I've heard you were strange. You always say the weirdest stuff right out of thin air, like you're listening to another voice or something." The rumbling of the other students behind and around them made it difficult to focus on her words because her voice was soft. Behind them, some boys started throwing wads of paper and shooting spit wads. The bus driver picked up the microphone to tell them to settle down or he would write warnings.

"I hear other people's thoughts. I see the colors around them and can hear the call of their soul. I don't like what I see or what I know. Sometimes it's hard to keep it to myself. You're not happy with who you are and you want to fit in. Why spend all your money on something as superficial as clothes just to fit in?"

"Don't you want to fit in?" she asked, moving her light brown hair away from her face.

"Yep, but I never will, so I don't worry about it." Xander shrugged. "I'm too freaky. Kids are afraid of me." He frowned.

The girl adjusted her skirt again as if she was willing it to grow longer. "China, over there, said if I did, she would help me meet this boy I like." The girl looked down at the floor. He felt her sadness in his chest, sucked his lips in and started chewing on lower one.

"And now she doesn't want to pay attention to you," he said after a bit. He turned his attention to the girl across from them. She was sitting with the boy who had been thinking about breaking into cars earlier. He saw a vision of China laughing at the new girl and turning her back on her.

"Look, for what's it worth, they aren't worth your time. Hey, what's your name?"

"Kimber. You're Xander, right? I've heard that you make up stories about people, and blame your problems on them. I've also heard that you fail your classes because you're too stupid to see the right answers, even though you can answer the teacher correctly before exams. I heard you made some kid disappear."

"Gee, it's nice to know you pay so much attention to the stories you hear." He turned away from her so she wouldn't see the hurt in his eyes.

The bus started to speed up after picking up all the students. They were near the high school now. Kimber looked at him. He felt her gaze, but didn't want to talk to her.

"So, is it true? What I've heard?" she asked, pulling her hair back away from her face.

"Yeah, some of it. You know I can read thoughts. And I'm not interested in school, that's why I don't do well. I'd rather be anywhere but here."

"Yeah. Me, too," Kimber replied. "I just want friends."

Xander turned his head, scrutinizing her, and nodded his head. "My mom says you have to be friends with yourself first."

The bus pulled up in front of the high school and the high school students stood up, pushing and shoving each other. The boy sitting across from them kissed China and got off. She stayed on. She glanced over at them.

"Oh, hi, Kimber, I didn't see you over there. Why are you sitting with that loser?"

Kimber gave her a weak smile. "He isn't a loser, China," she returned in a low tone. She turned her head, "So, what's it like?"

"What's what like?" he answered, blandly glancing over at her. Meeting her eyes, felt a twinge of recognition and looked away again.

"To see colors and pictures above people? How can you do it?"

"I can't control it and don't always see them around people. I've always been able to, though. I get accused of making stuff up most of the time because no one likes being confronted with their 'shadow,' as my mom calls it. I can't describe what it's like. It's something you have to experience."

"Their shadow?" Kimber adjusted her book bag on her lap.

"Yeah, the bad side of them. I can't explain it; it's just something my mom talks about," he muttered. She looked away.

*Just try,* Geoffrey urged. Xander shook his head, telling him to mind his own business.

The bus picked up speed as it went around the first roundabout and continued to Greenhurst Road.

Xander got out the statue and examined it in closer detail.

China patted the seat next to her. "Kimber, sit over here. Brad got off at the high school."

"No, the bus is moving." Kimber looked over at the statue. "What's that?" she asked. "Did you make it?"

"It's just something my cat dragged in," he joked. She giggled.

"Kimber, get away from that kid before he eats your brain or starts making up weird stories about you and they start coming true," China urged.

Kimber ignored her. "You're funny. The cat dragged it in," she repeated. The other kids quieted down as the middle school came into view.

"I'm serious." Xander looked at her. "My cat, Clarence, did drag it in last night. It fell from the sky." The kids sitting around them turned their attention to them.

"Statues don't just fall from the sky, Veh!" It sounded like all the bus said it at once even though it was just one or two people. They started chiding and mimicking him. Xander saw an image of himself shrinking to the size of mouse and running away.

"Seriously, it did fall from the sky!" he protested.

The bus pulled into the bus unloading area at the side of the building. Xander's heart fell to his gut, sad that a morning when no one was paying attention to him had turned into another day of taunts and verbal abuse. He put Geoffrey in his pocket. *Just as long as Butch leaves me alone it'll be okay,* he thought as he got off the bus and headed to the library. Kimber followed him, as did the girl with the piercing green-blue eyes who had been sitting up toward the front. Xander remembered that she'd kept looking back at him, smiling.

Kimber caught up to him, following him to a table. "Hey, I believe you. I believe it fell from the sky."

"Why?" he asked in an angry, daring tone as the other girl put her messenger bag on the table.

"Let me see it," she said softly. He took the statue out and gave it to her. She turned it over, noticing the scuff marks on the griffin's shoulder, paws and head. "See, there're grass stains as if it bounced a few times before it settled down. It isn't from here, either. It came from another world."

"How do you know?" Kimber asked the other girl.

"I can tell by touching him. My name's Sarah, by the way." She pointed to the statue. "Look, the words on the shield aren't like our written language! They're hard to see, but I can tell by the feel of the letters."

Xander and Kimber peered over her shoulder. Sarah gave the griffin back to him.

He pulled out some paper and explained, "I was going to put this over the words, then scrape my pencil over them to see what they said."

Kimber looked up, "So, what do you think, Sarah?"

"I think Xander has some interesting ideas. Though strange things happen around him." She smiled. Her blue-green eyes sparkled. Part of his heart melted, and his legs quivered. He sat down fast, before they gave out on him.

The two girls watched intently as he worked. The bell rang.

"We'll meet at lunchtime to discuss this," they all agreed, putting their books back in the bags, and leaving.

\*\*\*

On the way to his first class, pushing and shoveling through the chaotic mob of teenagers, Xander felt Geoffrey ask, *Why are you going to the trouble of scratching over my chest plate?*

*I want to know what the words say. Kimber says the language is different than ours,* Xander explained.

*I can tell you what the words say. You should have asked.*

Xander found his room and pushed his way through the wall of kids blocking the doorway. The whole classroom was abuzz, talking at once about the upcoming exam. Some of the students were standing next to their friends' desks. Others milled around by the heaters near the windows, sitting on top, while even more lined up by the pencil sharpener, grinding away on the wood. Sometimes all the noise gave him an overpowering headache; he had an urge to run out of the classroom screaming with his hands over his ears. He noticed so much how often someone would say one thing, while their inner thoughts were completely opposite of what they said.

*How did you get here?* Xander asked the statue.

*Where am I, kid?* the griffin countered. *I'm not from your world.*

*You're in a town called Nampa in the state of Idaho. You're on planet Earth.*

*Oh, that makes a lot sense.* Xander sensed the griffin rolling his eyes as he said the last words.

*So how did you get here?* Xander asked again.

*The Crow Judge dropped me through a wormhole. That's all I know.*

Xander wasn't sure what that meant, but he decided to wait until later to discuss it. Ignoring the burning question of what a Crow Judge was, he asked, *What does your chest plate say?* He took out the paper he had been using earlier and started scraping again, Geoffrey started giggling.

*What's wrong?* Xander asked, perplexed.

*That tickles!*

The teacher came in and started taking roll. "Okay, class, find your seats, sit down and take out your paper. Put your books away." He finished roll call, turned around and pulled down the screen behind him to cover the notes on the whiteboard. The whole class quieted down, except for Xander. All they heard, as the teacher started passing out the test papers, was the sound, *scritch, scratch, scritch* of Xander's pencil on the stone armor.

"What are you so busy with, Mr.Veh?" the teacher asked, putting the test down on his desk. The students all turned to look at Xander.

"Nothing, Mr. Adderson," he replied meekly. The class snickered.

"It looks like it must be something. Put it away and work on it later. Right now, you have a test. Let's see how well you can do." Mr. Adderson's cold steel eyes drilled into Xander. *Or how badly you will fail it this time,* he thought. The teacher's thoughts were so loud, Xander felt like he was yelling at him.

"Why should I do your test when you already know I'll fail?" Xander returned the stare, his jaw set and his eyes matching the teacher's expression exactly.

"I didn't say that, young man." The teacher tried not to soften his expression. Instead it became a bit harsher.

"You didn't have to. *'You don't know what it's like to be like me!'* Xander found himself saying, not sure where the words were coming from. "*'I have a lot on my plate, my wife complains about not having enough money to pay the bills, I work two more jobs in addition to this one and have to come here to deal with you miserable kids, and the one who reads minds and the unconscious thoughts I try to keep away from the students is the worst!"* Xander discovered he was standing up, and was yelling the words.

Everyone sucked in their breath. The teacher turned abruptly around, dropping the bundle of papers he was holding, jaw open. *How did he know all that? And I have an administrator from district coming to sit in on all my classes for performance review. This is the last thing I need.*

As though summoned, a gray-haired gentleman with horn-rim glasses and a suit with a bow tie walked in, saying, "Mr. Adderson, proceed with your day as if I'm not here." He looked around the room. "Did I miss something?"

"No, no, just Mr. Veh was venting about his frustrations. Take your test papers and books and go to detention for the rest of the period," he told Xander. "I'll be there in a minute to talk with you." The class giggled and smirked, all heads twisting around to watch Xander as he walked out the door with his stuff. He managed to stuff Geoffrey in his backpack and stomped to the detention room across the hall.

Detention was a small, all white room with a long desk attached to the wall, one chair, and no windows. Xander hated being in it since he couldn't see outside. Usually there was a guard or teacher in an adjoining room who supervised the students sent there, but not today. He took out the griffin and put him on the desk. He took out his textbook and binder, and put them down on the desk. He sat down, took out the test paper, turned it over and started writing.

*What're you doing?* Geoffrey asked.

*I'm flunking my history exam, as usual.* Xander doodled on the back of the paper, wondering why he had to say the unconscious thoughts of people at inopportune times. He wanted so badly to know why he was made this way. His mom often spoke of a 'Creator,' or 'Spirit,' as she referred to it, which made him special.

"Mom, special is for kids who are slow, can't learn and are born with deformities. I'm not special like that!" he remembered saying. The day had been sunny and they were heading to the swimming pool.

"You're an Indigo Child. That means you have a dark purple color in your aura field, have full memories of your past lives, and are closer to Spirit," she said, smiling.

"I don't remember anything about my past lives, Mom. I don't even feel this Creator you talk about. The Creator and past lives are fairy tales. All I know is I see colors, memories, and glimpses of what people do that they don't want others to know about. I hear their complaints and miseries, too."

*What's an Indigo Child? Geoffrey asked, interrupting his reverie. Your mom said you were one, and it makes you angry.*

*Stop eavesdropping on my thoughts!* Xander put down his pencil. He sighed. *Hey, you never told me what a Crow Judge is.*

*A Crow Judge is the invisible observer in my world. The Creator appointed them to help him monitor the spiritual laws and physical laws of my world. Don't you have Crow Judges here?*

*No, we have humans called police officers, lawyers, courts of laws and a bunch of other layers of crap and red tape. It sucks bad.*

*Red tape sucks? I thought it would be sticky. I've never heard of red tape having a mouth.*

*No, griffin!* Xander laughed. *It's a figure of speech. It's a hassle, that's all, to have to go through all that garbage. That's why the lawyers must interpret it for us. My Dad says so, at least.*

The door opened, and Mr. Adderson came in carrying another chair. He put it down and sat. "I see you're busy working." He looked at the paper. "You aren't working. You're still fuming about being misunderstood?" Mr. Adderson looked him with condescension, yet tried to empathize. "Look, Xander you're a bright boy. Anyone who can read minds is very smart. But you have to learn not to blurt it all out like that. You can't go through life telling everyone what they don't want to share. You have to change so others will accept you."

The teacher thought the talent belonged in a nightclub or in a sideshow act. Hearing the thought only stung Xander more. He felt tears rising, threatening to break over the barriers of his eyelids. "I don't know how to control it. I didn't know what I was saying. It just came out, like I went into a trance of something. Everyone hates me, even you and the other teachers."

Mr. Adderson smiled. "I don't hate you. I don't hate any of the students here. You just read me so thoroughly this morning it was like I was standing naked in front of the whole classroom. You have to learn to control it."

"How? I don't know how. I want to. Mostly, I just wish I could be like everyone else and not hear everyone's thoughts."

"You can't be like others, son. No one should be an exact copy of someone else. You need to be yourself. You need to learn to use your gift to help others, and learn to control it." He looked at the paper. "I'd also like to see you tap your brilliance and show me what you know about history. I know you know the answers to the questions, but you aren't even trying."

He caught a look at the griffin statue. "Hey, that's very good." He picked it up. "Did you make this?"

"No, my cat dragged it in last night; I guess he found in the yard and thought I'd like it."

"It's well made. Look at the detail of the armor, and the language is so different. Can you read what it says?"

"I was busy trying to when you interrupted my scribbling and I blurted out what I did." Xander felt his face grow hot. Mr. Adderson grimaced, and Xander thought he wanted to say something, but changed his mind.

"Let's see." Xander looked at the scribbled paper. He found a clean space, held it against the statue and started rubbing again. When he was done, he looked at the letters and scratched his head. He handed it to Mr. Adderson. "What do you think it says?"

"Hmm, I don't know that language. It isn't even based on our Roman or Greek alphabet."

Geoffrey mentally cleared his throat, *'Kingdom of Kent, one people, under the guard of Dragon, we abide by Albagoth and the Crow Judge.'*

Xander repeated it all. Mr. Adderson looked amused. "Dragons and Crow Judges?"

"Yes," said Xander. "Maybe I'm just imagining it." He mentally thanked the griffin for translating.

"What language is it?" the teacher rubbed his fingers over the letters, amazed.

"It's Kentese," Xander guessed. The bell rang. "It's from another dimension; I guess that sounds strange, but it's true."

"Uh, huh. Well, you'd better go to your other classes. You can finish the test in the morning before school."

Xander put his books away, stashed the statue in his jacket pocket and made his way to into the stream of kids once again, hoping others wouldn't notice him. He spotted a medium size boy wearing a school jacket, strutting down the hall with two cheerleaders on either side of him, looking proud and smug. Xander turned to go the other way, but he was too late.

"Hey, if it isn't Mr. Know All! Too bad you don't know all the answers to the test questions!" The boy made his way to Xander and put his arm around him. "Why don't we sit together in English. Maybe your abilities will rub off on me!"

Xander moved away from him, "Leave me alone, Butch," he said. "We don't even have the same class."

"Well, now, we'll have to fix that, won't we? Hey, I also heard you have a new toy to play with. I heard it's an ugly statue of a griffin. You know what I think? I think I'll be getting myself one just like it." The jock smirked.

"No, no, you can't. Sorry. It can't be found in stores." Xander stuttered.

Xander's next classroom was really close, so he managed to get out of Butch's grasp, but the kid grabbed his jacket hood and pulled him back. "If I can't buy a griffin statue like the one you have, you're gonna give me the one you have!"

"No, I'm not. 'Cause if I do, he'll break out the stone and tear your eyes out," Xander blurted out, hoping the bluff will be taken seriously. His heart raced as he braced himself for the bully to punch him or push him or show some sign of retaliating.

Instead, Butch just stood there, with his mouth hanging open. Then he started laughing, "You're just yanking my chain. Wait until lunchtime. You have until then to give me that statue or you're dog meat!" He started barking as he left Xander. Other athletes following behind copied his barks without thinking, and the cheerleaders laughed. The tardy bell rang, causing the hallway to clear.

Xander made his way to the desk near the window so that he could look out. The sun went behind the clouds. He wished he could go behind a cloud for the rest of the day, becoming invisible to all.

Glancing out the window, he saw a large crow sitting on a rock peering in. He had never seen a crow so tall, so black or quite so intelligent looking. Xander cocked his head to one side. *Hey, did you see that crow?* he thought to Geoffrey.

*No, I can't see through the stone. But I don't think Crow Judges are allowed to come to your world.*

The teacher came in, glancing at all the students as she took roll. Then she set up test tubes and chemicals, and pulled down the screen.

A student who worked with the PowerPoint display helped set up the computer and slides. She smiled at him. "Hi, Xander. Hey, I liked how you dealt with Butch."

Xander dragged his attention away from the window. "Hi, Kimber. He wanted my statue. Somehow, he got wind that I had it. He always wants whatever I have. Except, he doesn't want my lunch money because he knows I don't have any."

"No one carries lunch money anymore," she said, grinning. She was right, parents put money into the lunch account through the school's website similar to PayPal. "Have you named the statue? Or found out what language the words are? I bet it's in Norse Runes or something."

"I don't think it is runes. It's from another world. A place called Kent or something. The statue is a griffin named Geoffrey."

Something outside the window caught Xander's attention. It was that huge crow, again. It flapped its wings as if something was agitating it. Xander knitted his brow together, concentrating to see into the bird's mind.

*Get him out of there! Get that griffin out of there fast!*

*Who are you?*

*I am Connor, the Crow Judge of the World of Curá. You must leave now!*

*Geoffrey says you aren't supposed to be here.*

*Now! Leave now!* Connor flapped his wings and cawed insistently. At the same time, there was a loud *BOOM!* followed by the fire alarm going off.

# Chapter 4

*If it isn't one thing, it's another,* Xander thought as he and Kimber made their way out the emergency exit. They joined Sarah on the far side of the courtyard. Everyone was talking at once; girls screamed and boys tried to be strong and brave while shaking inside their skins. Smoke came out the building near the gymnasium as fire engines and police vehicles sirens whined on their way to the school.

"What happened?" their teacher asked an administrator who came to check on them.

"No one knows for sure."

Xander crossed his eyes and lifted his head. The movie running in his mind showed the administrator talking to another teacher, a secretary, and the SRO, when they heard the janitor say he'd caught Butch in the gym with some other kids, getting ready to set off smoke bombs. There were some boys setting them off in the restrooms, too. Before they could stop them, the bombs exploded.

The crow came over to Xander, flapping his wings. *Look, you're the only one who can see me. You gotta go. You gotta get out of here.*

*I can't. I don't know where you're from or why you're here, but I can't leave.*

*You must. There's a bully who wants to take that griffin away from you. He knows nothing about what the griffin is or what he can do. Has the griffin talked with you?*

*Yes, but hasn't told me a lot. Who are you? And why are you following me?*

*I'm Connor, the Crow Judge. I am the one who put Geoffrey in stone. You need to get out of here!*

Xander started walking away, and Connor followed, flying as fast as he could. Running steps came up behind them. *Don't turn around,* Connor urged. *Keep going. I'll protect you. Take Geoffrey out of your pocket.*

Glancing around, Xander saw that all the students in the large East Valley School were milling around while police officers questioned all about their whereabouts when the bombing happened. Kimber and Sarah had puzzled, worried looks on their faces.

The running sounds got closer. Xander started to run, too. He looked over his shoulder just as someone pounced on him, wrestling him to the ground,

"You aren't going anywhere until I get that statue!" Butch hissed.

"You gave me until lunchtime. It isn't lunchtime, yet!"

"I'm early, Veh! I rule this school! You know that! The administrators know it and my Daddy enforces it, too!" Butch grabbed his shirt, lifted him up and banged him down hard against the ground. He saw stars briefly.

*Take Geoffrey out!* Connor commanded. Xander obeyed. Connor moved his wing and chanted. At once a griffin twelve hands tall, white as fresh fallen snow, wearing regal armor, stood there. Both boys were suddenly speechless. Butch let Xander up, and fell to his knees, stunned to see the creature break free of the stone.

"You want me, Butch? You gotta catch me!" Geoffrey announced, flexing his muscles, extending his 12 foot wings and rearing up on his hind legs. "Climb on my back, Xander!"

He did, and they were off. Butch stood there, awestruck. As they flew up and over, Xander looked down to see the police flanking Butch, two grabbing his arms while a third handcuffed him.

Connor flew along beside the griffin. They flew a long way north of Nampa, to the mountains that surrounded McCall. They could see the snow-covered Brundage Mountain Resort, and the huge Payette Lake, which was so breathtaking that Xander was at a loss for words . . . and thoughts. His parents never took him there because they couldn't afford it.

Finally, they saw a meadow lined with trees at the north end of the lake. Patches of snow peppered the meadow. Geoffrey landed. Xander looked down from his perch on the griffin's back and slid off.

"That was marvelous! I've never flown before. It felt so free and awesome." He thought his words sounded lame. He walked over to the lake, as did Geoffrey and Connor. They looked in, and Connor was puzzled by his reflection not looking older.

"What's wrong with this reflection pond? Where is the older and wiser reflection? I have questions that need answers."

"I don't know of any lake that would show you that," Xander said. Getting down on his hands and knees, he cupped his hand, dipped it in the water, and drank. Around them more crows, eagles, song birds, and squirrels gathered, watching them. Connor and Geoffrey also drank.

"In our world, the Reflection Pond in Senilona shows us our older and wiser self. We get our questions answered. Where do you go to get answers?"

"Nowhere," Xander answered abruptly, then thought about it. "Well, sometimes I go to my Mom or Dad. Other times, I find a chatroom on the internet to talk. Most people want to get me banned because I'm so strange." Xander felt a stab in his gut. He knew he was exaggerating his own hurt, as he remembered online chats where he had hoped to find others who were like him, only to be accused of seeking attention. No one believed him, yet a person can be anyone they want to be online. Still, Xander knew he could not escape himself.

"You aren't strange. You're the Indigo Traveler. You are needed."

"Me? No, I can't do anything right. I'm totally useless. I can't even pass a test."

"You aren't trying," Geoffrey and Connor said together.

The Crow Judge looked around him as more crows gathered, sizing him up. "Hi, I'm Connor, what's your name?"

"Caaaw, caw, craw, haaaa," they echoed each other, nodding together. One picked up a twig and offered it to him.

"I don't understand the old language. Hasn't Albagoth taught you all the new?"

Xander listened to them. "Hmm, one says he is called Lyman, the other says his name is Berryhunter, the one with white feathers mixed into the black is known as Wisewoman. She's the one who wants you to take the twig. She says if you accept it, it means you two will build a nest together."

Connor flapped his wings and let out a startled caw. "Me? Build a nest? I don't have time! I'm a middle level judge on the highest Crow Court in my land! Mating is for the older Crow Judges!"

Xander looked at them. Geoffrey shrugged his shoulders. "They don't know you're from another land. They can't understand your accent or words." The crows flew off. Wisewoman stuck around, still trying to offer him twigs. She flew off, then came back with a branch from a berry bush.

"That looks tempting now; I'm hungry," he started to eat; Xander stopped him,

"Don't eat those, they could be poisonous. I've heard that some of the berries up here in the mountains aren't edible."

***

They moved away for a bit, soaking up the sunshine and the clear skies.

"So, what do you mean I'm the Indigo Traveler? I haven't traveled anywhere really." Xander threw a pebble into the lake and watched the ripples.

"You wonder who you are and where you came from."

"I wonder why I can do what I do but no one else can. My mom says there are other kids like me, but I haven't met them. She said others are taught not to be this way, so they block it out or suppress it. Once I was playing with a friend who understood and accepted me, and he moved away the next day. Everyone says I made him disappear or that he moved away because of me. But I don't think it was my fault."

"You have a power no one else has. You have something my world needs. The Creator came to me, gave me permission to come here to watch over you and Geoffrey. When the time is right, we will go back."

"Go back where?" Xander picked up a twig, broke off small pieces and tossed them into the lake.

"We will go back to Geoffrey's and my world. There is a war over there, and you are needed to help stop it."

"How can I stop it when I can't even stop the bullies from picking on me?"

"Look within yourself, Indigo Traveler, you have greater power than you know. Do not rebel against yourself. Rebel against that which denies you for who you are."

Xander walked around, and Geoffrey and Connor followed. He sat by the lake, drifting back in time to when he and his mom were in a store that sold crystals, magic books, candles and walking staffs. She always loved going to those stores; the energy in them sent chills up his spine. Because he was always asking why things were as they were, she would take him to one store and another looking for a psychic or spiritual healer to help him. "He's an Indigo Child; a star child. He'll be overwhelmed by what you say. He will be a rule breaker, never follow the path you set before him. He will be restless, angry and frustrated, and will have many dealings with the law," one told them. Xander remembered her because she was dressed in a silk sarong, wore a large purple crystal around her neck and spoke like her voice came through a long tube. He wondered why there were many entities floating above her and her aura was black with red spots and a few gray areas. He saw no white—most people had white near their body.

This woman's words upset his mom; yet she was ready to believe them until he spoke up. "You're evil," he told the woman. He saw clearly the movies in the head area were of her and her sons. "It is your sons who are in trouble with the law and you think I will be, too, because my colors are the same as theirs. You're wrong." The woman's face turned bright red, and she fumbled for words, but found none to reply.

Another so-called psychic at another store said, "He is the Indigo Intergalactic Traveler. He will unite worlds, creating peace in the land and be the friend of dragons and griffins." He remembered her words, too. Her aura had rich golden hues with purple and the movies above her head were peaceful, showing her resting by water and taking long walks in nature. His mom thought her words were symbolic.

The sun started to set. Xander knew his parents must be frantic with worry at where he could be. He climbed on Geoffrey's back and they flew back to Nampa. He felt refreshed after spending the day in the forest. Connor's words echoed in his mind.

Connor landed in the tallest tree in Xander's yard. Geoffrey slowly shrank as he turned back to stone, and Xander slid down his back. He turned to go in the house. His mom came out as soon as she saw him through the kitchen window.

"Where have you been? I heard about the bombing and went to bring you home, but no one could find you!" Erin, Xander's Mom, grabbed him and hugged him, holding close. Xander struggled uncomfortably, twisting out of her arms and staring at the ground.

"I'm fine, Mom. I just walked away. No one saw me or even cared that I disappeared. Everyone was preoccupied with finding Butch and making sure the kids that mattered were safe."

"I don't know how they could lose you like that! That boy they accused of setting the bombs said, 'He flew off on a griffin.'" His mom laughed.

Xander laughed, too, "Yeah, that's really funny, Mom." He bent down, picked up his new friend, put him in his jacket pocket, and headed inside. His mom followed on his heels.

"You didn't say where you were."

"I was all over, Mom. Don't worry about me. I'm fine. I was safe. I just hope Butch will be in the juvenile hall for a few days."

\*\*\*

Kimber and Sarah accompanied Xander to the library. Butch was already in there, waiting for them, though the three friends tried to ignore him.

"Hey, where did that overgrown eagle take you? I've never seen anything quite like it before."

"I don't know what you're talking about, Butch," Xander muttered. "How did you get out of juvy so quickly?"

"My Dad's an attorney. He bailed me out saying there was a mistake. I was innocent and anyone who is jealous of my prowess on the field would be able to disguise themselves as me."

Xander looked above the jock; saw the whole plan he had from early yesterday morning until when he put into action. Only problem, he also knew the school had cameras in every corner of the building. There were some places that didn't pick up anything. Butch knew how to skirt them, too.

"Nobody can prove I did it," the bully sneered, with his head tilted back, jaw jutted out, daring him to try.

"And you can't prove you didn't do it, either. I've heard the janitor caught you setting the bombs off." Xander ignored Butch's attitude.

"Look, I want that statue. I want to know how you got it and why you get stuff like it." Butch grabbed Xander's jacket. "I also want to know how you made it break out of that stone and how it grew like that."

"Leave him alone!" Both girls stood up. Butch looked up and down at the two girls. Kimber was dressed in jeans, a sweater, and athletic shoes, looking more comfortable than the other day. Sarah was in her black Tripp pants and Marilyn Manson t-shirt.

Butch sneered. "You're gonna let two girls fight for you?"

"Yeah, what's wrong with that? I am not a fighter, Butch. Leave me alone. You aren't getting the statue. It isn't anything special. My cat found it and brought it to me."

"When you address me, you stand up! I'm tougher and stronger and no one denies me what I want!" Butch lifted Xander up off his seat. "And god knows I've got more brains than you."

"Leave him alone! The statue isn't yours. You have no right to it." Sarah stepped forward, her hands balled into fists.

"What're you, She-Hulk? Look, I don't hurt girls. My Dad taught me girls are fragile. But you want to be tough!" He pushed her. "I don't have an issue with you. It's this freak over here!" Butch lifted Xander up higher. The bell rang.

"This isn't over, Veh. You will give me that statue before the day's end."

"I left it home today," Xander said, wiggling, trying to pry the bully's fingers from his sweater's collar. He glanced over and saw that the librarian was heading their way. "Mr. Brown is coming. Put me down! That was the bell."

"Yeah, I'll put you down!" Butch tossed Xander across the floor. He landed, crashed into some table legs, and slid across the carpet until the bookshelf stopped him.

As he lay there, Xander wished he knew more about fighting. He felt himself trembling from fear, but didn't want to show it. He stood up, and Mr. Brown and the girls came over to check on him. *It could be worse*, he thought. *Butch could've punched me in the face.*

"Are you okay?" they asked together.

"I think so," he rubbed his backside and his head. "Where did Butch go?"

"He went to class. But don't worry; I'll report what I saw. I'll see to it the principal knows." Mr. Brown smiled. "And I'll write tardy excuses for you three, too."

Xander walked to his first class feeling a bit shaken. His vision blurred and cleared several times, his back hurt and his mind was spinning. He went to the front of the room, feeling all eyes drilling into him as the teacher stopped lecturing to watch him, too. After he gave the tardy slip to the teacher, he found an empty desk near the window. He sighed as quietly as he could, closing his eyes and wishing he could be tougher.

*I don't belong here*, he thought. He looked around at all the other kids writing notes, hanging on the teacher's every word. They all wore the same or similar style of jeans, shirts and backpacks bought from Hollister or Macy's or some other fancy store. They all laughed the same, liked the same lame popular music and TV shows and frowned on anything out of the socially accepted norms. *Butch must know I don't belong here and that's why he picks on me.* Xander opened his eyes and looked around the room, catching a few of his classmates staring at him. He imagined they also were asking themselves why he was here. *I feel like I was dropped here from outer space, like Geoffrey. I wonder what I should do.* He glanced out the window, expecting to see that crow, Connor, but didn't see him.

Closing his blue eyes, Xander fell asleep. He was walking in a strange land where the skies were orange and purple with gold streaks. There was a little girl who was about his height, but appeared younger in the face, with blonde hair. She had one eye in the center of her forehead and another one vertical on the side of her face. In the background, Xander heard the clashing of swords, and what sounded like bombs exploding.

"People are dying. My daddy doesn't want me. My brother is lost. I'm lost and alone; too young to be out here. Where is the traveler who will be here? Connor told me he would come. It's been two years now."

The dream switched scenes to an underground maze with twists and turns. A minotaur sat in the corner, strumming a lyre, singing a ballad of the Indigo Traveler. He looked up, straight at Xander, stopped strumming, and opened his mouth. A sharp piercing ring came out. Xander's eyes flew open. Disoriented at first, he realized it was the bell to change classes.

As he packed up his bags, Mr. Adderson came over to him. "Are you okay? Mr. Brown wrote on the slip that you had a run in with Butch. You fell asleep in class. I think you need to see the nurse."

Xander looked down at the floor. "I'm okay." He picked up his books, not wanting to look in his teacher's eyes.

At lunch, he looked around the cafeteria at the other students, wondering what it would be like to be so happy, to feel like he had genuine friends and fit in. Kimber and Sarah joined him.

"What's wrong?" Kimber asked.

"Are you feeling okay? You may have a concussion or something," Sarah said.

He looked at them, then stared down at the tuna melt, tater tots, and mushy green beans. "Have you ever felt like you don't fit in?"

"Yeah, all the time," Kimber replied. "That's why when China suggested she could help me fit in by buying all those fancy clothes, I jumped at the chance. Only problem is, I'm not superficial."

"What makes people tick?" he asked. The two girls shrugged their shoulders. A food fight broke out in the neighboring table. A wad of mushy green beans rolled in a tuna melt soared over, slapping Xander in the back. The kid who threw it laughed.

"The crazy kid got it good!" they shouted.

"Ignore them," Kimber said. "They're just immature and don't know anything."

He nodded, not really paying attention. He looked over at them, saw their auras were rich in blacks, greens, and mixed in with base colors that surely meant they were not aware of their connection. He looked down at his own aura; saw rich purple hues, with the deep dark violet known as indigo. He knew there had to be something more to this life of his. Everything felt so empty and mindless, like those two boys playing with their food.

"Did you bring your griffin with you?" Kimber asked. "Butch wants him very bad. I heard he's trying to start a rumor that you stole it from him."

"He can't have it. Geoffrey won't stay with him," Xander muttered, moving slowly, as if someone had pushed a slow-motion button. In the distance, he heard the girl from his dream calling to him. He didn't hear anything else. He started praying: *Creator, if you are real, show me what to do. Lead me on the path. I don't know who I am. I don't know how to use my abilities. I don't belong here in this school and I want to leave this world. Nothing feels right. I don't know what it even feels like for it to be right. Dreams have power. Words have power. The girl in the dream doesn't look right. She looks odd with two eyes. Why should she be able to reach me?*

Xander walked out the cafeteria door that led to the outside. The warm October day hit his face, and the other kids who had finished eating were milling around. Boys were jumping from stone mound to stone mound, playing follow the leader, while others were racing up the grassy hill a way off. Middle schoolers were too big for swing sets and monkey bars, but they still had energy to spare. Nothing roused Xander from his stupor. He walked as though he was under a spell.

Connor appeared to him after he crossed the road away from the school. "Indigo Traveler, where is the griffin?"

Xander shook his head, hearing the crow's voice. "In the pocket of my jacket." He pulled Geoffrey out. The traffic buzzed by, scaring him. "How did I cross the street without stopping for the cars?"

"I put a protective bubble around you. You aren't well, but will heal in the other land. It's time to go. Put him on the ground so he can return to his normal self."

Xander did as he was directed and Geoffrey broke out of the stone, growing to his normal height, then stretched his wings, legs, and hindquarters. Stretching his wings out, shaking them, then pulling them in and shaking like a wet cat, he opened his beak and let out a *veer*, sounding like an eagle.

"Yes! I still remember the ancient language of my eagle ancestors!" he exclaimed.

Xander climbed on his back and they lifted off.

The air felt refreshing against Xander's skin, like a brisk shower after mowing the lawn on a hot summer's day. The cars, buses and pedestrians looked like ants crawling through their dirt tunnels underground. His gut said something important was about to happen, but, he didn't know what to expect. He was embarking on an adventure beyond his wildest dreams. He held onto Geoffrey's back armor. He felt secure.

They soared up to the highest atmosphere, up through moist clouds, which parted as if welcoming the interruption. Connor flew on ahead, pausing at the highest altitude, treading the air like a humming bird, though only one wing was going. With the other, he opened a wormhole and they flew through.

The wormhole was like a tunnel. It buzzed with electricity; there were no lights, just a sort of energy like a million insects were competing for the only human there. Xander closed his eyes for a moment; it felt as if they were spinning like a biplane doing aerobatics.

As he spun around, flipping head over heels, he hung on tighter to Geoffrey. He sensed his spirit soar out of his body, freely traveling to the end of the wormhole before the rest of him. He saw the girl with the odd large eye in the center of her head and the second eye along the side, like a Picasso painting. "You are safe," she told him.

Next, he felt his cat, Clarence looking at him, "Your way is clouded with uncertainty. Trust your gut. Watch out for the mountains that move on their own."

Xander opened his eyes to see the land rushing up to meet them; an urgency to break the fall surged through his body; he lost his grip, flying off. Geoffrey tried to pick up his speed to catch him, but managed only to get a shoe, which easily came off in his claws. Xander hit the sand bottom-first and bounced. He laughed as he tumbled. Geoffrey and Connor came to a stop at the same time.

The Indigo Traveler gazed up at the sky, seeing gray clouds in the shape of question marks in a lavender sky. That seemed strange.

"What do you see?" Connor asked, peering at him with wonder.

"You are a spiritual advisor, you know this world. You see through me, you tell me what I see," Xander countered.

"Each traveler to this world sees something different. I can only read the people of my land, Xander. I can tell you what to see, but that won't mean that it is right for you," Connor replied.

Xander considered his words, still looking around at everything. Slowly, he sat up, his head and the land spinning like a top. When it stopped, he glanced at the sky and still saw the puffy question marks. He told Connor what he saw.

"Each traveler to this desert will see something different. I see my fellow Crow Judges sitting on the clouds," Connor said, "but I know they aren't there. I just sense their presence from where they observe from the Justice Center on my world."

"Does Albagoth reside there, too?" Geoffrey asked, looking around to see as much as he could of this land. He had never been in this part of his world before.

"No, Albagoth resides in a whole different space." Connor flapped his wings and sighed. "I miss my world, sometimes."

"What do you see?" the Indigo Traveler asked his griffin.

"I see Kent, Prince Tayson, my sire and dame, and my Grandsire. They look angry and disappointed in me." His voice broke. He took in a sharp breath.

"You acted with your fear and gut," the Crow Judge told Geoffrey. "Once we get our bearings, and the world stops

48

spinning, we will get some food and travel to your village, where your Grandsire can teach you to forgive yourself."

# Chapter 5

Jaden wandered in the desert feeling lost. Being only four years old, she didn't know how long she had been out here. She had visions of finding someone who would help her. He would be riding on a pure white griffin with powerful catlike paws and a marvelous yellow beak. He would be tall, for a human, with pale skin and unkempt black hair, and would be wearing very strange clothes. Also, his language would be different. She glanced up at the sky; it was purplish with orange streaks at that moment. Intuitively, she knew she had to be creative on how to find him. Or maybe she was just supposed to pull up a rock and wait for him to find her.

She saw a rock standing by a plant with multiple arms and spikes all over it. She went over and turned around to lower herself onto the stone, not realizing how far she had to go to sit on it. She felt something catch her arm, like pinpricks. She jumped in surprise. She turned to see that the plant was holding her elbow. It had two large yellow eyes and a mouth open in a smile to show small seed teeth. She screamed.

"I didn't mean to startle you. Just helping you sit down" he said. "You're so pretty. You could be a princess dressed in that fancy silk dress."

"I am a princess." She tried to smile, startled that he said she was pretty. "You really think I'm pretty?"

"Yeah, your eye color is very bright, kind of like the sky." The plant boy bent his torso over to look up. Jaden followed his gaze.

"But I have two eyes and I'm only supposed to have one," she frowned.

"I just thought that was a beauty mark. I've never seen another being like you before. You aren't a plant person like me."

"No, I'm an Arimaspian. I've never seen anything like you, either," she blinked her eye, backing away. "I'm Jaden. Do you have a name?"

"I'm Cranny; I'm a Criatia. I live in the garden over yonder. We aren't supposed to walk out without an elder with us, but I like to explore and see if travelers from other worlds come by. One of my offshoot friends said one would come. I'm waiting for that person. Are you a traveler?"

Jaden thought of the boy with the griffin from her vision. She shook her head. "No, I'm not from another world. I'm from the village way over the mountains. My papa sent me away. He angered the Crow Judge and he punished me for it. My papa started fights with a peaceful place way over the other mountains too far for me to walk." Her voice broke and her eye teared up as her second eye fluttered, almost opening.

Cranny's inner chambers went out to her. He wondered how to help her. "Are you hungry or thirsty? I don't know what you eat. We Criatias put our roots deep into the soil and draw out the nutrients from it. We can find water that way, too. Do you have roots?"

Jaden looked at her hands and feet, then sadly shook her head, "No, I don't. The cook usually feeds me roast pig, chicken, fresh bread, puddings and the finest of vegetables. Even rabbits if the royal hunters can catch them; they aren't very quick. I don't know how to hunt or fix my own food. I'm only four years old!" She frowned again.

"Let's walk away from here," Cranny suggested. "Maybe we can find something you can eat." As they walked, they noticed the sky slowly turn gray with clouds of many different colors, and it soon began to rain. "Someone isn't happy," Cranny sighed. "I don't mind the rain. I always say the Crow Judges are crying because the Creator got angry with them."

"The Creator is never angry with them." the little girl smiled. Her second eye opened up. "Albagoth never gets upset. He says what happens is what happens." The eye closed again.

Cranny didn't know how to take her words, so he ignored them. He led her to some small bushes, hoping to find some edible roots she could dig up. "Do you know what the vegetables you eat look like while in the ground?"

The young girl shook her head, "I don't know. I never went to the gardens with the caregiver. I wasn't allowed to. Mamma said little princesses don't play in the dirt, and I was only allowed to see the flowers. My tummy hurts."

"I'm sure it does." Cranny felt helpless. He remembered he wasn't food, yet he was sure he could offer something of himself to her to help.

The saw a strange sight, like the sky was opening up, exposing pitch blackness as a funnel of golden hues mixed with white bolts of lightning appeared. They saw two creatures flying through the void. They weren't flying as much as spinning out of control. They landed with a thud. Jaden and Cranny glanced at each other, then rushed towards where the creatures had landed.

*** 

"I think the world has stopped spinning. Let's walk. Maybe we can find something to eat and drink." Geoffrey suggested.

Xander observed the sky's strange orange, pink and sick-yellow clouds lazily floating by, and rain the color of purple turnips falling. He didn't know if he was imagining this or what. He glanced at Geoffrey, who used his wings to protect his head from the rain.

Xander couldn't resist giggling. "What's wrong? I thought birds liked the rain." Geoffrey let out an irritated half-growl, half-veer sound from deep in his throat.

"I'm not a full bird. I'm mostly cat, and I hate getting wet. Especially when it's a sick yellow color! I usually bury anything that is so dark yellow it could be brown!"

"That isn't the color I see. It's definitely purple!" Xander exclaimed.

Geoffrey started to argue. Then he remembered. "We're in the desert, Xander. We're both right."

"How can we both be right? There's always a right and wrong." He glared at his new friend.

"My Grandsire told me about a place where each traveler sees the color of the sky or rain according to his troubles. It's our individual perception. You see purple rain because you deny you

52

are an Indigo kid. I see brown because I'm not grounded in my own worth." He turned to look the boy in the eyes. "The sky reflects our emotions."

"So did someone else cause the rain? Back home it rains when the clouds soak up moisture from the lakes, rivers and oceans and then clash with a warm front or something like that. Don't you have anyone here who studies the weather?"

"No, we don't. We just accept it for what it is. It's only in this desert that the rain and sky are colored. In my village, the sky is usually blue, unless there is a fire somewhere."

"Don't you have trees in this world? I haven't seen anything so barren in my life!" Xander looked around. Somehow, it didn't look like he'd imagined it would. Then, again, he had never stopped to consider what this world would look like.

Geoffrey didn't answer. Xander felt the griffin's thoughts drift back to the war he had left behind. He knew Geoffrey was wondering how much time had passed. It felt like he had only been gone one or two days. Surely the war was still taking place, but obviously, they were a long way from the battle.

*The mind is a funny thing,* Xander thought. *When at rest, all quiet and vacant, I feel peaceful. Here this land stirs up more questions. Not the normal ones I usually think, like who am I? and why do I have to do what my parents want me to do? Life is so boring. Do the chores. Clean my room. Pick up my dirty clothes and do homework. Make good grades and we will love you. All love is conditional.* He frowned at his thoughts, and his chest tightened, knowing he was exaggerating. *Love isn't supposed to be conditional. I'm expected to know what I want to be when I'm grown up. I don't know. I can't be who I am unless I change. Yet that means unlearning this ability I have to read auras and see people's thoughts. I don't even know how I learned it. Freak! That's what the kids call me. Freak of nature! I'm no more a freak than the next person.*

An image of Butch popped into his mind. *What makes him so special? Why do all the girls love him? He's the star of the football team and the basketball team. He's been playing since they were preschoolers. All the kids treat him like he's an epic warrior of the school. What would happen if he were sent into an actual battle? I'm afraid to see his field. The last time I saw his field, it was all muddled – there were swirling colors like someone spilled all the*

53

*primary colors and stirred them together. And all the images floating around were like a television set playing all channels at once, or just fuzzy like static interference. And he calls me a loser. I don't want to feel what I feel. I don't want to see what I see. I can't change! I can't help everyone!*

\*\*\*

The rain let up. Geoffrey put down his wings, set his hind paws back a way, his front equal with the back to form a rectangle. He shook himself, splattering water all over Xander. "I sure hope the day orb will come out and dry us," he sighed.

"Can you see the colors around people?" Xander asked. "Like I can?"

"No, not really. When I was in the stone I could sense the energy of the various people around me. There was one female, I think, who held me and mentioned the scrapes and bumps on the stone. She had a golden hue to her, and appeared to radiate an interest in you. There was another female who didn't hold me, but her voice caused a vibration through the stone that I sensed was bluer and calming. She, too, had an interest in you beyond friendship. I'm not totally sure unless I can see their faces. My Grandsire can teach what you know, though. He has taught many lessons to my friend, Sebastian. I just don't see the value in it."

Geoffrey thought for a minute. "Oh, there was a boy who wanted me. The one who threatened you; with him I sensed solid red mixed in with a lot of superiority. He thought he was better than everyone and he really hated you. I'm not sure why. He wants what he says he hates. I saw that clearly after I broke out of the stone the first time. What did you see when you looked at him?"

"I can't see anything around him. Butch scares me too much. His colors are scrambled and the images are, too." Xander's stomach rumbled. "Hey, where can we find something to eat? I'm hungry."

"Me, too. I don't know. We can wait until we see the forest in a bit. Or maybe there's a stream with some water life."

"You mean fish?" Xander asked. Geoffrey nodded. Xander saw two small objects walking towards them. One looked like a cactus and the other like a human. They were so tiny and fuzzy that he was sure he was seeing things. "Do you have cacti in this world?

If you do, we can open a cactus up to drink the water and eat the flesh from the inside."

"What's a cactus? Don't know about them. Do you see that walking plant creature? Or is the heat beginning to make me see things?"

"It is getting hot. I see them, too. Don't know what they are."

"We'd better fly away, Xander. Get on my back, we can go to my village where we can get food and see my Grandsire."

\*\*\*

"Pretty cat birdy!" Jaden exclaimed as she saw the griffin fly over their heads. "Bird has a rider! Look, Cranny, do you see?"

"That's a griffin, Jaden. He isn't that pretty, but I wonder about the rider," his voice trailed, "We're heading the wrong way. The lake we want to go to is the other direction." They turned around and followed the way the griffin had gone.

\*\*\*

King Titus, his gold and white robes flowing with each stride, paced the floor around the table, where his cabinet sat nervous and anxious for the meeting to be over. "So, Prince Tayson has called a ceasefire because he knows he is losing! His griffin disappeared two years ago. We know that griffin was of royal lineage and has disgraced his bloodline by fleeing the battle. We have taken the first mountain where there are rumors of gold, silver and rubies of the richest color of red," Titus rubbed his hands together. "But we have yet to get that young upstart of a prince to sign the papers giving up his father's right to the second mountain."

A smaller Arimaspian soldiered said meekly, "Sire, if I may, there are so many mountains in this land. And we know a dragon lives in two of the highest ones, and another one is where the gryphons have their village. We don't want to bother either of them for fear they'll tear us apart,"

Titus turned around abruptly. "You're afraid of the dragon? Why? I fear nothing about him! I know he guards the Kingdom of Kent, but he shall guard me! I shall make him fear me!"

"Sire, if I may, the legend says you have dragon's blood in your lineage. The dragon shared two hearts with two different princes. They pledged to abide in peace forever more. If one violates the agreement, the dragons will taint the errant one. Your two kingdoms being at war is contrary to this agreement."

"I do not abide by legends! My parents told me this tale. I see no reason or reality in it. If it were so, then the dragon himself would visit me, leading me and guiding me! He avoids me because he knows I am his equal." King Titus fumbled with the whip around his waist.

His wizard sat up, looking wise and knowledgeable. "It is not wise to disregard the dragon's legend, your Highness. The dragon remembers everything, all legends passed down. I've seen the vision in my gazing pool of one come from another world called Nampa. He wields a three-pronged sword that is tainted with the blood from two different dragons. Don't let him get close to you."

"No mere stranger from a foreign land will get close to me!" Titus roared. "Wizard, you know spells, you can protect me. You know . . . what does this traveler look like?" Titus placed his hands on the table, leaned across and stared with his one solid brown eye into the wizard's pale blue one, making the wizard to shift in his seat.

The wizard cleared his throat, "He is puny, and human. He isn't skilled in battle and fears his own shadow. But he has a power we haven't seen before. A power none of us have seen. Around him are the colors of Albagoth. The Crow Judge of our world has been assigned to guide him. He travels with an all-white griffin, too. We must not anger him. He is very powerful."

"But weak! If he's human, he can be captured and turned to my purposes. I can make him tremble in fear and teach him the ways of wealth and exploiting the poor for our gain. He can be the son that was taken from me!"

"Sire, I urge you, do not disregard the dragon and Albagoth. He smiles on this traveler."

"He is no more special than I am! If the Creator was so real, why hasn't he blessed me by giving my son back to me? I will stop at nothing until I have both my son and all lands of Kent! We are not blood brothers. No way can I be with brother to a human!"

"By the blood of the dragon, Sire, brothers until the end." The wizard recited the legend from memory. King Titus pulled his whip out and snapped it. The end struck the spell caster's face, and blood oozed from the wound. The other members around the table sucked in their breath and tried to back away from the table, not wanting to move any muscles.

"Weaklings! You are all cowards! Just like the tiniest mouse shaking in your skin when a cat appears around the corner. Outsmart the cat, you tell yourself, when no cat is near. The thought vanishes the second the cat is right in front of your nose! I will teach Prince Tayson to be afraid of me! I will teach all who threaten me to be afraid! The Creator himself will also be terrified of me! Just you wait! No one will rest until I have exactly all I need!"

# Chapter 6

The land below slowly turned to lush green grass with clumps of trees and shrubs. Xander felt woozy and his head hurt worse than it had. Putting his hand up, he felt dampness. He looked at his hand and saw blood. "I'm bleeding, Geoffrey. I remember that talking crow said I was injured before we came. He said I would come here to be healed."

"Yes, I know. I'm taking you to my village so my Grandsire can heal you. He's a healer. He knows how to heal humans as well as all creatures in this world. Don't stress," Geoffrey called out. The air rushing past them took most of the words away, but Xander understood enough.

Geoffrey scanned the land below, and saw a strange sight. "What are you looking at?" Xander asked.

"An Arimaspian child walking with a Criatia offshoot. I wonder where they're heading. It feels as if they're following us. That would be it strange. I'm not sure if it's a Criatia offshoot, though. Time will tell, I guess."

\*\*\*

The griffin village had minotaurs who lived with them in peace. They helped tend the gardens, hunt for food and tend to the young. Healer Astral, Geoffrey's Grandsire, had one working with him to help carry the sick to the shelter of the healing ward. Astral was also one of the teachers of the young, imparting the lessons they would need to be productive citizens in the village and spiritually in tune with the Creator. When called upon, the griffins and the minotaurs also served the Kingdom of Kent, since King Tonyar often gave them aid when they needed extra hands in the fields or gathering herbs for healing.

*\*\**

Astral sat in meditation, considering Geoffrey's absence for the last two years. He wasn't surprised when Geoffrey had abandoned his duties to Prince Tayson, since the young prince had quite an attitude and often looked down on the griffins as mere mindless and soulless animals. Yet the birth of a white griffin cub was a sign that something would happen to change their world. He remembered advising his son and his mate to be very respectful with this one. Geoffrey would not be the one to fight in a war unless he understood the higher calling of it. He was a sign that the peace was about to end, but Albagoth would see a way to bring the peace about again. Geoffrey would be a rule breaker, not abiding by any of traditional ways, and he did show this. He even denied the Crow Judge and the Creator, saying he had to see or feel them for himself. Astral knew they had to allow him to find his own way.

As he calmed his mind, relaxing his breathing until it was barely audible, Astral allowed his spirit to be free of physical confinement, soaring through the clouds. *Spirit of the Creator, I beseech you to guide my grandson back to us. Show me, if it is in the plan, where he is and if he is all right.*

His spirit traveled to the skies, and he saw Geoffrey flying to them, carrying a strange boy with bright indigo colors. Astral could tell the boy was injured. The boy had questions, felt lost and unsure of himself. Yet he had a tremendous ability to help heal others, though he was untrained in how to use it.

A voice, full of love and comfort, spoke. "I have great plans for both this boy from the world called Nampa and your grandson. They will both be guided by Connor. You, Astral, are to be a mentor. They are ready and open. They are the sign and promise of a peaceful end. Manitor, the dragon, is also expecting them. Be prepared to heal the warrior's injuries suffered in his world, made worse by coming through the vortex." The Creator's calming presence subsided.

Astral gradually came out of his meditation, feeling refreshed; his heart excited, yet glad that his grandson would be coming back soon.

Those words had come to him months ago, maybe even a year. Astral sat there today trying to relax, center himself, and move on. He had lost hope of ever seeing his grandson again. His mind was full of the war, sensing the Arimaspian King would be starting to renew his threats against all in the land. He knew the Crow Judge had been reassigned to another planet, and no other had taken his place. The Kingdom of Kent's wizard assured them Connor would return. Soon, they would hear more. There was concern, too, because they heard the rumor of the disfigured princess wandering around the desert, lost with no elder to guide her. Astral clicked his tongue against his beak, swaying his eagle head back and forth.

Outside his shelter, others in the village were shouting, cheering and rushing about. He stood, slowly stretching out his limbs, arching his back and flapping his wings. He wasn't as young as he used to be, and all his joints ached. He made a mental note to ask his mate to make a healing tonic for him later.

"What's happening?" he asked, watching everyone running all around. Two minotaur nurses hurried out with a stretcher. "If someone is hurt, why not tell me?"

"We didn't want to disturb you, Healer. We knew you needed your quiet time," one young griffin replied. "Geoffrey returned with a strange human who has a head wound. Geoffrey said he was injured at something called school. He said it was a building. How can a building hurt a human?"

Astral smiled at the young one's question, but his heart also jumped for joy to see his grandson again. He leaped into the air and flew so he could see where they all were. In the center of the village, Geoffrey was surrounded by his sire and his dame, who were telling everyone to back up to give them room to breathe. It was obvious the human was in bad shape; he was pale and could hardly keep his eyes open.

Astral landed. "Maxil, what's going on?" he asked, making his way through the crowd.

"Geoffrey's back, Father, and he brought a boy from another world. He said the place is called Nampa. The boy was injured. I think he has a concussion."

Astral went forward, nodding to the nurses with the stretcher to come on through. He looked at Xander, gently lifted him up and turned him over to see that the hair was matted with dry blood. Yep, it was like the vision from a year ago. The traveler was here. Astral held out his paw, ran it up and down the teen's torso and head, and put his eyes out of focus so he could see the colors around the boy. The energy was weak. The colors were faint, with whiter to pinkish purple or violet.

Astral folded his three of his toes around one, retracting the claw to raise the lid on Xander's left eye. "Yes, his eyes are not focusing and the whites aren't the right color. Take him to the hospital tent and prepare the herbs. Have one of the apprentice nurses take a bucket to the river to get some cold water. Also collect some water weeds to prepare a salve. I will be there soon."

The minotaurs placed Xander gently on the stretcher and went off. The crowd parted. Astral turned to his son, who was talking with Geoffrey in low tones. "So, my long lost grandcub returns. Do you know how long you've been gone?"

"Yeah, about two days, Gramps," Geoffrey said. "Connor, the Crow Judge, sent me through a wormhole. I landed in the Indigo Traveler's backyard. A feline brought me to him."

"It's been two years here, son," Maxil replied. "Time has gone quickly by."

"That makes no sense," Geoffrey replied, staring at the ground.

"Time is different in the other world, my son," Astral said gently. "We aren't upset with you. You are safe and look fine. Maybe a bit dirty from your travels. We will sit down to a good feast later. I'm sure you're so hungry you could eat a herd beast or two." He placed a gentle paw on Geoffrey's shoulders, patting him.

"Yes, that does sound good, Gramps." The young griffin met his Grandsire's eye; his pale blue eyes twinkled. "It's good to be back."

***

Xander stirred, feeling cool water being poured over him. He realized he was on his side and someone was washing the back of his head. His mind swam around, trying to remember what he done last. He vaguely remembered falling through a wormhole with the statue and that overgrown crow that could speak English. He heard voices sounding like they were coming through a vent a long way from him. He attempted to twist his body to get up when he heard a strange pattern of footsteps approaching.

"Don't move, Indigo Traveler. You're safe." A gentle paw settled on his shoulder. "You have a nice wound on the back of your head. Geoffrey said you were hurt at something called *school* or *East Valley. . . .*"

"Yeah, Butch, the school's bully, threw me down in the library. I bumped my head on the wall. It was just a bump, but my head feels like it's going to explode."

The griffin laughed. "It won't do that. Going through the wormhole did affect the bruise somehow. I think you two must have landed pretty hard and that caused the bruise to open up. My nurse is washing it now, and we will put some healing herbs on it. Just lie back and rest." Xander heard the paws retreat.

In the background, he heard Geoffrey asking how he was. Somehow, it also sounded like it came through a tunnel or tube. He heard the elder say "He will be okay, grandcub. Let him rest for a bit."

\*\*\*

Xander felt himself float out of the shell he was squeezed into. He drifted with the wind to a place that was all white, with tall buildings, city streets made of red and gold bricks, and large crows playing with pebbles and other objects. He saw a few men and women walking—but not really walking, more like gliding by. One building looked like a capital or judicial building, and had words written that were like the words on Geoffrey's shield. Xander wondered where he could go to get answers. Suddenly he was in a park standing at the base of a statue. There was a cliff nearby. He wanted to know who the statue was of, because there was no name engraved on it. He wandered over to the cliff and looked down to the valley.

"Hello!" he called, expecting to hear his words reverberate in the lush green valley.

"What are you doing here, Indigo Traveler from the world called Nampa?" came the reply.

"Aren't you supposed to repeat my words?" he asked, wondering where the other people were.

"Why should I? You aren't the boss of me! I have free will to say what I want and you can't make me go against it!" The words reminded Xander of thoughts he often had while sitting in school.

"Who gave you that freedom of will?"

"Albagoth did! He gave everyone the freedom to search for their own truth. Give voice to the voiceless."

That thought made Xander think of how he said aloud things that others wanted to keep to themselves. "But I have no right to voice what isn't mine to speak," Xander mused, feeling awkward.

"Bring to the light what is kept in the dark. The shadow can often be the light side of a dark person. Trust in the warrior when the peace keeper wants to be front and center."

Xander walked away, down a small path, and turned back, curious about this echo.

"You called me the Indigo Traveler. How do you know who I am? You don't have eyes."

"I don't have ears, yet I hear. I am an echo with a freedom of voice. I sense. I know each person who comes to the edge and speaks. I know the voice—your voice tells me who you are. Your rich colors surround you. See Manitor. He has a gift for you."

Xander scratched his ear, hearing a buzz around him. He wondered where all the traffic was, and realized the sound came from the sky, which was turning black with the flock of crows all talking at once. Some were cawing and others used words similar to Connor's. "Who's Manitor?" he asked the echo.

"He is the dragon who protects the Kingdom of Kent. King Tonyar and the ancestors of the Arimaspian kingdom have a contract. It's being violated. Albagoth needs you."

"Why me? What about the Crow Judge? And why can't the Creator see me? Why can't I see him?"

"Albagoth is a spirit and is all around and inside of you and each of his creations. Look inside yourself, Indigo Traveler. Travel to the scary place in the stillness of your own soul."

The words struck Xander between his eyes, driving him back on his heels as if something had physically struck him. "Ah – I—" he considered his words carefully. "I don't know. My mom spoke of meditating, but it isn't the same with me. Headache." He touched the back of his head and rubbed. "My head hurts." He slowly backed away.

A crow larger than Connor landed at his feet. It had white head feathers that appeared as if they'd been curled. "Did you put your talon in an electrical socket?" Xander asked without thinking.

The crow laughed a throaty laugh that was half cawing and half giggling. He looked at Xander with one onyx eye. "Indigo Traveler, you need to go back. This land is not for you to be in unescorted. Though you will return with Connor. He will escort you to the library of soul memory. Astral needs you. Connor will be back soon to guide you."

"Follow the golden path, Indigo Traveler. It is covered in stars, like those on your ceiling," called the Echo.

# Chapter 7

Alone in his chambers, King Titus reflected on his son's empty room. Remembering of his son's laughter and merriment as he chased his sister with a snake or rodent from the riverbed brought both a joy and sadness. Kontar was like him when he was young, except Kontar wanted to know what made the poor of their kingdom poor and why they had to give up so much of their harvest.

"The poor only know how to work hard, my son. They were not born of the privileged class, like you were," he had explained, suppressing his parents' teaching that the poor farmers were to be treated fairly.

He remembered walking with his Mum and Father through the town during a fall festival. Titus remembered feeling like an outcast, dressed in the finest silks and robes while the farmer's children were clothed in pure cotton, simple threads and tunic tops with laces. They wore homemade shoes, which he loved, longing to have some, too. His own shoes were made especially for him out of the finest leather of herd beast; his young, still-growing feet felt cramped, stuffed inside them like a turkey for a holiday meal. Secretly, Titus had wanted shoes like theirs. He had felt out of place in the village.

"When can we go back to the palace, Mum?" he whined. "Why do we have to be here among the common people?"

"We are here to share in their joy of bringing in the last harvest of the season." His Mum smiled. "We show them we care about them and share what we, too, have harvested."

"But we don't grow food, Mum. We are better than them. We rule them and they serve us."

"We serve them, Titus. According to the dragon, we are to serve the people, care for their growth and make sure they have enough for their families to live on. We do not take more than we need. We share with them, too. Our gardeners grow food and raise herd beasts. We give freely to them when their harvest isn't enough for them. It is our responsibility to help all."

Young Titus looked around, eyeing some youths his age playing with balls, and dogs chasing them. His Mum saw this. "Do you want to go play? They're your age, son." He wanted to, but was timid, seeing how different they were. "Don't be afraid, son. You need to remember that one day you will be able to be genuinely friendly with those boys when you both are grown."

"I want to. I wish I had a brother my age," he mumbled. He kicked the dirt as he shuffled with his head down. The boys looked up at him. Each of boys' joy had radiated in their single eyes, but tempered when they noticed their prince was coming towards them.

"Hi, my name is Titus. Can I play?" he asked, his chin against his chest, expecting them to reject him.

"Why are you dressed like a dandy? You can't play in clothes like that! My sister would love your outfit," the boy holding the ball said, laughing. The others roared. The words stung Titus.

"I'm your Prince. One day I will be your ruler!" Titus held up his head, chin out.

"You? A ruler? You aren't made of wood and don't have any numbers on yah! How can you rule when you're such a pansy! Do you know about hard work? I've seen your daddy out helping my daddy when the rivers flood and the village is in danger of being wiped out. Where were you?"

"My Mum won't let me out when it's like that," Titus admitted.

"Mumma's boy! You're a mumma's boy! No mumma's boys are allowed to play with us!" the others shouted. They all laughed and moved away with their ball, tossing it among them.

Titus felt sad, and angry. Who were they to talk to him like that? He fumed to himself.

He found his parents. His dad was busy talking with some of the farmers in the town square where a stage was set up. A minstrel band was getting ready to play. His dad asked what was wrong, and Titus said he had changed his mind about playing.

As he grew up, he watched those same boys grow up, too. His Mum had reminded him kids could be cruel, but Titus refused to forgive them. He watched them struggle to farm, saw them succeed, reaping rich, green crops and strong herd beasts. He wondered if they would remember him. A dandy, him? Yeah, he might be better than them, but he would not give anything to them. The seasons had been drier lately and the crops weren't growing as well. Yet his gardeners were able to bring the water up to his vegetable rows and his own herd beasts were stronger than ever. He refused to help the poor and neither would he venture to their feast days to help them celebrate.

His parents were pathetic in their love and caring for the villagers. They said it was the agreement between them and the dragon. The dragon, always born with two hearts, gave one heart to his great grandfather many ages back and the shared blood of the dragon, a different one, shared a heart with a mere human royal in the Kingdom of Kent. Peace reigned in the land, but it was going to end. Titus lusted after more land. He wanted to expand his kingdom. After all, the Arimaspians were supreme in height and strength, and their large single eyes saw more than the humans' two small eyes.

"What funny species humans are, always looking after those weaker than them. Let the weak take care of the weak. My parents bought into the dragon's jargon of peace. Keeping the peace isn't the way. War! Land, riches! There is never enough to go around," Titus roared out loud. One of his attendants heard him and poked his head in.

"Did you say something, Sire?" he asked, not sure if it was his place. King Titus was seldom in a good mood.

"I am just talking out loud, Kelvan. Just thinking it is time to renew our attack on that mountain. Have you heard back from the miners? Surely, they must have more findings to bring to me," he rubbed his hands together.

"No, Sire, no news from the miners. When we hear, we will let you know."

\*\*\*

Away in the Wizard's chamber, Seabon stirred his stew pot over the fire. He moved over to his spell books, herbs, incense and beakers, wondering what to do. It had been two long years. He worried about Princess Jaden, and he wanted more than anything to stop the advancing of his king's army against the Kent. He stroked his square chin.

Connor landed on his staff, which was inside a slender box made to hold it at the end of the table.

"You have a message, Seabon," the bird said in a noble tone. "The boy from the World called Nampa has returned with the pure white griffin. A myth is about to come to pass. Peace must come once more to the land. Titus needs to journey within before he can go beyond. Albagoth sent me back to our world to guide the noble traveler. Do you stand with the dragon of Kent? Or do you stand with your king?"

Seabon paused, considering the words of the bird. "You are not of this world any more than the stranger from the World of Nampa. How do you know?"

"I come from a place filled with wisdom, libraries of everyone's soul knowledge, showing the way to those who want to discover it, and where the Crows hold court. You are to choose."

"I cannot give my answer. I need time to see. I must look into the scrying stone." He went to check his stew; his stomach rumbled.

"You have seven days. The Traveler is ill. Astral cares for him. You must not share any of this with your king."

"The king's spies are everywhere, Connor. You know this as well as I do." Seabon went to his stew pot and stirred it again, tasting it. "My dinner is done. Come back in seven days and I will give you an answer."

"It is so," Connor fluttered his wings, gave a small bow and flew out the window he came in.

\*\*\*

Astral strolled over, stood up on his hind legs, put a front left paw against Xander's cheek for a few seconds, and moved it to his forehead.

"My mom used to do that when I was sick," Xander said. "You're checking my temperature, aren't you? You see colors, shapes and hear thoughts. Do you understand dreams?"

"Yes, on all you said. Dreams are symbols of the unconscious. Though there are times the dream is actually part of the soul going to another place to receive a message, like a vision quest. You were gone for a while, but are back." Astral got down, called one of his nurses to him, and asked him to check the leaves and herbal pack on back of the teen's head.

The wound looked better. Astral was pleased. "Are you thirsty? You're probably hungry, too. Jephra, go see what my mate has prepared for breakfast."

"Yes, Healer," Jephra, the minotaur nurse, smiled

The dwelling was made of strong wood, so Xander knew they had trees nearby. It smelled of incense and sickness, like a hospital. He glanced around from where he lay, wondering if there were more people. Someone called Astral's name from the doorway, and the healer walked away. Xander decided to sit up to try to see who it was. It was Geoffrey, who stood about the same height as Astral.

The white griffin came in with the nurse walking beside him carrying a bowl of something and a glass made of pottery. "We have some very good tuber soup and a cool glass of mint tea."

"Smells good," Xander said. "How long was I out?"

"About six hours. Grandsire says you were muttering something about an echo that didn't repeat your words." His tone was good natured. "I'm glad you're awake."

The nurse put the bowl and glass on a side table, "How are you feeling, Indigo?" she asked. Xander was struck by the nurse having human hands, hooves and the face of a bull, except she didn't have a ring in her nose. The colors around her were soft greens, and pastels, and the thoughts-in-picture-form were of picking more herbs, vegetables and tubers. "I'm fine" he responded. "You're a minotaur? I thought all minotaurs were mean and angry."

The minotaur giggled, "My son, Donnair, writes poetry, plays the lyre and is Prince Tayson's minstrel. My name is Bonnie, by the way. We have a mix of human and animal instincts. In human myth, likely from your world, we are monsters. But here, we are raised to be spiritual, healers and look for ways to leave our world better. Don't you aspire to the same?"

Xander accepted the bowl of soup. The soup was good. It had large potatoes, or tubers, orange colored slices, like carrots, and other large pieces of meat with spices that he'd never had before.

"Some of us in my world do," he told her, "but not all. But you have a concern for a one-eyed monster, or someone who is considered a monster. His daughter is lost. Can't we find her?"

A few minutes went by while he waited for the minotaur to speak. Xander sensed that his words had made her uncomfortable. Astral and another griffin, slightly smaller, with the eagle feathers on her head graying, came in.

"You speak of King Titus, the Arimaspian ruler. Some whisper about him being a monster, but we are careful so the Crow Judge doesn't hear. Though he can read thoughts. Indigo Child, this is my mate, Syria," Astral added. She's the one who oversees the cooks and the hunters."

Syria bowed slightly. "It's rumored that you are the one who will end the war the Arimaspians have started. Connor will guide you and Geoffrey directly. You're special, Indigo Traveler. You aren't like the other travelers who stumble through here. I'm honored to be in your presence."

Xander almost choked on the soup, not wanting to believe his ears. "I'm not the one to look to," he stammered. "I'm just a kid from planet Earth. I know nothing about any of that. Before we came here, I was seeing a girl who was supposed to have only one eye, but her face seemed to have a deformity. She said she was waiting for me." Xander looked from one griffin to the next to the third, and then looked up to the minotaur, hoping to see recognition on their faces. "You don't know what I'm talking about?" He saw question marks over their heads.

Geoffrey shook his eagle head, his beak turning up, "Actually, we're baffled that you saw a vision of her. But you and I saw her on the way here. She and a Criatia offshoot followed us here."

Xander shook his head. Images swam around his mind with the words but didn't connect. He remembered Butch throwing him against the chair in the library, and sliding toward a wall. He remembered sleeping throughout his morning classes at school and vaguely remembered walking out of the building. Geoffrey and a very tall crow had been standing across the road in front of the church. They were on a corner, perhaps. The images of flying through a wormhole brought back the nausea he had felt after they landed. "What is this world called? How did this young girl know to follow us? Where is she?"

"This is Curá," Astral said, cocking his head as he walked closer. "You're not looking too good. Images from your world and here are confusing you." He turned around to the others, "We'd better leave and allow the Indigo One to rest." As they left, Xander heard a young girl outside asking in a hushed voice if she could come in. Astral told her to wait.

***

*I don't know why I'm here,* Xander thought to himself. *My parents are likely worried sick about me. But I can't go home. Butch wants me dead, and Sarah and Kimber probably won't talk to me again. I must have looked weak to them because I didn't fight back. And Mr. Adderson might've lost his job because I revealed his secrets in front of everyone.*

He worried about what to do or how he was supposed to do what they said he was supposed to do. *I'm just a kid. I'm no one special.* His mind flashed back to the dream of a crow with curly white feathers on his head like an old-fashioned judge's wig. *What did he say? I can't remember it all.*

"It will come back to you when the time is right," Connor answered his thoughts, revealing himself. "Be sure to drink the tea. It was brewed with medicine that will assist you to heal faster. Albagoth wants you to travel within two days to the Kingdom of Kent."

"You've been here the whole time, haven't you?" Xander observed, seeing something knowing in the crow's deep onyx eyes.

"It is my role to observe all of the people and animals in this world to make sure all are obeying the rules and laws," Connor said, sending an image of him smiling because his beak wasn't flexible like the griffins of this village.

71

"But I was told you were to be my teacher and guide, or something like that." Xander coughed at the last words. He reached for the glass of tea. It tasted like mint, honey, and something like ginseng. His words echoed back in his mind, making him wonder how he knew that.

Connor paced a bit, cocking his head from one side to the other, considering what to say. Xander finished his tea, placed his cup on the side table and settled in a bit. His head didn't feel as bad as it had when he first woke up.

"I know that is what my superior on the Crow Court has told you and what the Creator has imparted to me, too, as I meditated," Connor said, "but I don't know all of what you need. I will ask Astral to assist in your training." He paused, and looked straight at Xander, who knew he was looking at his thoughts and soul.

Xander closed his eyes. "What do you see?" he asked.

"I can see aspects of your soul," the Crow Judge told him. "A division of sorts. I only see part of your life's plan. I'm not privy to the full knowledge. I see that you feel excluded from humans in your age group, and are not sure how to relate to them. I see symbols above you, and you are surrounded by deep purple, gold, silver and some lime green. The green is the sign of a healer, yet this part of you hasn't been awakened yet. I also see many questions within the deep purple colors as well as a few small streaks of red, which means you are angry and unsure."

Connor's thoughts faded from Xander's mind. It was as if there was a cloud over him. Xander felt a presence of love, and deep connection, but it was as if the Crow Judge was behind a closed door. He could not know that Connor was asking for Albagoth's help and blessing.

*What does he need to learn?* Connor was asking the Creator. *Show me.*

Albagoth responded to the Crow Healer's question. *Teach him how to shield himself, how to receive information and distinguish when to tell the person and when to keep it to himself. Show him how to fight. Prince Tayson can be the one to teach him that. The rest of his questions surrounding who he is as an Indigo Child will be for him to find on his own. When needed, give him the space to explore with the princess and the plant boy.*

"Who are you communicating with?" Xander asked as Connor came out of his private thoughts. "I'm not used to being blocked from hearing another's thoughts like that."

"I know how to shield myself. I was talking with Albagoth."

The teen nodded, considering his words. Feeling a sting, he frowned. "Why can't I talk with this Albagoth? Why are you so close to it and I can't be?" His eyes narrowed as his face set.

Connor walked closer to his cot and extended a wing, "You haven't forged the relationship with the Creator. You spend your time blaming the Spirit for all your troubles instead of seeing the good within and without you. I, on the other hand, because of my role as Crow Judge and unseen disciplinarian of Curá, need to work very closely with the Spirit of Albagoth."

"So, this Creator of your world also created my world?" Xander's tone was mixed with accusation, awe and confusion.

"Yes, he did, and many other worlds, too." Connor's tone was loving and kind. "Aren't you all taught about this Spirit?"

"On my world, there are very many different religions. My mom calls them faiths, and they all say they are right, condemning the ones that don't agree with them. My mom says they all have a commonality, and all lead to Spirit. But she and others don't include other planets or dimensions, such as this world. Most say their god is the same as they are. I think that would make god a human if he had the same likes and dislikes as they do."

Xander scratched his temple, then adjusted his blankets, longing to get out of bed and walk around. "What do you teach the people here? I mean, there are animals that talk, reason, and are accepted with equality here, and different races of people. I even sense that plant life may be able to reason. Surely, if your Albagoth could design and bring to life such a world as that, he could do the same on my world."

Connor smiled, nodding his head. "The bird life also reason and think, but they don't speak the same language as we do here. Your thoughts are well formed. I suspect there are few in your world who are of similar thoughts?"

"No, if I said any of this to my so-called friends, I'd be called crazy and condemned to hell. My dad would be uncomfortable, too, and my mom may consider my words, but she wouldn't know how to answer." He looked out the doorway. "Could I get out of bed? I want to stretch my legs."

"I will alert Astral. I have to make my rounds and will return later." Connor gave a short jump into the air as he flapped his wings and turned invisible at the doorway.

Astral and a different minotaur nurse came in, one who was about Xander's height, dressed in a simple tunic made from hemp or cotton, Xander guessed. Her feet were human, though they had a hoof type toe, and she wore sandals.

"I understand you want to stand up for a bit. Samantha will help you. You may want to relieve your bladder, too," he added. Xander put his legs over the cot as the nurse stepped up to help him. She was tiny, but had soft brown eyes, and a small mouth. Her face, while still bovine shaped, was also smaller, her hand dainty, with nails painted a yellow with golden sun images.

"Don't move too fast," she cautioned, her voice soft and comforting.

"I'm fine. I can move without your help," he barked, placing his feet down on the soft dirt floor, standing up and taking a step. He nearly collapsed. Samantha giggled.

"You aren't as sure of yourself now, Indigo One, are you?" Her lips turned up. "Now maybe you'll let me help you some? I'll hold your elbow. As soon as you're steady, I'll let you go."

"Yeah, I guess that would be okay," he replied, admitting defeat.

"The day orb is bright today," she told him.

He blinked and squinted. The shack didn't have a lot of windows. Though the orb did feel warm and comforting.

"Back home, we call the day star a sun."

"We also have a night orb. What do you call your night orb? Is it a star, too?"

"We call it a moon and it orbits our planet." Xander looked around the village. It looked primitive, like something he would see in Africa back home, where people still lived in tribal units. There were groups of female minotaurs tending cooking kettles, which were hung from triangular wooden posts over a fire. Other groups of women were pounding what looked like cornmeal or wheat into a powder to make bread. The younger minotaurs and griffins were playing games, while an older group was gathering wood, herbs, and vegetables from a garden area. Xander was surprised to see the hustle and bustle.

"What about school? Don't your young learn social science or other stuff?" he asked.

"Yes, when we are old enough to sit, listen and discuss we learn what is expected of us. We learned how Albagoth created all the worlds and the rules and laws to live by. We learn to respect the Crow Judge's appointment as our guardian to make sure all is abided by. Healer Astral teaches us for the most part. We spend a year with him learning all this. Afterward, we choose what our task will be for the village or, if we are chosen, go train with the human kingdom of Kent. If we are chosen, we are taught the dragon's additional laws. We are taught to respect all we meet, whether plant life, human life, griffin, Arimaspian or gryphon. They are the cousins of the griffins here, but look different. They have a full eagle body, except for the torso and hind legs of the lion. They also have mighty wings."

"I see," he muttered, trying to organize all she said. He spotted a girl, about the size of a ten-year-old human child but seeming quite young, with a couple of young griffins and minotaurs. There was also a strange plant creature with them, who appeared to be impatiently tapping one group of roots.

"What do you see?" Samantha asked, looking puzzled.

"I mean I understand. That's a lot of information to remember, Samantha. May I call you Sam for short?"

"I'm not short!" she huffed. "I'm as tall as you, though I've heard you're still growing."

Xander backed away, seeing her energy emit what looked like steam from her nostrils. "I'm sorry. In my world, we break a name up into a nickname or shorten it so it's easier to remember. My name is Alexander, but my mom wanted me called Xander instead of Alex. I think it's a British nickname."

"Oh, I see." Sam's face flushed a bit. "Um, what's British?"

"It is a country in my world. I guess it could be considered a different world, because their culture is so different than where we live."

"Your world is called Nampa. Is it a big place?"

"Not really. I guess it may seem like it, though." The little girl turned around, Xander could see her large round eye in the center of her forehead and the smaller eye on the side of her face. It was closed, but started fluttered a bit. She fell back on her heels, and then got her balance and began pointing at him excitedly.

"Who is that girl pointing at me? She's dressed different than the minotaur children and she isn't a minotaur."

"That's Princess Jaden, of the Arimaspian kingdom. Her father turned her out because she can see and talk to the Crow Judge. He blames her and the Crow Judge for the gryphons taking his son, his heir to the throne. She wants to talk with you. Do you want to see her? Are you strong enough? Maybe we need to find a place for you to sit down." Sam led him to a large boulder and helped him sit. "How are you feeling?"

"A bit shaky, but I think I'll recover. Um...." He looked at his clothes, just noticing he wasn't wearing his jeans from the other day. Instead he had on trousers made of some kind of rough plant fibers that were a tan color like hemp. They felt rough, but were also kind of comfortable. "What happened to my t-shirt and jeans?"

"Dames Syria and Crystal took them down to the wash ladies. They smelled like smoke and ash. Geoffrey had to bathe, too. When your head wound heals, we'll take you there, too. Are you still hungry? We have some luscious fruits that are in season." Jaden ran up to them, curtsying. "May I speak with the traveler?" she asked politely, looking up from her curtsy.

"Princess, you don't have to do that to me or to the traveler." Sam smiled, patting her on the shoulder, and then offering to help her sit.

"I'm Jaden, Traveler. I'm glad you're feeling better. Humans from your world are puny compared to humans here." She smiled. Xander was taken aback by her observation, not knowing if he should be offended by it or chalk it up to a child speaking her thoughts without thinking.

"What do humans here on Curá look like? I haven't met any yet. But know I'll be meeting Prince Tayson soon," he answered her. Crossing his eyes and centering himself, he looked above the young Princess to see her colors. They were rich in gold, purples, and amber mixed with pinks and soft green. He saw that her thoughts were about trying to see into him, too. She scrutinized him at the same time. Suddenly, her second eye flew open, revealing a startling purple eye, and it frightened him.

"You scan without permission, stealing information not freely given! Shield yourself, Indigo Traveler! Shield yourself! Must learn proper methods, ethics, and not take without permission!" She blurted out. Her tone changed from a childlike innocence to sounding older than her young years. The eye closed. Jaden bowed her head. Her main eye closed as she exhaled. She raised her chin up and smiled. Her words hit Xander as if she had struck him with an iron skillet.

"You are a student. The master teacher will come to lead you. Cranny must take you to the pond that shows the inside, what you cannot see for yourself. I've been waiting and looking for you for two years. You can stop my Father, make him take me back. Make him love me." She paused, trembling, as tears began to well up to her eye, spilling over the lower lid.

"You're not an Indigo Child, but you are a seer," Xander told her. "Your father is afraid of you 'cause you see into his heart. I don't know if I can make him take you back." He paused, staring at the ground. "I'm sorry, Jaden, for looking at your energy field without asking. It's a habit I've had since I was a youngster. I do it without effort, yet do it on purpose." He paused again. "Um, who's Cranny? And what is a cranny?"

A plant creature made his way up. He had been standing in the background, listening, trying his best to wait patiently even though he was obviously excited about talking to this new traveler.

Cranny smiled, showing his seed teeth, though one was turning black with tiny white spots and was now larger than the others. "I am Cranny, Traveler. I am pleased to meet you. An offshoot in my garden's pod told me to wait for you."

Xander saw without effort that it wasn't really an offshoot, but Connor who had spoken to him. "Cranny, you can't see the Crow Judge, can you?" he asked.

"No, no one can see the Crow Judge unless they are in trouble. I only get in trouble with my garden's elders because I don't listen too well." He drooped one of his limbs so that it almost touched the ground. "I'm not supposed to talk to strangers who end up here. Unlike you, many of the travelers who come through don't know how they got here. They usually disappear and no one knows how they do that." He pressed his lips together. "Do you know where they go?"

The teen from the world called Nampa smiled, leaning back on the boulder. He guessed the plant creature was about the age of a three or four-year-old on his world. He was amazed by the creature's ability to talk, think and consider. "I'm guessing they go back to where they came from. They likely come here to learn lessons or something." He looked around, noticing there weren't any white griffins, except one. "Where's Geoffrey?"

"He's with his sire and dame, tending to his younger siblings. He will be over when he's dismissed. He knows you two will be traveling to other areas here on Curá as soon as Healer Astral says you are strong enough to go." A bell rang out. "Evening meal is ready. Come, you will meet the rest of the village."

# Chapter 8

Two days later, Geoffrey and Samantha came into the healer's shack with Xander's clean jeans and t-shirt. It was early in the morning, but Xander still felt tired. He was unsure what to do with himself.

"After you get dressed, we will meet with my Grandsire out by the community fire. He said something about Connor meeting up with us, and Jaden and Cranny will be accompanying us as well."

Xander sat up, threw his legs over the edge, took the jeans from Sam, and put them on. She gave him the t-shirt, and he pulled it over his head. His own clothes felt good to him, like having an old baby blanket for comfort.

"Now, where are my shoes?" he asked, looking around. Geoffrey and Sam looked at each other. He noticed she wore sandals that were simply made. He squatted down, looked under the cot and saw his shoes. He pulled them out, grinning. "These were on my feet."

"What're they made from?" Sammy asked. "We've never seen material like that." She bent down to sit on the floor in front of him, watching as he slipped them on and stuffed the laces under the tongue of each shoe.

"Canvas and rubber. Canvas is made from a plant, I think, and rubber is processed somehow. Though there is a rubber plant that grows somewhere on my world." He stood up and his stomach rumbled. "Is there anything for breakfast?"

"Yes, follow us," Sam and Geoffrey said. Xander helped the female minotaur up, and they walked out of the tent. As he followed them he thought of walking exactly like they did. When he'd been in elementary school, they played followed the leader, copying the leader's every move. He smiled, but suppressed the impulse to do it.

Cranny, Jaden, Astral, his mate and Geoffrey's sire and dame were gathered around the community center, which had a central fireplace surrounded with rocks and stone benches for the minotaurs or human guests to sit, with gaps for the griffins to be next to them. While they found seats, Geoffrey's sire asked Xander to accompany him to the stage. A few other villagers gathered to listen to them. They were served some hot porridge with spices, butter and eggs mixed in.

"We gather this morning to bid farewell to one of our own, Prince Geoffrey, his new human protectee and two village guests, Princess Jaden and Cranny, the Criatia." Cranny, who was off to the side where he could dig his roots deep into the soil, waved a limb as those gathered looked at him. Geoffrey's sire continued, "We wish them well. Our healer, my sire, will be traveling with them since the Indigo Traveler will be his new initiate into the art of seeing spiritually and understanding his place within the Worlds he is called to visit."

Xander sat back, paused in his eating, and considered. He hadn't realized Astral was going with them, yet vaguely remembered that the healer was supposed to train him to learn more about shielding himself so that he wouldn't pick up other's thoughts so easily.

"After they all finish their morning meal, they will be leaving."

Xander swayed, his eyes closed involuntarily as he felt something or someone call to him. He felt a tug on his inner spirit that became more like the entity was yanking him out of the confines of the physical body.

*I summon you, Indigo One, to come to me. I have a blade with a story behind it. Heal the divisions in this world, Indigo One. Come to me to learn more.*

The voice sounded very distant, as if it spoke through a tube. He couldn't see an image with it until the very last: a blade, long, sharpened edges surrounded by white, with red streaks toward the middle. The sensation of something hot and moist brought him out. Xander opened his eyes to see Geoffrey staring at him with concern.

"Are you okay? You don't look too well," the griffin whispered. Xander nodded, blinking his eyes and rubbing them. His mind wandered to the vision, longing to know who had talked to him. He felt a pang in his gut say a dragon, but he dismissed it. Dragons couldn't be real. Then, again, maybe they were, because griffins were real.

***

The travelers had been on the road for two hours and were far from the village. Xander had packed Geoffrey's armor in a large sack with some spare clothing the minotaur ladies had given him. They acted very motherly toward Xander, concerned for his health and welfare.

"Now, when you meet Prince Tayson, remember to bow. Follow Geoffrey's lead. Be sure to remember your manners. You do know what those are, right?" Dame Syria said. The other minotaur ladies nodded in agreement. Xander rolled his eyes, saying he did.

"You young people are all alike, no matter if you are plant, human, Arimaspian, griffin some other being."

"Yeah, I suppose so. I know: Don't roll my eyes; it isn't polite or respectful."

Xander thought there wasn't much to see on their journey since the land was mostly flat and boring. No small towns or rest areas or historical sites. He wondered why they weren't flying, since it would be faster. He didn't know where they were heading first.

Astral gave him a slight grin. "Cranny wouldn't be able to sit on me. His needles would be too painful for my old back; Criatias need to have their roots touching the ground or they wither and dry out."

"Oh. Um – how did you know what I was thinking?"

"I can see the images and hear the words through mind speak. Most healer griffins are trained to tune in when needed. Geoffrey, though, being the rare white griffin, comes to it naturally. I had to start training him at two or three months when he began repeating and answering thoughts. I've also needed to teach him to shield himself because he would start to take on another's feelings, thinking they were his own."

Xander thought a moment, "I've done that, too, I think. When I was younger, I used to call the other kids freak and say they were scared of me because I heard their thoughts so loud in my mind, I thought they were my own. One day, a boy asked me how I knew what he was thinking. I couldn't answer him. I just had to say the words were so loud I thought they were mine; except he really didn't scare me and I didn't think he was a freak. I realized those were his reactions to me. What was I supposed to do?"

"We will have our first lesson when we get to the Reflection Pond," Astral answered, glancing at the others the party with them. He looked back at Jaden, who was lagging a bit. "Would you like Geoffrey or me to carry you for a while, Jaden?"

"Yeah, my feet and legs hurt. I'm hungry, too." She rubbed her eye and the side of her face without the second eye.

"I have some dried meats and tubers," Xander offered, pulling the pack to his side so he could reach in to get some of the snacks. "I could use something, too. Anyone else?"

The others shook their heads 'no'. Xander gave Jaden a piece of the dried meat and a couple dried tubers, which were like potato chips, except they were larger, flat and had different herbal seasonings on them. Geoffrey paused to let the little girl climb on his back.

"We should be near the first rest stop soon," Astral said.

Xander wondered when Connor would be joining them. His thoughts wandered to home, hoping his parents weren't worried about him. He missed Kimber and Sarah, too, and hoped they weren't worried. Butch he could do without. Though he was curious what would happen once he got back home without Geoffrey. What would the bully do then?

"Time will reveal all things, Indigo One," Astral whispered for his ears only.

\*\*\*

Connor flew over Kent Castle towards the cave of the dragon. He saw the mighty Manitor stretched out under the day orb's noon warmth. The golden light accented the dragon's green, violet and red plates, and his tail was wrapped around his forty or fifty-foot body so that Connor couldn't tell exactly how long he was. The Crow Judge smiled, grateful for his ability to grow big enough to look into Manitor's huge blue and gold eyes or to shrink to the size of the crows in the World called Nampa.

He felt a ping in his gullet that reminded him of the reason he was visiting Manitor. As he neared, he saw the mighty dragon lift his head, squinting into the day orb's light.

Manitor stood, stretching his body and flexing his wings as he readied himself to meet his special guest. He greeted the Crow Judge with a friendly roar as he landed on the ledge. "Welcome, Honorable Connor. What brings you to my humble abode?"

"Greetings, brother Manitor. I have sensed the vision you sent to the young Indigo Traveler. He is not aware of who sent it to him. I wanted to make sure you know exactly where all the blades are that will be made into one sword." He raised his voice in a question.

"Aye, I know very well where they all are. I have my ancestor's main blood-soaked blade within my possession and the other two are scattered. The Indigo youth.... He is not a child anymore, Connor. It is called adolescence in his world as well as among the human community here. Yet he needs the scrolls that tell the story of the way the two kingdoms were before my ancestors shared the hearts and before the crows were lifted to the esteemed position of judges over our realm of Curá."

"I am aware of that." Connor's left wing twitched. "Who has the scrolls? Are they in King Tonyar's possession?"

Manitor cocked his head, blinking. "Hmm, it seems to me you should know this. Aren't you supposed to know all about everything on this world? Perhaps you need to speak to your Superior Judge back in the other realm."

Connor felt a bit uncomfortable with Manitor's words and tone. For once, he wasn't sure how to answer the mighty dragon, who was at least a century older than him. Something sparkling caught his eye and he glanced off in that direction as he considered exactly what to say.

"I don't know everything, Manitor. Albagoth put limits on all of us. In most activities of Curá, I know what's important or am given a vision of what I need to know. The most important task at hand is for me to know where that scroll is." Connor paused as the glittering particle moved to away from him. For a brief moment, the sky opened up and he felt Albagoth touch his mind, quieting his inner distress about what to do. He was shown a cavern deep in the underground away from where Titus was digging. For a moment, he saw where he had to go to get the information. Another soft but intense touch of his heart and gullet let him know he wasn't to retrieve it, but had to lead Xander there somehow.

Connor's vision and conversation with his main boss were suddenly interrupted as Manitor lifted his large muzzle and put it as close to Connor's eyes as he could.

"You have that faraway look, Connor. Come back before I lose you." The old dragon told him.

A white inner lid from under each eyebrow came down over each of Connor's onyx eyes. Then he looked at the dragon, and jumped back, a bit startled. "I was just conversing with my boss," he said in a low voice, "I was shown what I needed to know." Human voices rose up from down the mountainside. Connor turned his body halfway to see what was going on. "Do you ever go down to converse with King Tonyar?"

Manitor nodded his head, lifting himself up. "When I need to. Mostly his wizard talks with me. He's concerned about the ceasefire not lasting. He worries that the Arimaspians will be renewing their attack soon. He says their wizard has sent messenger pigeons to him relaying the plans. I worry the Indigo Traveler will not be ready to assist us when the time comes. My brother with the gryphons says Kontar is getting restless. He wants to help his dad, but he's also fully aware of the agreement with my ancestors. Part of the young prince is worried that his own heart will fail if his dad will not abandon his quest for more land and riches."

"In four days, I'll be going back to speak to the Arimaspian wizard to see where he stands." Down below, Connor could see the humans and villagers hurriedly planning something. He was concerned. "I'd better go down and see what's happening." He turned to the overgrown reptile. "I'll be in touch with you as soon as I can." He bowed his upper body in honor to the mighty dragon.

"I wait to meet the traveler," the dragon replied, bowing his head in return. As Connor flew off, he turned his long body around and went into his cave.

\* \* \*

Prince Tayson, his knights and several servants were gathering in the village square arguing over the price of goods and the tools being forged by the blacksmith. Connor saw, to his amazement, that a new blacksmith was working, and that he was the cause for the concern. The blacksmith was accused of forging new weapons and selling them to the Arimaspian representatives.

Invisible, Connor got close enough to Prince Tayson's ear to inquire, "How do you know he's doing what he's being accused of?" Tayson, a slender youth in his late teens, with a narrow face, small nose and high cheek bones, glanced at Marcus.

"Did you ask me how we know?"

The knight shook his head. "No, Sire, it wasn't me. Though I heard the same question. Perhaps we need to ask those who are arguing to show us the proof." Tayson, who usually tried to do the right thing, yet at times jumped to conclusions without enough evidence, considered it.

"Yes, I think I shall. If I do not come to the right decision, my father will be upset with me, and if I make matters worse after that the Crow Judge will make himself known." He pressed his thin lips together and stretched them out in thought.

"Quiet everyone. One at a time. I need to know who saw what and if anyone actually saw an Arimaspian here in this village," he shouted, and everyone settled down.

The new blacksmith, who was in the middle of the village square, with Prince Tayson across from him and all the others around him, put his tongs down. "If I may, your highness, I have not done anything wrong. I'm just making a living for meself and me family. I make swords and such. I am not doing anything treasonous like selling to the enemy." He glanced nervously around him. "I sell to those who have the money, or cattle or something of value to trade. I sell to humans, not those overgrown one-eyed freaks!"

Prince Tayson crossed his arms over his chest, "Hmm, okay. But you aren't selling these weapons to my men or anyone on our staff. I oversee those in charge of designing and building new swords and fighting equipment. We contract with the Alchemist blacksmith over yonder. You are a new face."

"I've not been here long. I do not know who the men are who come to me. I don't question how they will use the tools they want me to make. I just do as I'm told."

"That isn't good enough. You see, we're in a war. Even though it is currently a ceasefire, we are all on our high guard. You will keep a record of who comes and goes. If you do not, and we find proof of these accusations, we will drag you before my father, King Tonyar. Is that clear?"

The blacksmith shuffled from one foot to the other, rubbed a soot-covered hand over his already black streaked face. A pained expression crossed his face, "Yes, Sire. Except, I do not read or write."

"I see." Prince Tayson looked around, "Does anyone here know how to read or write? Is there anyone who can work with our new blacksmith?" A young villager about fourteen raised his hand, as did some other youths. "Okay, then, you two, come forward and consult with the blacksmith. Everyone else, go back to your duties. I have other matters to attend to."

The crowd broke up. Connor flew beside the young prince as he walked with the four knights and a servant, listening to their words.

"I hear that there is a new traveler in the village of the griffins. I hear he has your old griffin that abandoned his post. What do you make of this?" asked the servant.

"I make out that he will be a warrior like no other. My wizard advised me that he would be able to read the unseen thoughts and energies around all living creatures. I'm supposed to teach him to battle with sword or have my best swordsman teach him. Tell me, where did you hear this?"

"A minotaur traveling through with wares from the village stopped me the other day. He usually travels with other humans. I was just wondering if you knew any of this. The minotaur said he came in hurt. It was said he was injured in his world before the griffin brought him back."

Tayson looked at his servant more closely. "I wouldn't believe all you hear, Casper. I've seen some of the strange travelers that end up here. None can say how they got here. And this traveler is supposed to be different than them? The others never meddled in our affairs, so what gives this one the right to meddle in them? If he came here specifically to solve our problems, then he'd better turn around and go back to his own world!"

The prince quickened his step, leaving the servant far behind. The knights stared at Casper harshly, as if demanding to know why he had to be so difficult and upset their prince. They quickened their pace, too.

Connor wasn't pleased with the young prince's reaction. He landed, realized he was still larger than he needed to be, and shrank to the height of the prince. Looking into his mind, he anticipated where he was going— his chambers— and met him there.

Prince Tayson took off his shirt, still mulling over the villagers accusing the new blacksmith of treason and the words of his servant. He vaguely remembered seeing some Arimaspians coming through town, hauling carts as if they were selling wares. He didn't trust them anymore. Not like he used to. He wished he had the abilities of his wizard, Sylvester, so he could see into their minds to find out why they were here in Kent. If it was to spy or ask others to make weapons for their side, then someone had to answer for the treason. His thoughts went to his first griffin coming back. And the griffin was bringing a so-called Indigo kid who was supposed to be a hero! Tayson didn't believe that.

Connor lifted his head up in challenge, choosing to reveal himself to the young prince, "Tell me, young prince, what is keeping you from defeating the King?"

Tayson jumped, turning toward him. "You.... You're the one who spoke to me in the crowd asking for evidence! You're that Crow Judge! Why haven't you stopped King Titus's raids on our land? He's destroying mountains! Ripping up the beautiful green grass, digging for Creator knows what!" He threw his shirt halfway across the room.

"I cannot interfere until he takes a life. The Crow Court has already acted, removing his eldest heir. That hasn't stopped him. It is up to you, Tayson, to stop him. And yet you haven't. You chose a rare white griffin to be your protector, did you not, knowing the myth about the white griffin?"

"Yeah, but I don't believe in myths!" Tayson glared at the black crow. "You're supposed to be a myth, too! What is it you want?"

"I want to remind you of the legend of the white griffin. Humor me, Tayson. When you were young, we played together. Now you're almost a man, you're angry at me. I cannot force Titus to stop his crimes against the Dragon's agreement with him, this kingdom and the Spiritual Laws of the Creator. Tell me the legend now, please." Connor's tone was even, peaceful. Tayson relaxed a bit, remembering when he was young and the Crow Judge came to visit. He smiled.

"I thought it was a childish memory that was part of my make-believe," he sighed. "But you were real all this time?" He softened, looking with recognition at his visitor. Moving his head to one side, he considered. "The white griffin is supposed to bring peace. He's also supposed to travel to a land far from Curá and bring back a stranger who has the sight and knowledge of a wizard or healer." He looked out the window of his chamber, watched the golden finches flit from one branch to another on the shrubs, flapping their wings and chirping. He smiled, exhaling. "I chose Geoffrey because he was white, beautiful and I wanted to ride on a beast that would amaze and awe the enemy. I was sure they would be so spellbound by his height, color and all, that he would paralyze them from attacking us. I didn't even consider the meaning behind his color."

"And that is the reason he left you," Connor replied.

"And you still punished him, though for leaving without telling me?"

"I had to obey what the Crow Court and the Creator dictated. It was for that reason that the Indigo Traveler is here. And you don't want him here, do you?"

"I want to be able to solve my own problems without help from outsiders!"

"You make yourself an outsider by your thoughts, Tayson. The Indigo One is not used to the rules here. Agree to work with him or decide to work against him. The choice is yours." Connor left through the open window.

Tayson threw his shirt at the wall. He wanted to rule his life and his own kingdom without the Crow Judge giving him words of advice or direction. After all, wasn't he supposed to have free will? A knock came to his door, and a servant came in. She bowed. "Your highness, your father requests your presence in the council chambers."

Tayson nodded so she would know he'd heard. "I'll be right there." He turned away, crossing to his wardrobe for a clean tunic.

# Chapter 9

Xander's thoughts wandered to his home. He missed his mom, often imagining she was calling for him, asking where he was and if he was okay. He also had dreams of his cat, Clarence, informing him of the day's activities.

*Today my staff sat in front of that thing with the bright light where pictures and squiggling lines appear. She pressed those buttons very fast. I could tell she was crying again. She misses you. Her mate was upset, too, blaming himself for working so hard. Two of your friends, of the female kind, came by the house to talk the other day. No one from the place you go to every morning knows how you left without anyone seeing you. I heard someone was blamed for it, but the name didn't register with me. I got a picture of a boy with scowl always yelling at you and taking your things. He pushes you around. Master, you need to come home. I can't go to where you are,* Clarence advised, *I can't protect you when you aren't with me.*

Xander remembered waking from the dream, happy, yet sad. He wished he could communicate with his cat. He wasn't sure how to reach him. He made a mental note to ask Astral when he got a chance.

Something brushed lightly against his cheeks, bringing him out of his own thoughts. He looked around to see that Geoffrey was way ahead, Jaden still riding on his back. His own legs felt heavy and his feet hurt. *We've been traveling for almost a day and half,* he thought. They'd stopped several times to eat, rest and sleep, but it was taking longer than he'd anticipated.

Cranny moved up to him. "Mind if I walk beside you? I'm walking all alone back here."

"Sure. You just walk too slow." Xander grinned. "I thought you were up with Jaden and Geoffrey."

Cranny glanced up at the traveler from the other world. "We haven't had much time to talk."

"Do you miss your people, Cranny? You've been gone longer from your people than I have mine."

"Nah, I haven't been gone that long— maybe a week. I'm old enough to travel where I want. I could even find another Criatia to cross-pollinate with if I wanted to." Cranny smiled, winking, "if you get my drift."

Xander blushed. "Um, I don't think you're old enough for that. Your seeds are still white. I'm guessing they turn black with white spots when they are considered adult teeth – I mean seeds. Don't your kind have flowers that bloom?"

He really didn't know what he was talking about, but he could hear his grandma's voice in his head lecturing him on being careful with girls and not doing anything to get a girl in trouble. She'd said he was too young to be a dad. Remembering her words only made him angry again, even though that lecture had taken place three years ago when he had no interest in girls and knew no girl in her right mind would like him. A thought out of nowhere said Sarah liked him in that way, but he didn't believe it. Sarah, with her gorgeous blue-green eyes, made his heart sing.

"I don't think I'm too young." Cranny pouted. "My elders say I am, though. They don't like me going out of the garden without one of them and they're upset because I like to talk to travelers, like you." The plant boy looked up at Xander with large orange eyes, like an innocent child. Xander's heart melted.

"Your elders have your best interest in mind. I know elders can be annoying though. My own parents don't like me to leave the house without telling them where I'm going, who I'll be with and when I'll be home. It's a pain. I think I'm old enough to do what I want, too. What is it that your elders are afraid of?"

"They're afraid a traveler may think I'm food or have a store of water inside, and will cut me open and hurt me. I'm not food, nor do I have water they can use inside of me. The moisture that runs through my chambers is only for me."

"I see. On my world, we have plants called cactus that look a lot like you. They grow in the desert and people who get stranded there know some of them have water inside. We're taught which ones have flesh inside that we can eat. Some of the cacti bloom–

they have flowers that come out their limbs– and that's how they drop their seeds or pollinate. I don't know how old the plant has to be before it happens."

Cranny thought for a few minutes, considering the human teen's words. "I understand what my elders were saying. I thought they were just warning us out of fear that didn't have any reality to it." They walked awhile in silence.

The day was pleasant enough, with a slight breeze, and the sky was a mixture of colors. Cranny glanced at up at Xander. "So what do you do that your elders don't like?"

"I read minds, and sometimes I say what someone is thinking without their permission. Most of the time I don't mean to; it just pops out. I hate it." Xander frowned. "I don't even know why I have these gifts. I wish I could talk to this Albagoth to find out why I was made this way. I'm hoping I can find out."

"Maybe this world and your world need more humans like you who aren't afraid to stand up to rules that are unfair," said Cranny.

"But your world has fair rules. Or I think it does." He thought a minute. "I've heard that Jaden's dad kicked her out, though. That's unheard of in my world. It makes me angry, in fact!"

"So, can you help Jaden get her dad to take her back?" Cranny asked, hopefully.

"I'm not sure," Xander paused for a minute, considering. "Geoffrey said it had something to do with a war."

Astral landed beside them. "War? Are you talking about the war? There's been a ceasefire, but the war isn't over. King Titus wants to take as much land as he can to expand his kingdom. That is against all our spiritual and world's laws. He's also digging up ground and mining under some mountains looking for valuable stones and minerals that he believes are worth a lot. I don't understand why he wants them. Our world doesn't run on money but on trade for good. If I understand it, King Titus wants to change how we've always done things, and make some thing valuable that aren't really good for anything."

"War is bad no matter what the reason is," Xander said, shaking his head. "There has to be another way to deal with it. Who's in charge? Who can stop him?"

Astral shot Xander a look. "Well, Prince Tayson wants to, but doesn't he have enough power. His wizard is assisting. We've asked the dragon to get involved, since he knows the secrets of the Arimaspian and Kingdom of Kent's connection. But he refuses to get involved until the myth is fulfilled. The one about the Dragon blood's blade."

Xander and Cranny just stared at him, not understanding. "The blade will be surrounded by two other special blades unique to the purpose, but it is the center blade that is most important. It has to be sealed in dragon's blood. The myth talks about the one person who can wield it."

Astral's words hit Xander as if they had solid form. He wondered if he was the one who would wield this awesome sword. *No, it can't be me. I'm not from here. It has to be Prince Tayson. Maybe I can convince this prince he has to be the one to find it and use it. Surely, he knows more about combat than I do.*

Up ahead, Geoffrey and Jaden stopped, turned and looked back, "Hurry up, slow pokes! We're almost at the Reflection Pond!"

Astral looked at Xander. "If you like, you can ride on my back the rest of the way. I'm sorry," he told Cranny. "I'm afraid you'll have to walk."

"That's okay," Cranny replied. "Criatia don't get tired like humans do."

Astral lowered himself to the ground, lifting his wings up and over his head so Xander could climb up and have room for his feet. After the boy was settled, he moved his wings back in place.

"Be careful of the feathers. Don't hold them too tight. And, by all means, don't let anyone else know I let you ride me. It's a matter of pride," the healer said with a light joking tone. Xander laughed, telling him not to worry about it.

***

The air began to feel a bit moister the closer they came to the Reflection Pond. Xander noticed that there were few birds flying around, and few insects, too. The trees were off in the distance, not very close to where they were. He guessed this was like a desert. He felt a heaviness set into his chest, as the weight of everything he didn't want to think about came flooding to the front of his mind. He wondered, once again, if his parents even knew he was gone and were worried about him. He saw visions of the kids at school laughing at him, skipping around in a circle, calling him names. He wasn't sure if that had really happened, but under the heat of the day orb, it felt so real. The vision brought up a searing heat from his gut, which spread throughout his body. He wanted to lash out, yell at them for what they said. The memory switched to all the teachers, Mr. Adderson and others, and his Dad, who had told him he had to change. No one liked him the way he was and no one could ever like him. He wanted to lash out at them all.

The faces of people— Butch, unnamed children he went to school with, teachers, his dad and the various psychic readers his mom took him to— swam in front of his mind's eye, growing large and distorted, taunting him, "You're weak, Xander. You're nothing but a weakling who can't do anyone or anything a bit of good! Why even try? All you can do is guess what you see in us. How do you know it's true? What if it isn't really us you're reading? What if it's all about you? And you're saying what you don't want to see in yourself!" They all sneered at Xander. He felt like a tiny insect under their accusations. He thought maybe they were right. He remembered his grandma telling him once that other people knew him better than he knew himself. She urged him to listen to other people.

*No, Grandma! Others do not know me better than I know myself! You are the one who is wrong!* he thought back to her.

As he came out of the dream, he wondered just how well he knew himself. Sometimes he felt like he was just drifting through life, not coming to any decisions on his own. Yet he knew one thing for sure, he didn't like being able to see through people. Though it wasn't all people he met, just certain ones. Still, he wanted his Grandma to be wrong. He had to find a way to get to know himself better than others did. He welcomed the offer Connor and the healer had made to help him learn how to shield himself.

Astral shook himself and flexed his wings to stir his rider, who had fallen asleep. Unconsciously, Xander felt the probe of the griffin's mind, and woke from his dreams. He stirred, catching himself from falling. He yawned.

"What happened? Why did you shake yourself? I almost fell off."

"My back is beginning to fall asleep," Astral complained. "We're almost at the Reflection Pond. Geoffrey has been walking with us for a while."

Xander glanced over to see Jaden smiling, still perched on the white griffin, and Geoffrey smiled, too.

The breeze picked up, lifting small sand particles into the air and carrying them away to a new home. Cranny didn't have any problem with the sand since his eyes had a natural protective clear skin over them, but Xander and the others ducked their heads down, covering their eyes to keep from getting them filled with grit.

The air felt alive with electricity, or some kind of energy that Xander couldn't name. He had never felt anything like it. It was as if everything had a spirit or aliveness of its own. As the sand blew past his ears, he could hear it whispering, singing songs about freedom. It sounded like each particle was saying, "Finally, I am free to travel to another part of Curá."

The teen shook his head, deciding he was imagining sand being able to think or have self-awareness. Yet beside him was a walking, talking, plant creature that reminded him of a cactus. Maybe anything could be possible.

"It's not far now until we get to the water," Astral said, turning to Geoffrey, who walked beside them. "Xander, I'm going to stop so you can get down. My old back is going numb." He paused, Geoffrey stopped, too. They both lay down so their riders could get off.

"Can you walk the rest of the way, Princess?" the young griffin asked. "It isn't far."

"I think so." She smiled, took a deep breath, and then exhaled. She lifted her hands up to see if she could catch some of the sand blowing past. "The sand looks so pretty. It doesn't feel good in my eye, but I love the sparkly colors under the day orb's light." Jaden danced around, twirling as the sand storm seemed to fall just on her, reminding Xander of little kids twirling in the rain back home. He smiled, wishing he could be young like that again.

"Let's move. I'm sensing Connor will be meeting us soon. We don't want to be late," Astral said. They all got in line behind him.

Cranny glanced at Xander, grinning. "Can you really see images around all living things?" he asked.

"Yeah, I think so." He held up his right hand, hoping to catch some of the sand. "I've never seen anything like this. The particles have voices. I can hear them singing and talking as they pass my ears. Can you hear it?"

"Not really. I could when I was just sprouted. As we get bigger, we're told it isn't real. The sand doesn't breathe, so it isn't supposed to be able to talk or have soul." Cranny paused, considering. "Actually, I don't think we Criatias have souls either. Yet we talk, think and move around."

"Everything is supposed to have a soul," Geoffrey interjected, "Even the grains of sand blowing past us. Only the most sensitive ears can hear their voices, though. It's a form of mind speak because they don't have mouths. They're too small for that."

"How did you learn to do that?" Cranny asked Xander.

"I didn't. I've always been able to see them." Xander exhaled abruptly. "Some kids are intrigued when they find out I can do it and others are scared. Sometimes I wish I couldn't do it at all."

Cranny shook his head. "I know, but I'm flabbergasted that you don't like being able to do it. It upsets me that those on your world tell you not to be who are born to be. I mean, what's the worst it can do to you?"

"It can make me feel like an idiot, like I just fell to my planet of birth from an alien universe. I don't know much else. I know we've been over this so much. What else did you want to know, Cranny?"

"I wanted to know, um, could you see colors around me? And what they meant."

Xander looked at the plant boy, considering his energy field. "With so many other bodies and energies so close together, I can't really tell what your energy is saying. Can we just talk about something else?"

"You are an alien who fell to our world," Jaden said. "I think you are a wonderful alien and can learn to like yourself the way you are."

Cranny frowned, upset that Xander couldn't see his energies. He wanted to know what was around him.

*No one understands me,* Xander thought to himself. *Sometimes I think I don't know where others stop and I start. I blend in so much with others. I wish I didn't. I just don't want to feel anyone's feelings and hurt, or even know what they did the night before. I don't have my own life. Or my own thoughts. Maybe I don't have a right to have my own stuff. Maybe I really am an alien in my own world. What if those people laughing at me are right? Maybe I'm crazy. Maybe I am seeing myself in the other people.* His mind went back to the neighbor boy who got on the bus at his stop. He saw the boy's memories of breaking into cars and stealing things. *I don't steal from others and have no desire to, so why would I see an image of that in him if was truly me? I just want to live in peace.*

The sound of Cranny and Jaden's excited giggles and running feet and roots stirred Xander out of his thoughts. Looking ahead, he saw a large body of water. The water excited him, too. Xander hadn't really been around water much. In his world, he went to swimming pools and occasionally went fishing with his dad, but he had been so young the last time that he really didn't remember. He just remembered seeing bears outside their tent and one of them had sensed his fear. The bear said she didn't eat little boys unless they tried to hurt her or her cubs.

"C'mon, Xander, climb on, we're going to beat them!" Geoffrey exclaimed as he lowered himself so the teen could get on. Geoffrey flapped his wings as he took a running start and leaped into the air. The expectation of getting to the water first lifted Xander's spirits. They managed to just barely beat Jaden and the plant boy.

Geoffrey took a dive into the water without warning him, scaring the teen at first. He had barely enough time to hold his breath. The water felt cold, yet warm. He could almost hear a heartbeat, which he was sure was his own at first. His hair, which almost too long, floated all over, getting in his eyes. He pushed it away with his right hand, opened his eyes and saw the strangest sight. A man who looked just like Xander, except older, was floating without effort and not even holding his breath. Xander thought he had to be at least thirty-five or forty since he had a few wrinkles and his sideburns were beginning to turn gray.

"Hello, younger self. I've been waiting for you," the man said. Xander's heart dropped.

"Are you real?" He reached out a hand to touch the other person. The man felt real, but also it was like touching jello.

"I am real enough. You have much to learn." The older self-smiled. "Usually, the searcher views us from the shore instead of from inside the pond."

Xander cocked his head, puzzled how they were communicating. He wasn't actually speaking, but he was asking questions and searching the person in front of him.

"I'm telepathic, younger self. Much like you communicate with animals on your world. I don't breathe air, like you do, so I can talk under water." The doppelganger started to say something else, but the water around them erupted as a something at least as big as Xander plunged into the water. Throwing the teen to the side, it grabbed him by his shirt and yanked him up. The doppelganger merged with the ripples, flowing away in circles, only to reassemble as the water merged with itself and settled.

Xander wiggled under the tight talons of a huge bird, he guessed, carrying him to Albagoth knew where. The cold air shocked his skin after being submerged in the water for only a few minutes. He didn't know who had him. He could see the ground underneath them. Geoffrey, Astral and Jaden were pointing up and seemed scared, while Cranny watched with awe. The ground suddenly seemed close under him, and then further away, as if he were on a trampoline, over and over again until Xander felt dizzy and nauseated. He wiggled, trying to feel better. He closed his eyes, but it only intensified the feeling.

"Don't look down, Indigo Traveler," Connor warned him. "Hold still so I don't lose my grip. It's like holding onto a wet, slippery fish."

Once on solid ground Connor, still invisible, let go of the Earth boy. The Crow Judge shook himself and marched over to Geoffrey. He removed the invisibility with a thought, appearing very dark and angry.

"How dare you dive into the pond with a rider on your back! You didn't even tell him to hold his breath! He could've drowned! What were you thinking?"

Geoffrey ducked his head in shame. He pulled one of his wings, still dripping wet, over his face, "I wasn't thinking, I guess, your honor. I just wanted to wash that flying sand from my feathers and fur. Are you going to turn me back into a statue?"

The young griffin's words seemed to melt Connor's anger. He smiled. "No, Geoffrey. Just remember to think next time, okay?"

"Yes, your honor," Geoffrey bowed slightly, stepping forward. "I'll be more careful next time."

From where Xander had just been plopped, he glanced from the Crow Judge to each of the griffins, Jaden and the cactus boy, not sure what to think. The blowing sand had stopped, for now. He got to his feet.

"Connor –um – Your Honor, I'm not hurt. I was just shocked to land in the water, and shocked more when you grabbed me and yanked me out." He paused, considering what he had experienced under the water. With his head cocked, he walked cautiously towards the pond. "I saw the strangest image of myself as an adult. Surely, I was imagining it!"

He tentatively walked to the edge and looked in, expecting to see the water and his own thirteen-year old face staring back at him. Instead it was the same face he had seen a few minutes ago. The face smiled up at him. *Greetings, again.*

"Can everyone see him? He looks just like me, but his sideburns are gray!"

Connor and the others walked up beside him and peered in; Connor spoke. "Traveler, we each see an older version of ourselves. I can't see what you see, but I can sense what he tells you if I concentrate, unless the reflection blocks me from knowing."

"I see." Xander turned to him, "But you're the judge of this world. Surely you are supposed to know."

"It is not my place to know what your soul needs to counsel you on. Unless the Creator dictates that I have to know to further guide you. Part of what you will learn is from this body of water. The rest will come from other places."

"Such as?"

"Don't know. The Creator doesn't tell me all I need to know on each subject who visits here beforehand. You, Xander, are the first traveler I've been assigned to guide, teach and travel with. Yet I have to divide up my time with you with my other duties, too."

"I am here to teach you more about boundaries," Astral piped up as he sat down. His old legs were not able to stand for very long.

A chill slowly crawled up Xander's spine and grabbed his shoulders. He looked away from the pond. Seeing his older self was eerie. He walked away and sat down under a tree, pulled his knees up, wrapped his arms around them and hid his head.

Cranny found a swampy area to plant his roots and slurp up some water and nutrients from the ground. Jaden played around in a smaller pool, splashing as only a little kid could do. Connor and Astral talked for a bit.

Geoffrey walked over and turned around a couple times, trying to smooth down the stiff coarse grass. Once satisfied, he sat down beside Xander. He opened his beak and panted like a dog as he looked around. "It's overwhelming, isn't it?"

"What is?" Xander looked at the griffin, his fur and feathers sparkling in the rays coming down between the branches and leaves.

"Being in a place like this that is so different from your own world. I wasn't in your world for long, and couldn't see really. I experienced it vicariously through your thoughts. It was strange, but I could see what you were seeing and could hear some of what you heard."

Xander looked up at him, surprised. "So, could you see my visions and hear the thoughts of my teachers before I spoke them?"

"Yeah, I think so. I saw some human male with a piece of cloth hanging from his neck, with one hand twitching. I sensed he felt very nervous and scared, worried some other adult would fire him or discipline him for not having complete control of his classrooms. I also sensed that he had mixed feelings about what you said. He felt awed that you could see his worries and also angry that you had to state them on this one day. He wanted to call you names, deny them."

The griffin looked off across the pond. "The two females who talk with you are true friends, Xander. One of them— the one that makes your heart race— I sensed she likes you, but doesn't know how to approach you about it. She likes to be around you, though. She will beat up anyone who tries to hurt you. Trust her, Xander. Trust her, confide in her and don't brush her off. The new female is intrigued by you and wants to know you better. You told her the truth about the other kids and she respects you for it."

One word came to Xander's mind as he sat there, absorbing what the white griffin said – empty. He felt empty and frightened of that reflection pond. He loved swimming, but that pond scared the living bejesus out of him. He felt empty. He just wanted to tune everything out and see what surfaced. He also wondered why Geoffrey was telling him all this.

The griffin fidgeted. "Um, hey, I'm sorry I didn't warn you before I dove into the pond. That blowing sand irritates my fur and feathers. I wanted to get it off of me. Also, I love getting wet." Geoffrey sounded ashamed as he made excuses for his behavior.

"That's okay, man," the teen said meekly.

"He's not a man, he's a griffin," Jaden exclaimed, overhearing their conversation. She walked over and plopped down.

"Jaden, it's a figure of speech on my world." He smiled.

"Figure of speech? How can speech have figures? You mean like statues put into words?"

Xander grinned. "I can't explain it. It's just something we say."

The day orb was beginning to set. Astral and Connor came over. "I think it's time to for your first lesson, Indigo Traveler," the elderly griffin stated. "Come over here away from the others so we can concentrate on what you need first."

Xander nodded, stood up and followed Astral. Connor hopped over to observe. He wanted to see how Astral did his teaching and also add his own thoughts as he could.

"Okay, I want you to empty your mind," Astral started.

"Done," Xander answered, feeling bored. He rolled his eyes as he turned his head to look across the pond.

Connor turned to look at the healer. "His problem is not the problem we think it is. He doesn't feel he has a purpose or a reason to have his own thoughts. The line is blurred. He sees himself as an extension of others."

Xander snapped his head around, "You mean I'm not?"

"I wonder if we should have a human here to help me understand where this boy is," Astral whispered to Connor.

"No, you can learn about him by looking within him like you do with your students here in Curá." He shook head as he spoke.

Astral thought for a few minutes, considering his plan of action. He walked forward, wagging his tail slowly as if he was stalking his prey. He got up to the teen's eye, lowering his head so he wasn't taller than the human boy. He wanted to see eye to eye with him. As he stilled his mind, letting go of preconceived notions, he focused on understanding what Xander felt, experienced and how his home life was. He saw a rush of experiences that threatened to blow his mind. They came so fast, he wasn't sure where they came from or in what order. Then, all at once, they stopped. He heard a voice inside his mind, the presence he knew was the Creator: *Don't look inside him too deeply, Healer Astral. Give him enough information so he will thirst for more. He needs to see his own good and not allow himself to take on others' thoughts of him. Ask him to define himself. Ask him for his own strengths. Teach him how to hear the Divine Voice within, the seed that was given to him when his soul agreed to go into this body."*

As the words ended, Astral saw a vision of a tree with roots that weren't planted very deep. When the wind blew, the tree moved in the direction of it. He could tell this boy from the World called Nampa was like that. He allowed others to imprint their own feelings and thoughts on him and he wasn't willing to decide how he wanted to be or who he was. Yet Astral could also see that he had made a clear decision not to fight. He also didn't want others forcing him to stand up for himself. He was afraid of fighting for himself because he thought he was worthless.

The image changed. Suddenly the tree was firmly planted in solid ground, with deep dark indigo colors surrounding it. The journey for this talented traveler lay deep within himself. The tree wasn't shallow, but had a rich life deep inside that he was avoiding. There were vague, blurry images moving among the colors, but Astral couldn't make out where they were for sure.

Xander closed his eyes, wondering what the old griffin saw in him. He felt a warm, loving presence come over him and heard a voice within his head he hadn't heard before. *Don't close your eyes, Indigo Child, Astral needs to read you. If you close your eyes, you will be reading him.* He opened his eyes. The voice sounded warm and friendly, and it felt like whoever spoke had known him for a very long time. *Deep within you, you need to search. Follow the Crow Judge and others, but do not do what doesn't feel right to you.*

*I don't know what you mean. Nothing feels right to me,* Xander responded. The presence was gone.

Astral lifted a paw and slowly moved it up and down, scanning him from head to toe. He felt warm towards his head and upper body, and no feeling at all within the lower half as if he was totally numb or cut off.

"Tell me, Xander, what are your strengths?"

"I don't have any," he said, slumping his shoulders and moving his gaze from the old griffin.

"You are like a tree without any roots. You drift with the wind, picking up on all kinds of thoughts that aren't yours, but you soak them in and decide they're right. Tell me about your sire and dame."

"You mean my parents?"

The old griffin nodded.

"My mom works in a massage therapy business and likes to take me to psychics to see if they can help me get out my bullying and find my inner strength. Most of them don't see the real me, though one said something about me going on a long journey and finding what I need there." He paused, considering. "My name doesn't suit me. I'm not sure where to find what I need." He looked back at the old griffin and the Crow Judge. "The psychic said I was wise for my age and an old soul. She said I came to help bring peace to many lands, but first I had to awaken the desire to find the true self deep within me. To admit that I have the god/or Creator deep inside already. She said I am at war with myself."

Connor nodded. "What do you need most to know?"

"I need to know how I can make peace with myself when I get other people's anger, and their hatred, and I'm treated like I'm a monster. I mean I feel like I'm a monster."

"No, you aren't one," Astral, Connor and Geoffrey stated at once. "You have a great potential."

Xander looked away, feeling tears suddenly filling his eyes. A few managed to spill over, and he wiped them away.

"My mom loves me. She just doesn't know how to truly see within me. She says I'm special. My dad is always at work. He's a construction worker and welder and often is away in another state. When he's home and I get in trouble at school, he usually expects me to be the one who started it. He doesn't listen to my side. If I happen to see his thoughts and answer or speak them, he jumps down my throat more, demanding I take it back."

Xander paused again, looking at the water. "I want to know why this loving Creator gave me a dad like him. He hates me. I can see how stressed out his job makes him. But sometimes he isn't that kind or loving. And he also doesn't listen to my mom when she talks about her spiritual practices. They're so unlike each other. I don't really feel like I belong to them, because I'm so different from them both. I don't really look like either one and I'm just so strange." He stared off at the pond, considering the reflection he had seen about an hour ago. His clothes were almost dry and his stomach rumbled.

"We'll find some food soon," Connor said, sensing the teen's restlessness.

***

Astral felt overwhelmed by the traveler's experience. He asked within himself what he needed to say or for some insight into his sire and dame's emotions towards him. He sensed rather suddenly that the boy's dame's love was overflowing and so was his sire's; yet Xander had cut off his feelings. Something else wasn't entirely right, but that door was closed.

"Your sire and dame have a great love for you, Xander. You aren't allowing yourself to feel it, though. You aren't allowing yourself to even consider yourself worthy of anyone's love. How can you achieve what you desire if you don't love yourself?"

"I don't have any goals for myself. My goals are what my parents want for me. My parents want me to be a good student at school, but I'm not achieving that because I have to spend so much time watching my own back. My mom wants me to meditate and talk with that being she calls Spirit, but how can it love me when love is based on what I achieve and do and not who I am? I've heard so many people tell me who I'm supposed to be that I'm very confused. I came here looking for answers and all I've found out is that you all expect me to be a savior and stop a war. I don't know how to fight. I don't want to fight. Why does it have to be me?"

Connor and Astral looked at each other, shrugged, and looked back at him.

"I think we'd better find some food," Connor said. "I'm sure everyone is feeling hungry." Everyone agreed except Cranny, who had been getting his fill from the soil and picking off the insects that landed near his limbs and mouth, unaware of what he was.

***

Night came. Xander and Geoffrey took a walk away from everyone. The air smelled of salt water and the sound of the pond moved up on the side bar and back out was like a miniature sea. Up in the sky the evening orb shone full, lighting some of the path, and they could see dots of lights blinking on and off. Xander stopped.

"Do you call them stars? The dots of light, back home we call them stars."

"Yeah, we call them that. Have you ever tried to imagine a line between them to make out pictures? Sometimes I think I see my sire and dame or my friends. I miss Sebastian and Donnair. Do you miss anyone from your world?"

"Yeah, I miss my cat and my own bed. I miss my room. Let's sit down." They sat on a slight hill looking out. "We have several star constellations that form images that appear at different times of the year. Each country can see them, I think. Sometimes, we need a telescope to see them better."

"Here, we see what we need to see in the night sky. Sometimes there's words that appear that only the individual can see."

"Isn't that scary? In my world, if only one person can see something, everyone thinks they're crazy. That's why I don't like my gift. I hear voices that no one else can. Sometimes I pick up on stuff the other person won't admit to."

"Here, if we hear something no one else does, we usually say it's the Crow Judge; even if it might not be." Geoffrey giggled.

"Why wouldn't it be? Don't you all see him like I do or like Jaden does?"

"Connor isn't always visible, Xander. Most of the time, he is unseen so he can observe without us stopping what we're doing. I'm not sure why he isn't invisible now."

Observing in the dark, invisible to their eyes, Connor heard. He grinned to himself, knowing he needed to address this, but now wasn't the time. He felt a nudge inside him, down to his gullet; the Crow Court superior reminding him of his duty to bring the Traveler to their world.

*But he hasn't talked with his reflection,* Connor responded.

*That can wait. You also need to go to King Titus's wizard. The seven days are about up. See what his decision is. Trouble is brewing in the mining camps. Titus's patrols found a metal object roaming the desert and put it to work. Check on it. Give direction to this Indigo Traveler. He is still lost. If he stays in the dark, he can't help us or himself.*

Connor felt like he was being corrected. *I'm aware he is still feeling lost. I'm not sure how to help him, Your Honor. I've never dealt with a human as his guide before. Give me an idea of what to do.*

*Take him with you to check on the mining Titus has going. Take the young griffin, too. Leave the others with Astral.* Connor could sense his superior's face and white feathers looking at him, as if he was standing next to him. He took a deep a breath and let it out slowly, wanting to respond in a short, curt manner, but not doing so.

*Yes, Your Honor, I will do as you say.*

Astral called Xander and Geoffrey to bed down for the night. They had blankets and a warm fire to huddle around.

Xander lay awake, missing his room, where he felt safe. He felt kind of safe here – he felt warm inside, staring up at the night sky and seeing the familiar stars moving in circular fashion, as if they were synchronized swimmers or dancers. Some blinked on and their neighbors blinked off, changing colors. He closed his eyes, opened them and imagined lines between several groups. One group looked like his cat, Clarence. He imagined breathing life into the image to animate it. The cat stood up, arched its back and walked over to another group, which reminded him of his mom. The cat stars rubbed against his mom's legs; she bent down and picked up the cat. Another group reminded him of his dad, complete with a beard and balding hairline. He came over, put his arm around his mom and they smiled. Xander's heart sank. He missed his parents and home more than he ever thought he would.

# Chapter 10

Xander felt funny, like he was floating in air. He saw a spiral staircase like a double helix leading upward. He followed it up into the sky, through fluffy clouds and other objects he hadn't seen before. The stairs led to a city like he'd none never seen before. The sky was clear, and smelled of roses and fresh baking bread like his grandma used to make before she got sick. The path was made of cobblestones that didn't look worn at all. There were few people around, yet he could see large crows rushing here and there, some with scrolls under their wings. Some were walking together. A few humans, one or two Arimaspians and what looked like young crows sat in a group being taught under a tree with massive branches that came down into the ground as if they were walking somewhere else.

There were large buildings, too. One looked very official, with a million steps. Xander found it effortless to climb them. He wished physical education was that easy. Near the top two large griffin statues stood on either side. He decided to go inside to see what it was. He hoped it was a library. He loved to read, when he could; but lately he hadn't been able to still his mind to follow a story.

Inside, at the front desk he saw a large crow with mostly white feathers looking very official, holding a stylus in his wing, writing on a scroll. Pausing to look at a reference book, the crow glanced back at the scroll to scribble some more. Xander tried to read the words, but he didn't recognize the language. The crow looked up, annoyed.

"How may I help you?" he asked, in an irritating, scratching voice that sounded almost like he was cawing in-between words.

"Um, I'm not sure where I am or how I got here. I was in Curá and then this staircase came up and here I am."

"Oh, excuse me, Indigo Traveler." The crow sat up straight, sounding less annoyed. "Connor is supposed to escort you here. Where is he?"

"He was asleep with his head buried under a wing last time I saw him." Xander remembered "This way, young Indigo Traveler," the crow said, scooting out his chair and walking around the long desk. He held a ring of keys in his wing.

They walked into a large room with multiple tables, and kiosks full of various creatures including birds, humans and other animals, and humanoids he hadn't seen before, sat with headphones on. Some simply listened. Others typed on table tops like computer screens. Xander wondered what this place was and what they were viewing. The walls were totally white, with no pictures; yet it felt peaceful.

The crow librarian led him to a room marked Hall of Records. He unlocked the door, and opened it. Another librarian was inside waiting. The other librarian was a taller bird, l like a stork, with round frame glasses and a striped vest with a gold chain hanging from one pocket to the next.

"Ah, Alexander Michael Veh: Indigo from the World called Nampa; I've been expecting you" the stork said, looking him up and down. "I do believe you've forgotten to bring something."

"I did? What did I forget?"

"You forgot your body. You need it , young traveler."

Suddenly he was falling down from a very tall cliff and he couldn't control the descent. He woke up abruptly with a silent scream echoing in his mind. Xander sat up, Jaden was still asleep next to him, but her head was now buried on Geoffrey's side with his wing around her keeping her warm and safe.

Standing, he walked over to the reflection pond. He wondered if the dream was truly a dream or if it was something more. His mom told him dreams had meanings. She claimed to know when one was actually an out of body experience. Yet he never thought of himself as an astral traveler since he never remembered leaving the body. He remembered laughing at her, dismissing it.

He sat on the bank, dangling his feet in the water. He remembered Astral touching his belly with his right paw but nothing had happened. He wondered why he did that. The reflection wasn't visible in the night orb's light; but just thinking of it sent chills up and down Xander's spine. He sensed something flutter down from a nearby tree and land next to him.

"Having a hard time sleeping, Indigo One?" Connor asked, startling the teen. Xander glanced to his right; the pure black crow blended in with the night time, yet he could see the outline of the Crow Judge.

"Yeah. I miss home. I miss my parents and my cat. I even miss that bully, Butch. I don't know why, though."

"The absence of what we're used to makes the heart grow fonder. There's a connection between you and that bully boy that you have to figure out. Once you understand it, you can solve the issue and he won't bother you anymore."

"I see," Xander said noncommittally, because he really couldn't see it. *I'm not really connected to that wuss, Butch.*

"All things are connected, Master Indigo One," Connor answered his thoughts.

"Yeah, I've heard that before," he muttered, pulling up one knee to his chest, wrapping his arms around it and rolling his eyes. He was glad the Crow Judge couldn't see his face. After a pause, "Why did Astral touch my belly with his paw?" "You're cut off from your emotions. Astral's healing touch was meant to awaken that part of your body. Did you feel something?"

"No, I just felt his sandpaper pads touching my skin. He needs to put lotion on them," Xander smirked at the thought of a griffin putting his Mom's Mary Kay lotion on.

"You will have to find your own way to awaken that part of your system," Connor told him.

"I was wondering why my reflection looks older than me. And where did it go?"

"The beings that inhabit the pond have the ability to take on the appearance of whoever has a heavy heart. You have a very heavy heart. Though all the weight you carry does not belong to you. The beings are likely resting at this time of day."

"That makes sense," Xander agreed. "Wish I could sleep."

They sat in silence for a while, enjoying the sound of the rippling water, insects flitting around and others chirping to their mates. After a while, Connor spoke again.

"I'd better go see Wizard Seabon at the Arimaspian castle. You all be careful following this path; it's close to their borders." Connor, turned, took a running leap into the air, and flew off.

\*\*\*

Seabon sat up staring into the gazing stone, watching a machine he'd never seen before traveling alone in the barren sands of Senilona. It was yellow with orange trim.It had a long arm and elbow that ended in a backward shovel that looked like a hand. A board shovel on the back of it looked like it could move a mountain.

The old wizard sat back on his stool and rubbed his hands together, imagining what it could be used for. It occurred to him that the machine was moving without anyone in it. That didn't seem right. He looked again, waving his hand over the large orb, commanding it to bring him in closer to see. Sure enough, no one was inside it.

He smiled, talking aloud to himself. "I wonder how Albagoth could've created something like this. Surely it is from another place, but no one is with it. It is lost and may not know where it is. Then again, it might not have an awareness of who it is or how it got here. I will tell the king first thing in the morning."

A breeze blew in the open window, sending loose sheaves and open scrolls all over the floor. Seabon got up from his stool to gather them up, and sensed a presence in the room. It was a large presence. Then he remembered that his seven days were about up.

"Good morrow, Crow Judge," Seabon bowed. "I wasn't expecting you."

"No, you've been busy, I see," Connor said, observing the scrawling script of formulas, tubes of potions and herbs jars scattered around the room and table. "You're trying to come up with a way to turn ordinary stones to gold. He crossed to the gazing crystal, which still emitted a bright white light. When he looked in, he saw the different sight. He saw Xander, working in the mines and Jaden trapped in a dungeon with a minotaur youth he recognized as Geoffrey's friend. He heard a machine honking and whistling, struggling under the whip of a massive, yet not too bright, Arimaspian guard. Connor had no idea where that machine came from, yet he sensed the machine was trying to help Xander get free from the torture. The scene switched to the Gryphon mountain village, and Kontar, King Titus's son, demanding to be reunited with his father. Yet he was divided; he worried about his sister. He wanted something to end. The Crow Judge couldn't tell what.

*Life, Connor. Life is what you make it. You can't help everyone. Get Seabon's answer, then go back to the others.*

"What's your answer? Do you stand with the Kingdom of Kent and the Creator? Or do you stay with the Arimaspian Kingdom?"

Seabon turned around slowly, washing his hands as he thought. His eyes darted back and forth, considering what would be the better of the two. He loved working with the cold-hearted King Titus. He loved seeing the villagers whipped for no reason and watching the slaves working their skin off in the mines. But he understood the covenant the Arimaspian and Kingdom of Kent had with the Dragons of long ago. He knew Titus was in grievous violation of it and if the chosen one with the brilliant indigo coloring was real and found the dragon blood sword, his king will fall and he would go down, too. He couldn't decide.

"I sit upon the high wall, Your Honor. I cannot decide. I beg you to give me another seven days. Or longer. There is much to plan. My king's men prepare to attack soon, as well as seeking lost travelers to imprison." Seabon hid his deepest desire. "Tell me, have you heard of the traveler with the bright indigo colors?"

"If I tell you, what are your plans?" Connor walked close to the wizard, his keen instincts tingling to be wary of him. He lowered his gaze slightly to see within the wizard as if he was prey to be devoured if he didn't answer correctly. He could see an image of the mine and a faceless figure working hard inside that had the colors of the boy from the World of Nampa. "How did you know about the?"

"I have my way. I'm a wizard, after all, trained to see into the near future. Often travelers come through quite lost and alone. They never quite make it to the reason they came here. Many don't even know how they got here. And the loving Albagoth that you so wisely work for often forsakes them. King Titus, in his wisdom, looks out for them. We take care of all lost souls." Seabon's mouth twitched in a crooked smile with his eyebrows turned downward so he looked more angry than happy. Connor straightened his back and grew so he looked the evil wizard in his two eyes (since he was only half Arimaspian).

"Watch your step, Seabon. Albagoth never forsakes those brought here. There is a reason for all that happens. Watch your accusations."

"I heed only one voice," Seabon said. "It is my own and my king's."

"That is two voices," Connor corrected. He looked around, quieting his inner thoughts to get a handle on what to do. The room was large. Shelves with many jars of herbs, tinctures and other leaves, berries and liquids as well as drawings, plans and diagrams of the constellations in the universe were pinned on the walls. "I will not give you any more time, Seabon. Your time is up. One seven-day period has passed, and I sense you have no plans to go against King Titus."

Connor vanished from sight and flew out the window, leaving Seabon in turmoil, wondering if he should've agreed to be a spy for Albagoth against his king. Surely, if he did, he would die at Titus's hand – the kind of death no one would want to endure.

Seabon wrung his hands as he paced the floor, worrying about what to do. Would this Crow Judge cause problems with the plans? Indeed, the plans weren't fully in place yet.

***

King Titus sensed something was wrong, it wasn't normal for him to wake in the middle of the night. He had a nightmare that his son, Kontar, had decided to work against him. Kontar led a group of gryphons, humans and a traitor Arimaspian to meet with the mighty dragon who was the sole surviving ancestor to the dragons who had made the covenant with his great grandfather many times removed. Kontar was accompanied by a boy from a distant world who flew on a pure white griffin and carried a mighty three-blade sword that blazed under the day orb's light. The stranger pledged to end the abuse.

Titus wiped the sweat from his brow and closed his massive eyelid, praying to the unseen Creator, even though he really did not believe it existed, that his son would be on his side. *Surely, it's just a dream. My son understands what I want to do. He's been gone from my household for two years, though. How I miss him. I must get him back, even if it means stealing him from those awful gryphons! Creator, please don't let my son turn his back on me!*

"King Titus," Connor answered for Albagoth, "you know what you must do to get your son back. You must adhere to the agreement the dragons made with your ancestors' eons ago. You need to stop tearing up mountains looking for riches that will serve only yourself and your kingdom. Share your wealth with the poor in your land. Teach them how to provide for themselves. Unite once again with the Kingdom of Kent to work together for the betterment of both kingdoms."

"Why do I need to respect these lowly villagers? They haven't done anything for me! All they want is for me to help them with the work they were born to do! I hate them all! I wish them all gone from my life!" spat King Titus as he paced the room.

"Your words are very strong, King Titus! Is this really what you want? If it is, it can be arranged."

"What do you mean, it can be arranged?" The mountain sized man turned to face the visible Crow Judge, who stood looking him straight in the eye.

"It means the Creator can arrange for them to no longer be under you anymore." Connor said calmly.

"You mean— take them away from me?"

"I will not be the one to say exactly what the Creator has planned. It is your decision, Titus. You have free will. But sometimes, if one isn't following certain spiritual laws, that free will is forfeited."

Titus uttered a roar of hot anger from the depths of his belly. "What does that mean?" All his muscles tensed.

"That is up to you to decide," Connor smiled as he disappeared and flew out the open window.

# Chapter 11

Connor met up with Xander in the forest. "It's time to take you to another land, kiddo. We need to get Geoffrey to go with us."

"What about food? My stomach is growling and I'm sure the others are hungry, too. This land doesn't have any Golden Arches or Crown Burger places," the teen complained.

"We will find food to take back to the others, and then you and Geoffrey are coming with me. The librarian Artemis sent me a message that you came to visit but forgot something vital to your entering the sacred documents. Remember, as you thumb through them, to look for the scrolls of the dragon contract between Kent and the Arimaspian Kingdoms. You must find those. They are as important as unlocking the secrets of your own life's purpose."

"Okay." Xander rolled his eyes, dismissing the importance of that. "I don't understand how some dusty old scroll contract is going to help me here." He winced as his mind threw him a curveball picture of his old friend, Milo, who had disappeared many years ago after they played in the park together. He shook the memory out of his head, but the vision came back strong with a sensation that Milo was trying to reach him through mind speak.

Connor found a berry bush and wild herd beasts to send toward Astral, Jaden and Geoffrey. They all ate. Even Cranny tried a few berries, though he felt guilty for eating a fellow plant life.

Connor told Geoffrey and Xander to prepare to leave, and when Xander had climbed on the griffin's back, he escorted them to the upper regions of the sky and through a wormhole that led to the Crow Court world.

As they flew through the wormhole, Xander was amazed at the varieties of stars, small planets, and different geometric shapes and sizes they saw. They even passed the double helix staircase he had seen in his dream, which made him wonder if he really had visited this place without his body.

They came out of the wormhole, landing in a park with a statue of a large crow with the inscription, "In Honor of the first Crow Judge."

"Did you know him?" Geoffrey asked Connor.

"No, he lived way back before I was hatched. Albagoth chose him because of his noble spirit. He saw him negotiating and mediating arguments between animals and other beings. He saw the wisdom he used and decided all crows had this same wisdom. So he created the Crow Court and asked this one, Davon, to be the head. The Creator set up the spiritual laws and Davon, along with others, wrote out the laws they had to enforce for each plane and world. On Curá, we also asked the dragons to assist us because they have two hearts and a few serve to watch over Kent. Xander, one of your tasks is to find the scroll with the dragon's contract between the Kingdom of Kent and the Kingdom of the Arimaspians."

"Why me?"

"Because the Creator and the Dragon of Kent have requested it. Follow me to the Library of Records."

Connor led them through the white cobblestone street, passed young crows being taught by taller crows under a tree, and humans, minotaurs and other creatures Xander thought only existed in mythology stories going about their day. He noticed that some of the beings stopped when they saw Geoffrey, and bowed with respect and awe. A few of the young hatchlings would interrupt class, and with open beak and wing pointing say, "Look, a white griffin!" Classes would then erupt in loud talking mixed with the old language cawing until the elder crow got their attention back.

"Why are they pointing at you?" Xander asked.

"I am a symbol of peace and goodwill, a legend to my people. No one expected to see a white griffin born in these times. Prince Tayson knew the legend, but still chose me to be his guardian and fight by his side. It's against my nature to fight in battle. Yet I cannot bring peace by myself. I also realize I need to fight, sometimes. I need to enter this fight and risk the results. I don't like being a symbol like this. I want to run away again. I don't want to handle this alone."

"You aren't alone, Geoffrey. I'm with you." Xander reached out and embraced his tall griffin friend. Geoffrey looked at him, smiling and nodding his approval.

The buildings were large and much of the city was white, except for trees that looked like willow, though some had large trunks with the branches drooping down on the ground. Xander could visualize them pulling up their roots and walking down the road. He giggled at the thought – then had a weird feeling of thinking that once before.

Coming up on their left was a tall building that reminded him of the capitol in Boise, Idaho, except it didn't have dome on top. It had millions of steps leading up to it that started from very long rectangles and narrowed as they went up. On each side two griffins made of marble lay with their wings folded at their sides and tips pointing upward. Xander remembered it from his dream.

They turned and went up the stairs. This time, Xander felt the pulling of each muscle in his legs as he climbed, and his heart began to beat out a call to war, begging him to stop each time he lifted his foot. Connor and Geoffrey didn't bother with climbing, they just flew up.

Connor led them inside and they walked through the open doors. Sitting at the front desk was the same crow with the white and black feathers, busy scribbling on the parchment.

"Greetings, Connor. Where were you last night when your charge came in without his body?"

"Huh?" was all Connor could say. He acted like someone had kicked him in the gullet. "Richmond, you're getting too old to sit there! My charge isn't able to travel without his body."

"If you say so. Master Artemis is waiting for you all," the information crow replied.

"You are supposed to be above snide remarks, Richmond. If the Judge Superior finds out, he will discipline you again. I'd hate to see you outside working with the hatchlings that don't listen to any elder." Connor straightened his back, holding his head high.

Connor led them around the corner, passing the large room with all the tables and kiosks. "What is this place? A library?"

"This is the Hall of Records," Connor explained. "This is where you will get some of the answers to your questions. You will go in with Artemis Stork and I will take Geoffrey to another area. He has questions to answer, too."

The stork opened the door before Connor could knock with his beak, "Greetings, Connor, Master Indigo Traveler and the long-awaited White Griffin. I'm so honored you brought your body, this time.," The old stork smiled. "Come in, Indigo One. Connor, take the White Griffin down to the next silent research room. Someone is waiting for him." Connor nodded and ushered Geoffrey away.

"You're strange for a bird," Xander observed.

"How so?" the stork asked, looking over his frames, which bothered the traveler.

Xander shrugged his shoulders, not knowing how to describe what he felt.

Artemis led the way to a small room built like a sound room where recording artists would record songs. It was complete with a switchboard and mixer knobs, switches and buttons to flip either up or down. Turning to the left, though, Xander saw walls of books, and dividers, which held folders and files and other tin cans with an emblem like a circle with a cross. He guessed they contained reel to reel film or audio tapes. He touched one and felt an electric current run up his fingers and into his arm, shocking him.

"It shocked you. That must be your audio file, young one. Do you want to know more?" Artemis asked.

"Come this way. This room has been reserved just for you." Artemis picked up the large tin reel-to-reel and carried it to the room. "This is where you will learn what it means to be an Indigo Child and see how your life is intrinsically entwined with the white griffin. It is not every time that the white griffin is entwined with a child from another world. So the bonding for you two is very unique. It is not often that a white griffin is born, either.

Xander sat down in the booth. Artemis drew the shades to hide the control room. Then he went into another room to put the audio film on the projector. He spoke to Xander over the intercom, "This isn't just an audio tape. It has moving pictures. Once I turn it on, you will understand. There are more records here for you to research when you are ready."

Xander sat down on something, hoping it would support him. It had a pedestal, a cushion and a back made out of Formica, bright orange. He wondered if it would glow when the lights were off. It was shaped almost like a hand, but the fingers were fused together.

"Face forward, put your hand on the arm of the stool," Artemis directed.

Xander looked on either side of him. There was no arm attached to the stool; a low buzzing sound came out of the side of the back as something made its way out and lowered into place on either side so he could rest his arms. The ends of the rests had molds of hands that would fit four fingers and the thumb. Xander thought it was strange that his hand fit them.

"Each hand mold is made for the traveler who comes. We have foreknowledge of each one, but never know exactly when he or she will arrive. Now, relax as I turn down the lights and flip this on."

A bright light and a whirring noise like wheels spinning came from in back of Xander. The light flickered a bit while a narrow black string image danced around. Then a picture of a large room with a desk and books came into view. Xander relaxed, wishing he had some popcorn with lots of butter on it and a soda. A person walked in front of the desk, turned, and sat on it lopsided, smiling. He was fairly tall, narrow faced and small boned. He wore a white dress shirt and tweed jacket.

"Greetings, Shawndre. You are thirteen now and feeling quite out of place on the planet you chose to live on. You chose to be an Indigo Child in this lifetime and are quite stuck on exactly what to do. You see and hear things no one else does, and are uncertain why you do or what to do with them. You're numb inside, hoping it will stop the psychic events. It won't until you learn how to turn on the gift and turn it off. It is also important awaken the feelings in all your body so you can feel, and begin to grow your awareness of Spirit once you're back on your home world. Do you have any questions for me?"

"Yes, why are you calling me Shawndre? Who are you? How do you know so much about me?"

"Ah, yes, I forgot to introduce myself." The man smiled, bending down a bit as he laughed. "I'm Sirrayna. Everyone has a soul name. Yours is Shawndre. I'm you before I went into the body you now have. I am knowledgeable of our plan for this life, so we recorded this message before you went to the World called Nampa."

"How can you interact with me? This was filmed before I came here," Xander asked, puzzled and a bit scared.

"We anticipated your responses when we filmed this and the sensors your hands are on help me to know your chemical reaction."

"Like some kind of hologram or virtual reality game?"

"Sort of." Sirrayana crimped his face as he considered those terms. "I'm not quite familiar with those words, but will agree with it. Now, to answer your main questions I want to remind you of why you came. You are an Indigo Child so you can assist to awaken the people who are drawn to you. You are on your world to change how things are run. Question your school rules. Love those that hurt you and do your best to see within the bully at your school. He needs your love the most. You are telepathic because that is how you will communicate with Spirit or Albagoth and also those who are there to assist you that you cannot see all the time."

"You mean, like Connor, the Crow Judge?"

"Among them. But also, the spirit guides you have yet to meet. You also need to awaken your feelings so you can help heal those with injuries no one can see."

"I'm afraid to feel, though. When I feel, I'm overwhelmed with the pain. I can't explain it. No one believes, they can't see anything wrong . . . "

"It's because you're an empath, Shawndre. You are feeling the pain of others. Ask Healer Astral to teach you how to distinguish the pain of others from your own pain."

"I feel threatened by others, too. Even though I know instinctively that I'm really in no danger."

"Believe in yourself. The Creator is all around you and part of him/her is within you, too. This is the part you need to open up in your heart and tummy." The speaker paused for effect, closing his eyes. Xander couldn't sense anything from the film itself, yet felt something probing him inside, outside and all around him. The speaker opened his eyes. "Yes, I see. I see you do have some of this stomach area opened so you do follow it. But you aren't always speaking from it or trusting what it tells you."

Xander's mouth flew open. "So, how do I fix that?"

"You can't unless you really desire to make the change." The man on the screen closed his eyes again. The film flickered. A most amazing thing happened: The man stood up walked forward; the scene flickered like Jell-O when someone put a finger in it, and Sirrayana stood before him, smiling. Xander didn't know if he should scream or wrap his arms around him. Instead, he sat back as far as he could on the stool, and lifted his hands off the molding, hoping the man standing there would disappear.

"Sorry, I needed to leave the film for a bit. You need to relax. Now, stand up. I can still sense you, Shawndre."

The man from the film walked around the chair, then stood about twelve inches in front of him, "Now, stand up and face me." Xander did. "I'm going to scan you with my hands."

"Why?"

"When we scan a person with our hands, we're sensing their energy levels, hot or cold areas, and also where something isn't right." "Healer Astral did that yesterday with his paw. And he punched me in the stomach. It hurt even though his claws weren't extended. He doesn't know his own strength."

"I bet. The old griffin was a youngster way before you came into body. In the spirit world, you used to play with him when he was cub. You don't remember that."

"Why not? If I lived other lives, why don't I remember?"

"Each soul goes through the waterfall of forgetfulness. If you were to remember your plan for your life, that would make the lessons you have to endure too easy. It would be like cheating on a test at school."

"I don't cheat. I just read the teacher's mind when I want to ace the test. I don't know how I do it; I just concentrate on what he was thinking as he prepared it. Sometimes I can sense his moods just by touching the paper before me."

"Ah" he said. "That has to be fixed, too. You still have that area in your stomach that is closed off. Take a deep breath and hold it," Xander did. Sirrayana put one hand on the traveler's shoulder and pressed the other on the stomach. All at once, Xander felt a bolt of electricity surge through his body from his stomach up through his head. Another went down his legs and out the bottoms of his feet. He wanted to faint, yet the jolts were invigorating.

"Wow! Now what?"

"Now you sit back down. Later, you will begin to remember odd parts of your journey and life's plan. You will also learn where to find the dragon scroll. When you do, go visit him. With the dragon scroll, you will find the blade with the dragon's blood tempered into it. You must have this if you are to awaken King Titus's memory of his tasks. He is far off course."

"I've had a vision of someone else telling me this, too. Though I didn't see a clear face, it looked like a reptile."

"Ahem!" They turned to see another man on the screen. HIs hair was the color of straw, what Xander's grandma would have called tow headed. "What are you doing down there in the physical world? Get back here!"

"Tyler, I will be right there."

There was something familiar about the new man, but Xander couldn't place it. His eyes were bright blue, like the ocean. His features were round, cheek bones chiseled, and his nose medium. But his mouth turned up in a friendly smile when Xander felt he should be sneering. And the hair color was all wrong, too.

"Butch? What are you doing there?"

"Hi, Shawndre. No, I'm not Butch. But he's my alter self in this life." Tyler cocked his head to one side as Sirrayana turned and jumped back through the Jell-O wormhole. "You wonder why Butch is teasing you? Or abusing you? He's jealous of what you are. Part of him wants to befriend you and part of him wants to punish you for having all the neat gifts in this lifetime."

Sirrayana turned around, the two friends smiled. "Do you want to know how to be his friend? Love. Send him love."

Xander crumpled up his face and shivered, "That sounds so girly and soft! Dad says I need to fight him. I say he just needs to leave me alone."

"Then understand him. When you get back to your world, use the lessons Astral and Connor teach you to see within Butch. Kill him with kindness," Sirrayana added.

"And look for a lost soul trapped inside a metal body. Only you can free this lost soul."

The tape flickered off and he heard a flip flip flip noise as it the end went around and around. The lights came back on.

Suddenly, Xander felt as if he had just woken up from a long dream. Only he knew it was very real.

*Look for a lost soul in a metal body,* he thought as he walked out        of        the        room.

# Chapter 12

*Look for the lost soul trapped within a metal body*, Xander thought as he left. Geoffrey was waiting outside, sitting at a desk with Connor. He was going through something on the screen embedded in the table. Xander went up to them, "Well? How did your session go?"

The griffin looked thoughtful. "It was interesting. I learned I have to face the conflict of fighting in a war even though every part of my being screams against it. How did yours go?"

"I learned I have to come to terms with myself, open up the feelings I've shut off and accept myself as I am. I'm also supposed to search for a lost soul trapped within something metal. Whatever that means." He shrugged. "So, what next, Connor?"

"We go back to Curá."

\*\*\*

Milo traveled the lonely desert, not knowing where he was or how he got there; his four wheels crunched the sand and pebbles as he rolled on. He remembered the lost boy he used to play with before he was trapped in this metal body. The boy no one but him liked. He could read minds, he could heal and somehow, that boy's wish for a digging machine had turned Milo into one. The next thing Milo knew, he had been visited by some etheric being that whisked him away.

Now he was stranded on this world and so very alone. He missed his parents. He missed his brothers and sisters. Stranger than not, he also missed school. He'd been a digging machine for such a long time that he couldn't remember how old he was. Though he thought he was in his teens.

He felt something heavy strike his crooked hand shovel. He looked out through his headlights, trying to figure out exactly what it was he'd hit. He couldn't see anything but some large objects that looked like moving mountains coming his way. He quivered in fear; mountains weren't supposed to move or walk, yet these two were.

As they grew closer, Milo realized they weren't mountains at all, but beings with one large eye in the middle of their foreheads. They wore armor, carried shields strapped to their backs and swords strapped to their waists, and sandals with laces that went clear up their large bulky legs. They appeared to be in a jovial mood, smiling and pushing each other.

"Look, that must be the machine King Titus told us to be on the lookout for. It will bring us honor to bring it in before him. We must wrap the chains around it and haul back," said the one the taller one.

"Nay, we're supposed to take it directly to the mine in the gryphon's valley. We'll use it to make sure they know we intend to bring down their home in the sky," said the one with the scar down the side of his face.

The scar-faced one pulled a large rope of chains from around his waist, made a lasso and swung it overhead like a lasso. Milo grunted, trying to tell them he wasn't for slavery, but all he could manage to say sounded like the honking of a horn as steam came out of the pipe next to his windshield.

"I'm a boy!" Milo screamed, wishing they would hear his words. "I am not a machine!" He sped up, trying to move forward and out of their way. They yanked harder and Milo accelerated some more. His engine began to grind and strain. The two soldiers pulled harder, and Milo lost control. He put down his stabilizers, to help keep him in place. Doing that lifted him up some and he shifted the gears to his backward hand shovel, extending it so it knocked them on their noggins. The two monsters tumbled over like dominoes. They lay there for a few seconds, rubbing their heads.

"It's your fault!" scar face yelped. "If you had let me have control, we wouldn't have gotten clobbered!"

"No! It's your fault! Somehow you triggered that bucket thing!"

"How could I? I was standing by you the whole time!" They began punching and shoving each other.

Suddenly, they stopped, as an idea came to them, "Who's driving that thing? No one is in there, so how is it moving and fighting us?"

"Maybe that invisible Crow Judge is at the controls?" Scarface asked, shaking in fear.

"If it is him, then we're in trouble!" said the other, also shaking. "Why don't you check? Maybe if you wave your hand over the seat, you can feel it."

"No, I'm not going any closer! I don't want to mess with a Crow Judge! I heard he turned a griffin into stone and sent him to a galaxy far away from Curá. I don't want to be turned to stone."

"Like fire and brimstone, you will be, Curly. Okay, I'll go with you."

They both stood up, walked over and one waved a hand inside the cab. Not feeling anything, he shrugged. The other one decided to sit in the seat and figure out how the machine worked.

"I've never seen anything like this before. So, how does it work?"

The other one shrugged.

Milo put his stabilizers up and took off, leaving the other one eating the sand and dust. Milo wasn't about to stop for anything. As he drove on, his mind raced, wondering where to take this fool inside of him. Curly, he guessed was his name. All at once, he felt something like a vision come over him: his old friend, Xander Veh, the one who had turned him into a machine; somehow, he knew they would be seeing each other again.

***

King Titus fumed. Somehow, his two bungling soldiers had managed to get the machine back to the castle. He didn't know how, but he could tell the machine was going to be more trouble than it was worth.

"Get that machine to the mountain mines! With this machine, we will be able to find more gold, silver and maybe bring the whole dwelling down to size so I can get my son back!"

"Sire, I advise against it," Seabon spoke up, shaking his head. "You know the rules. You need to adhere by the Spiritual laws and the contract the Dragons put down. When you make peace with Kingdom of Kent and stop this foolish war and looking for wealth in areas that aren't yours, you will get your son back."

"How dare you stand against me! You must adhere to *my* rules! The spiritual laws and the contract that worthless dragon made with my ancestors are outdated. I make my own rules! I will conquer this world and get where I want to be without Albagoth and others!'"

"And when you do, Titus, the heart that beats inside of you will stop. That heart is still related to the dragon. He can sense when you aren't obeying the contract."

"Don't try to scare me," King Titus roared, though he did feel his heart tremble a bit. He didn't want anyone to see his fear. "I will have your head!"

"Titus, your Highness." The wizard bowed from the waist and looked up. "It is not my place to create fear in you. It is my place, though, to steer you in the right direction. The villagers need a wise king who will help them, show them how to revere Albagoth, honor the spiritual laws all the time. You have left the teachings of your parents and your tutors from your childhood. You've beheaded all the tutors who teach the old laws and hired new ones who are rewriting them to show your bias. It is time to realize this is a grave mistake."

King Titus moved freely, his blood boiling. "You have been influenced by something else! I need a faithful adviser who will back me up. You sidetrack me from the subject at hand! What do I do with that strange machine that is chained in the stables? I say take to the mountains! What do you say?"

Seabon stroked his chin as he thought. He was perplexed, wondering how Connor would direct him to speak. He tried to imagine a conversation with him, but couldn't. Instead, he heard a little boy speaking inside his head, *Hey, wizard, I'm trapped inside this metal body. Can you get me out? There is a lost bunny that needs my help. I mean, a lost friend. He can tell you what happened to me.*

Seabon was startled by what he heard. *You mean you're a boy trapped in that machine?*

*Isn't that what I just said? My name is Milo. I remember that. Others call me Digger, because I can dig holes and move dirt. Can you help me?*

*Lost boy? What do you mean you lost a friend?* The wizard responded.

*He's about my age – hey, I'll send you an image.* Milo sent him a mental image of the Indigo Traveler. Seabon hadn't talked to this traveler, yet, but he had an idea who he was.

"Your Majesty, you have marvelous insight. Yes, indeed, we should take this machine to the mines. And that traveler others are spreading rumors about, we will have to find, capture and send to the mines, too. I personally will help transport this metal monster to the proper mining site."

# Chapter 13

Xander, Geoffrey and Connor were in Curá, walking towards the Reflection Pond.

"This is where the last battle took place, Geoff, after I placed you in the World called Nampa."

Around them, they saw blood still stained into the sand, broken swords, javelins and other weapons of war; even a few broken shields. Xander felt a mixture of awe and revulsion.

"Tell me, Connor, when will I learn about my shields? How to put them up?"

"It will be easier if Astral tells you. Your soul-self opened your feelings up. I sensed your distaste for walking through a former battlefield. Now that you can feel, Healer Astral will be able to show you how to erect your shields and also help others."

"Are they physical shields?" Xander visualized carrying around heavy metal disks everywhere he went, thinking they would be cumbersome, but help a lot with what he did.

"No." Connor smiled, and Geoffrey laughed, too.

"They're invisible. Only you can feel and employ them. You will be able to take them down or open a window in them. Nothing will get through unless you want it to."

The three traveled a bit further in silence. Xander, more than the others, enjoyed feeling the cool afternoon day orb shining down on them; the sky was a pleasant light violet with streaks of gold and pink. In the distance, he saw a disturbance like a herd of mountains heading their way. They were pulling something large behind them that rattled and clanged. The sound echoed throughout the quiet valley.

"Danger up ahead, Connor!" Geoffrey shrieked. "Arimaspians. At least twenty of them. By the look, they are rounding up strangers to take to their mining camps for slave labor."

"Relax, Geoffrey, I'm with you. They won't hurt you two with me here."

"I don't trust them. They don't respect your authority. I've heard it from Prince Tayson and others. We need to go! Xander, climb on my back, we'll take to the air!" Before they could, the herd of Arimaspians surrounded them.

Connor grew to their size, but that didn't frighten them, "Do you know who I am?"

"You be the almighty Crow Judge! We aren't afraid of you!"

"You damn the whole nation of Arimaspians. You—and they— will be disciplined severely for imprisoning me!" Connor roared.

"King Titus will be so proud when we bring you in! Put him in the cage!" Curly shouted. They grabbed for him, but he turned invisible and flew away from their grasp. "Where did he go?"

While four of them were frantically looking for Connor, four others caught Xander and put him in a giant size cage, like what zoo animals were put in for display. Geoffrey fought them, trying to fly off, but they had a large net big enough to catch a whale on Earth and caught him easily. He was stuffed into the cage with Xander.

"You numbskull! You let the Crow Judge get away!" one of the Arimaspians shouted, hitting Curly in the shoulder.

"Me? He's disappeared!"

"It can't be that hard to find him!" another shouted as he took his sword and alternated between slashing it through the air and thumping it on the ground, "Here birdy, birdy birdy!"

From the cage, Xander and Geoffrey cheered for the invisible Crow Judge and taunted the soldiers, "You'll never catch him! He's tricky!"

"Shut up, you!" Curly ran his sword back and forth over the bars, making a *blllblll* sound.

"Make us!" Geoffrey shouted, jumping up on his back paws, unsheathing his claws.

"Yeah, make us!" Xander repeated, sticking his fingers in his ears, wiggling them and sticking his tongue out. Somewhere in the back of his mind, he was wondering about the change in his behavior. Back home, he would have been too timid to threaten bullies like these soldiers; yet these men were twenty times taller than Butch and the same amount stronger than he was. He was sure he and Geoffrey were like insects to the Arimaspians, yet he didn't feel afraid.

"You two are quite the funny case. You really think we're afraid of you?" Curly sneered. "You've got nothing to frighten us with. Besides, we could squish you all under our feet without even trying! Now, just tell us where the awful crow went! Our king wants him for his dinner!"

"So, you're gonna make him eat crow, eh?" Xander mocked. "On my world, that means he's eating his words because he's ashamed of what he did!" Xander giggled.

The guards stood up straight, and exchanged nervous glances which turned to worried looks. Each slowly shook their head 'nooo'; each of their single eyes showed complete and utter fear.

"Um, we better not make him eat that crow, then. King Titus would never admit he was wrong. We would be executed if we ever told him he was," the soldier with one ear said slowly, his single eye open as large as platter big enough for a hundred-pound turkey.

"Yeah, you can't afford to lose the other ear, Dillard," muttered another with two fingers missing.

"Let's forget him. King Titus will get him another time. Right now, we'd better turn around and take these prisoners to Mining Mountain."

They plodded on slowly. "With such long legs, you'd think they could walk faster," Xander told Geoffrey. One of the soldiers heard them talking, came up to the side of the cage and banged on it with his sword. "Stop your yanking!"

"Hey, don't worry about us!" Geoffrey said snidely.

"Yeah, we aren't talking to you! You're bothered because you aren't included in the conversation," the teen added.

"I ain't afraid of you two!" he retorted.

"Maybe you should be," Xander suggested.

"I'm much bigger than you! Shall I remind you?"

"Well, I can see into your heart and soul, you big ugly monster!"

"No, you can't! Only a Crow Judge or Albagoth can do that!"

"Give me your hand!" Xander yelled over the loud racket of the wheels going over the rocky ground. Curly, though, could only fit one finger, as thick as a tree trunk, between the bars.

The minute Xander touched it, he felt intense electricity flow into him. He saw vivid images of the Arimaspian with his wife, children, and fellow soldiers and in front of the king. He sensed Scarface's fear of his king and his own desires to rebel against him. The last scene he saw was of Scarface and another soldier capturing a backhoe that moved without anyone in it, and a wizard telling the Arimaspian king where to put it. Something was familiar about that machine. Suddenly, he had a tremendous longing to find it. He knew the digging machine was the lost soul he had to find.

"Well, what did you see?" Curly inquired.

"You don't always agree with your king, yet you are too timid to stand up. You respect the Spiritual Laws your parents taught you and it bothers you to see your king dismantle them."

Curly backed away from the cage, "You.... you really do see into me. How did you? What are you?"

"I am the Indigo Traveler from the world called Nampa. I came to remind King Titus who he is, and that the Creator of All World's spiritual laws are to be followed."

"Should I be frightened by that?" The soldier laughed. "I say not! No one will make King Titus change his mind! He is not someone you want to reckon with. That's why Prince Tayson called for a ceasefire and ran with his tail between his legs." He laughed again.

"Yeah, that white griffin of his went AWOL on him! It was supposed to bring him good luck," said another soldier, joining in the laughter.

Geoffrey glanced at Xander with his feather brows lifted. His ear tufts drooped slightly.

"It was scared of its own shadow, that one! The legend of the white griffin being a herald to end war just is hysterical!"

"Yeah. About as hysterical as me telling King Titus my true emotions!" Curly put in, slapping his knee.

"The white griffin is a myth, you say?" Geoffrey stood up on his hind feet, changing his front claws to talons. "What do you all think I am?"

"A white griffin." They all laughed. "But you aren't *the* white griffin!"

"You mean you've seen other white griffins?"

"No." The soldier put his finger to his lips, his eye rolled up as he thought.

"You idiot!" the soldier next to him shouted, hitting him over the head with his shield. "White griffins are very rare!"

They all stood still as it dawned on them. "Um . . . didn't Wizard Seabon say something about a traveler from another world coming with a white griffin?"

"Yeah, that's right. We were supposed to take them directly to the mine and put them to work."

# Chapter 14

Connor flew as fast as his wings could go until he got back to the Reflection Pond. Astral, Jaden and Cranny were gathered around, relaxing. Astral was worried about where they Xander and his friends had gone and how long it was taking them, so he was relieved when Connor materialized in front of them.

Connor felt frantic, but relaxed, knowing Albagoth had events firmly in control. Yet free will did reign. He also realized that the Arimaspians were taught to disregard the spiritual laws; that frightened him more.

Astral rose on his haunches. "Where are my grandcub and his new charge?"

"Calm, Healer Astral. It will be all right!"

"What do you mean it'll be all right?"

"Xander and Geoffrey were captured by the Arimaspians. They tried to catch me, but I escaped. We need to go and get them out. I flew above them for a while to hear their plans. They're taking them to the mining mountain."

Astral took to the air, not waiting to hear another word.

\*\*\*

Prince Tayson paced back and forth in front of his father's conference room with his hands clasped behind his back, holding a message in one hand. Only his father, King Tonyar, was with him, waiting for others. He scanned the message again.

"Father, we can't just wait for this attack! King Titus has gone too far! He's capturing stray travelers who aren't any threat and taking them to the mines! My men have spotted them doing this! One of our scouts even overheard that he is planning on sending some troops to attack us! We need to act now!

"Tayson, we can't just attack. We have no proof of this. We must wait until proof comes," said his father in a calm tone.

"No, Father, we can't just sit back and wait! We must do something! We must fortify our city and protect the villagers. We have villagers who travel from place to place selling their produce and crafts. We can't just wait for someone to come in . . ."

"I agree. We strengthen the gates into our kingdom, but we will not send troops out yet," King Tonyar stated. "Have you any information on the new blacksmith? Is he still selling arms to the Arimaspians?"

"I don't know for sure. Last I heard, two of my men saw some strange Arimaspians with him talking and exchanging items in trade for well-crafted steel swords, battle axes and shields. But this is just a common blacksmith. He used no magic, not like our royal blacksmith." Tayson paused. "Father, what about the Crow Judge? Surely, he knows what's going on. Why isn't he stopping this maniac Arimaspian king?"

"There are some things the Crow Judge cannot solve, and this is one of them." The old king stood up, his gray eyes dimmed with concern for his son. "You must relax. You're wearing me out just watching you pace." He smiled kindly. "On a different note, I spoke with the dragon the other day. He cautioned me to stay in the palace and await more information for our noble Crow Judge. He spoke of a traveler from a different world that will be helping us stop this abuse of the spiritual laws and his agreement between us and him. He said Connor is leading him here. You are to teach him to fight."

Tayson leaned his head to one side and let out a frustrated sigh, "Yes, I know. The Crow Judge visited me last week. He informed me that the strange traveler is going to stop this problem." The prince crumpled up the message and punched it with his other hand. "Why should I train someone who never saw a sword up close? Where on the planet Curá could any boy not learn how to fight? And why have *me* train him?

King Tonyar smiled, walked to his son, and put a comforting hand on his shoulder. "Because you are of noble blood, son, and one of the best swordsmen in the human village on Curá. This young traveler is from a world where fighting is left for the men, not the boys, and certainly not mandatory for them to know. He's also quite timid and a seer. In most societies, seers and healers are not trained to fight. They are trained in their specialty's gifts. This young traveler is to be trained in both ways. We can help him and back him up in battle. Now, I suggest you go take a long walk to settle your mind, heart and soul."

Prince Tayson bowed his head, his heart sunk to the bottom of his gut. "Yes Father. I will."

***

Under the dim torchlight of the cave, Digger moved slowly, dragging his bulldozer shovel on the ground, while the Arimaspian slave driver pulled on a strong rope, making him go forward. He refused. Another slave driver slashed at him with a long whip, wishing the machine had flesh like the humans.

"You act like a stubborn child! I don't know how you move without a being inside you! The wizard says you've been bewitched, which means we ought to be afraid of you! But I ain't afraid of no one!"

"Except King Titus!" the others roared, laughing.

"Aye, we all are frightened of him."

A rambling, noisy crunch, crunch, crunch from outside the cave drew their attention away from their straining and punishing Digger. As soon as the chain was tossed away, Digger hit the accelerator and took off down the cavern, not sure where he was going.

"Hey, stop, you stupid machine!"

"Don't worry about that thing. Curly is back with more slaves," said the other.

It wasn't Curly; it was another group of workers, including human kids who had strayed from their parents, renegade guerrilla rabbits who were arguing with their captors, Arimaspian teens who had disobeyed their parents and a few Criatia offshoots who had been out looking for Cranny.

"We can't use those plant creatures! They have needles and hurt us too much," said the guard with the whip.

The other looked around, "Where did that stubborn machine go? Hildo, you let it get away!"

"Me? You're the one who dropped the chain!" They began shoving each other.

"Stop fighting and help me get this crate unloaded!"

"When we get out of here, I demand to speak to your commander! How dare you capture me, Rabbito, leader of the Guerrilla Dust Bunny Commandos! I'm a famous outlaw in twelve worlds! All bounty hunters would love to get the reward for bringing me in. But only one can. Which of you is man enough to do it? If none of you are, then release me and my gang."

The guard hit the bars with the hilt of his sword. "You are going to be the famous miner in these parts! Settle down and stop your belly aching!"

"Maybe we should get the King down here."

The others shrugged. "Isn't Wizard Seabon supposed to be bringing him here? We're due for an inspection soon."

*** 

Deeper and deeper, Digger traveled down the dark cavern under the mountain, following an echo of hammer and chisels. On either side, there were slaves chained together chipping at the walls, and rock fell like rain of pebbles and gravel. Others loaded up large wheelbarrows so high in that they couldn't even over them. He realized that he was supposed to be the one digging the walls in the denser areas. He wasn't willing to do that; it made his human heart shiver with despair. Digger was frantic to be free of this place. He prayed for help to find the one the wizard called the Indigo Traveler; he was sure that boy was the one who had turned him into a backhoe. Yet he didn't blame him. He was a kid with a good heart and an interesting outlook on life.

Somewhere down the line, Digger saw a tiny bright light and heard what sounded like another wagon coming up. He slowed up, deciding which way to go. More guards were wandering around watching over the slaves' work; he moved forward slowly.

"Aren't you supposed to be digging?" one asked him. "Where is the slave who is supposed to be using you?" He stopped the backhoe with one foot. Digger trembled from the top of his smoke stack to the bottoms of his four wheels. "You're just a dumb machine! You can't talk. He looked around to the slaves, "You, over there, drop that pickaxe and come here! You can use this thing to dig and move more rock!"

"I don't know how to work it," the worker replied. He was slumped over, his shoulders rounded from the hard work and deep feeling of hopelessness.

"Figure it out!"

Digger heard more prisoners being let out of a cage further down from the exit opening. He felt deep in his carburetor that the one he was waiting for was among them. He pushed down on his gas pedal once again, but the guard held him firmly under his foot.

The slave climbed into Digger, looking at the controls levers, not knowing anything about them. "I've never seen anything like this before. Who made it?"

"We don't know." The guard blinked his single yellow eye, wiping the sweat off his brow. "Just figure it out."

"Where did it come from?"

"Stop asking questions! Some of us were roaming the deserts and found it. Look, just figure out how to move the shovels and start digging. The king is due here sometime today and we have to find plenty of gold, silver and other metals to show him. If we can't, we'll in big trouble!"

***

Xander and Geoffrey were unloaded. They fought with all their strength to escape their captors; they tried to distract them, but the giants had them outsized. Far down the long dim corridor, they heard an engine vrooming, sounding like a large construction vehicle. Xander wondered why and how one got here, but his intuition told him that it was the lost soul. *He's a goner*, came to his mind; but that didn't make sense to him. He managed to kick one of the guards in the shin, which only tickled them. Geoffrey stooped down so Xander could climb on his back, and they flew down the corridor, Geoffrey sometimes turning on his side as he banked right and left to avoid the guards who were swinging chains, whips or pickaxes at them.

"Down there. Do you see that backhoe?" Xander asked.

"What's a backhoe?" the griffin responded, puzzled.

"It is a machine made to dig holes or pick up dirt and all kinds of large and heavy objects. Back on my world, the construction workers use them a lot. You remember my dad, don't you? He's is a construction worker and uses backhoes a lot."

"No, didn't meet him. Never really met your mom, either," Geoffrey said as he climbed up toward the ceiling, avoiding the guards, who had pulled a net out of a cubby hole. "I don't remember much about your world since I experienced it encased in stone. I hope to go back so I can see it more."

"Yeah, that would be terrific if you could." Xander held on. As they neared Digger, they could see a man covered from head to toe in the black dust inside the machine. Xander feared the man was going to dismantle it. He couldn't let that happen. He felt an urgency to save the backhoe even though he didn't know exactly why. "See that person inside the cab? Can you stick your claws or talons out to grab him? We've got to get him out. Take me down closer."

"That person has chains around him. Do you want me to yank his chains?" Geoffrey asked, not meaning to make a joke. Xander laughed.

"Yeah, let's yank the chains on the guards!" the teen cheered.

To avoid the guards, the white griffin had to make a sharp bank. He hit the left wall, scaring some of the miners down below. Others stopped working and cheered for them, which invigorated them, spurring them on to continue fighting. The man inside Digger heard the cheering and saw the guards swinging nets, swords and pickaxes up at the sky. All they managed to do was bring more of the cave's mineral and rock down on them, getting the grit in their eyes, making them shriek with pain. The slave laughed and hooted, wanting the boy and his once-white griffin to succeed in escaping their captors.

Geoffrey finally reached the side of the machine and swooped down so Xander could disembark. As soon as he touched the roof, Xander got an image of a small boy with sandy blond hair, freckles and an impish smile. His heart skipped a beat. "Milo!" he choked out.

"No, I'm Geoffrey!"

"I know! This is Milo, my friend who disappeared. I remember now. I wished for a backhoe my size. But he isn't my size," he said, bewildered. He let that thought go, "Hey, you inside Milo! Get out!"

"Do you know how to work this thing?" he replied, half standing up.

Milo put himself in gear, bucked and took off so fast Xander was left hanging from the side and the man almost fell out. As he went roaring down the corridor, he bowled over the guards still fumbling with the nets. All they managed to catch was each other. Xander wished he had more upper body strength; suddenly he felt it in his arms. He swung himself up onto the roof and held on to each side of the cab. Geoffrey flew after them.

The slave looked up at him on the roof, "Who are you?"

"I'm the Indigo Traveler. Who are you?"

"Mason. I think that's my name. How did you get this machine to go?"

"I didn't. It has a consciousness, so it's moving on its own," Xander shouted over the loud racket.

They reached the end of the tunnel. Xander looked over his shoulder to see if anyone was following them. Digger/Milo went out into the bright day orb's light. He blinked his headlights a couple times to adjust, then shut them off.

Another wagon pulled up and suddenly the guards began scurrying around, acting terrified. Xander lifted himself up to see what was going on. What he'd thought was a wagon was the royal carriage, and the notorious King Titus was getting out of it. Digger turned up his gears, shifted and continued on, not realizing who the large one-eyed giant was, even though he was wearing a crown and robe.

"Turn slightly to avoid them, Milo," Xander urged.

Milo didn't listen. He went as fast as he cold, almost running down the king. He lowered his shovel to trip the king, but Titus jumped aside. The horses, much larger than the ones on Earth, reared up, whinnying and anxious, and threatened to run away. The guards fought to settle them down, while the king yelled in anger.

Once they were a safe distance away, Milo slowed down., Geoffrey helped Xander to get down and they both stood by the machine. The slave, Mason, got out.

"That was fun." He looked at his hands. "How did my chains come off?"

Xander shrugged. "Magic, I think. Milo was created by a wish. He has an ability: When someone wishes for something while they're touching, it happens."

"Oh! Well, thank you, Milo." Mason patted the backhoe gratefully. "Can you take me to my home?"

"Not sure. Where are you from?" Geoffrey asked.

"A planet a long way from here. I got here through a wormhole, I think. Don't exactly know." The slave looked around. Above them, they heard another sound, Healer Astral landed by them. He hugged his grandcub, saying how glad he was they were safe; though his grandcub was filthy dirty. They laughed, letting out the energy they held from the chase.

***

When King Titus got up from the ground, he was more than angry. "What *was* that thing? And what kind of growth was on top of it?"

"It was the machine Curly and Dameon found the other day," one of the guards explained.

"It was supposed to have been put to work!"

"We couldn't get it to work. It was stubborn. It wouldn't do anything we said."

Titus's heart raced; he wanted to separate their heads from their shoulders, but knew he couldn't yet. "What was on top of it? Was it a human child?"

"Yeah, it was that Indigo Traveler, Sire," they agreed meekly. "The one wizard Seabon has been warning about."

"I supposed you couldn't find any jewels or gold or precious metals, either?"

"We found some, but not much."

"But we found some renegade rabbits that want to work for you in the dungeons. We have them down in the other side," the guard with the whip around his body offered.

Titus smiled grimly. "Well, maybe this day has something good involved yet."

# Chapter 15

Astral, Geoffrey, Xander and Milo (still in backhoe form), started back to the Reflection Pond. They were excited to be reunited, though it felt like they had been apart for a long time. Xander felt tired and hungry, as did Geoffrey. They talked about what to do next. Xander remembered he needed to find the scrolls that told the story of how the Arimaspian and Kent Kingdoms were connected. But first he wanted to get back to see Cranny and Jaden.

The sky turned purple to orange as the day orb continued on its downward path to the evening. Xander stilled his mind and touched Milo's hard metal shell, wondering what his friend was thinking and where he'd been.

"I can't tell you because I don't remember it all. It's all fuzzy," Digger replied through honking and toots. Xander understood.

"Who or what is that?" Astral inquired.

"This is a long-lost friend of mine, Milo. He has a strange gift. If someone wishes for something while touching him, the wish is granted. Though sometimes it doesn't work. I remember playing with him, and when he disappeared I was blamed for it. I wished for a backhoe . . . I had forgotten that until we were back at the mining cave and I saw him."

"I.... Oh, never mind," Astral changed his mind on asking. "We need to train you, Xander. We need to prepare you for the battle that will be starting again soon. King Titus is anxious to take over the Kent's land and I understand you have to be ready to do your part. And, Geoffrey, you also have to do your part."

"Yes, Grandsire. Only, I won't ever be willing to do my part."

"Nor I; I don't want to fight. Though I do need to learn." Xander thought a moment or so. "Can't you teach me while we walk how to erect my shield?"

"It's better to be someplace where we can be still, to center ourselves and visualize."

"I can visualize while I'm walking. My mom meditates while she drives. She's told me about that."

"It is better not to be walking or doing anything else while we meditate and erect shields, Cubbeo."

"Cubbeo? I'm not a cub. I'm a teen!" He looked at the old griffin with surprise.

"Relax. He calls all young ones Cubbeo. It's a term of affection." Geoffrey patted him. "Hey, can we fly? We'd get back quicker. Digger, can you reduce your size? Or travel faster?" Digger nodded his backward arm in response. "Okay, imagine you're at the Reflection Pond."

Digger did, though he wasn't sure how to get there. He sensed the directions through the white griffin and Xander's touch.

"Okay, Xander." Geoffrey squatted down, "Climb on and close your eyes." He did and the two griffins ran together, then jumped into the air. Digger bucked at the sight, wanting to call out for them to wait. Instead, he relaxed and wished himself to the body of water he had seen through Xander's touch. Moments later, he heard the griffins landing beside him. He opened his eyes and smiled as he saw the clear waters of the Reflection Pond, and the surprised faces of the friends who had been camping there.

The next morning, as they relaxed after breakfast, Astral and Xander went to a quiet spot away from the others. It felt odd that Jaden and Cranny were still there after two or three days. He had expected them to move on. Then it occurred to him that maybe they had been told to stay where they were.

Astral directed Xander to sit under a tree while he sat in front of him. Astral sat back, all the way on his backside, moving his back-lion legs forward and touching the pads together like a triangle. He directed Xander to put his feet together, too.

"What's the point of that?" he asked, thinking the old griffin looked uncomfortable and that the half-lion half-eagle looked silly with his feet together like that.

"It helps to relax and center you." Xander did it, even though he doubted it would work. "Now, bring the tips of your fingers together in like manner," the healer added. Xander understood because he had seen his mom sit that way.

"Now, take a deep breath and release it slowly. Allow your thoughts to flow down your body and out the bottom of your paws. Take another breath; let it out slowly. Focus on the middle between your nostrils and center between your eyes; that is your third eye."

Xander knew he meant his forehead since Astral was used to teaching other griffins.

"Imagine you are rooted to the spot, like a tree. Visualize a swirl of energies above your head; they are relaxing."

Astral's voice was even, calm, almost monotonous. Xander easily let go of the tension in his body, and his jumble of thoughts. Suddenly, he felt an urge to draw or write. He couldn't get to his backpack, though. He settled to watch as an invisible hand began to craft individual letters, as if he were watching a toddler show on television. The hand finished, and he read, *Peace begins with you. Two hearts in two different dragons were shared with two different people on Curá. The first dragon shared his heart with an Arimaspian prince. The second with a Kentese Prince. The original contract they agreed to was peace. This contract has not been abided by. You are the secret.*

His vision cleared as he felt his spirit rise slightly out of his body, dimming the strange darkness around him. It was broken up by a swirl of colors, and out of them burst a white griffin. At first, he didn't recognize it as Geoffrey.

*See the white griffin rise like a phoenix from the fire.*

Again, the vision cleared and Xander saw a sword with three blades. The two on the sides were smaller; the middle one was longer, streaked with red. He felt the sense of fire tempering the steel.

*Do not fear the dragon sword. Do not fear the dragon with the wisdom and the history who will lead you. A lowly prince is your second teacher. He is the pupil not sure if he is ready for the teacher to come to him. Wisdom resides in a young body. Embrace yourself. Embrace your path at this age: Never say too young, never say too old. All follow. The key will be found.*

A sense of peace enfolded Xander as he watched and listened to his inner guide. He didn't wonder who was speaking to him, because it all seemed right.

Outside of him, Astral paused in his guidance as if he realized his pupil wasn't fully aware of his voice. Gradually, Xander came back to his body. He took a deep breath and opened his eyes, smiling.

The griffin beamed at him. "Wonderful, though we didn't get to the shields. Okay, close your eyes again." The healer was patient. Xander did it, and relaxed easily. "Now, visualize yourself in a bubble. Put your arms out to set your boundaries."

"Boundaries?" Xander cracked one eye.

"The boundaries will keep people from getting into your space. You set the limits. Also, the shields that you will pull down will prevent you from picking up information on anyone unless they ask for it or it is necessary for you to know."

"Okay, I'm ready." Xander smiled, imagining a being inside a purple bubble. He set his boundaries to no more than a few yards from himself, hoping when he got home Butch wouldn't be able to get close to him. *He'll run into an invisible wall,* Xander mused to himself.

"Now pull down another shield, like a cap, I think your world calls it, to prevent someone else from sending their thoughts to you either knowingly or unknowingly, unless you need to be aware. Choose a color for this cap if you want to."

Xander imagined a baseball cap, like his dad wore whenever he went out. He smiled because it felt right.

"Okay, Indigo Traveler, you're ready." Astral sounded pleased.

Xander opened his eyes, feeling refreshed and secure.

"Now," said Astral, "When we get to the Kingdom of Kent in a few days, Prince Tayson will train you to fight both with swords and with your fists. We will be in battle again – sooner than we want."

\*\*\*

Connor landed back at the Reflection Pond, glanced around, saw Astral was working with Xander. He observed Jaden playing on Geoffrey, who was lying down trying to rest. She climbed on him and slid down his back, giggling. She found a pine cone and used it to brush his snowy white wings and fur.

"Pretty griffin. Wish you were mine. Wish I could keep you like a pet," she said, hugging him.

"I'm not a pet," he grumbled, trying to be patient. "I belong to no one except myself, Jaden." He lay his head down.

Connor saw the backhoe down by the edge of the pond, staring in it. He sensed a soul within it. He went over, wondering where it had come from. Surely Albagoth would not create something like this. He touched his wing to the metal frame and sensed the distressed soul of an earth boy inside.

"What do you see when you look in the water?" Connor asked.

Milo looked at the bird, an oversized crow, startled that it spoke to him. He saw his human form in the water, only it showed him an older boy than he remembered.

Xander saw the Crow Judge trying to communicate with his friend and went to see what they were talking about.

"Can you communicate with him, Connor?" he asked as he sat down between them.

Connor moved his wing and looked up at him. "No, not really; I sense this thing is sad."

"Milo, what's going on?"

*The pond is very freaky. I don't see how I look in this form. I see my face, but older. I want my human form back,* Milo said to Xander in thought form.

Xander told Connor what he heard.

"I see." Connor thought a minute. "The Creator hasn't told me about this thing. I don't know how to help or guide it. Where did it come from?"

"Milo is the friend I had who disappeared when I was five. I remember making a wish for a magical backhoe while we were playing. I called them diggers back then. Milo has a strange ability to make wishes come true, only it didn't happen right then. He must have turned into a backhoe later. I don't know how he got here."

"Maybe if you wish for him to be back in his human form he will change," Astral suggested, walking up to them. He sat down on the other side of Connor.

"Maybe," Xander said slowly. "Only I sense we may need him in this form later."

Cranny came up to them, yawning as he stretched his limbs out. "I think I need to be heading back to my garden. My elders don't know where I am and I've been gone for more than a week. Where are you all going next?"

"We need to move on to the Kingdom of Kent. I've heard bad news: The dragon grows restless and King Titus will be renewing the war soon. He wants the land and is anxious to expand his rule."

"When the time is right, we will find the answers to undoing the wish," Connor and Astral said in unison. They looked at each other and twittered like they were laughing.

Xander smiled. "When I do that back home, we say, 'Jinx! You owe me a soda!'"

"What's a soda?" Cranny asked, wrinkling up the space between his mouth and eyes.

"It's a sugary, fizzy drink."

"Is it good?"

"Yeah, but it isn't good for us."

In the morning, they broke camp, leaving the Reflection Pond behind. Geoffrey carried Jaden on his back. Connor and Astral flew above them as the others moved along the ground. Xander rode in Digger, which comforted the backhoe's soul. Milo shared a bit of what happened to him in the last twelve years, though it was sketchy since a backhoe's memory wasn't very good.

*** 

During a lull in the conversation, Xander half slept and half considered what he'd learned since arriving in this world. He recalled meeting his true soul-self and seeing him interact with Butch's true soul-self. It still blew his mind that they were friends and got along. He had to find a way to use this information when he got home. That is, if he got home. He liked it here, so far. It was relaxing and nice not to have his parents guarding his every move or to have to go to school. Though he missed Sarah and the new friend he'd made, Kimber. He wondered how things were at school. He hoped his parents weren't worried sick about him.

"Wake up, Indigo Traveler!" Cranny called. "There's something coming our way! Giants! I've never seen them before, but I've heard stories about them. I'm afraid." His voice quivered and his limbs shook.

Xander sat up. He couldn't see them clearly because they were still very far away, yet he could make out the long, lopsided gait of the Arimaspian guards and the sound of the wagon with the cage on top.

"Danger up ahead!" he called, hoping the griffins and Crow Judge heard.

Connor swooped down, flying parallel with them, "I see them. Don't worry. There is something good going to happen out of this. They won't see us." Connor chanted a spell, the only one he knew in the old crow tongue to turn them invisible. They drew nearer to the soldiers looking for stray travelers.

Geoffrey swooped lower to find out why they had disappeared.

The Arimaspian guards brightened up when they saw Jaden. They shouted for glee, "We found Princess Jaden! We will bring her back and put her to work like a common villager, and surely King Titus will be delighted. He will forget all about us losing that machine!"

Before Geoffrey could react, the guards had him and Jaden in the net. Jaden wasn't happy to be caught. "Don't take me to my father!" she pleaded.

"I'm so sorry, Jaden," Geoffrey wailed, feeling guilty for coming down.

"We aren't taking you to the castle, you ugly girl you! You are going to the mines to work for us. Your father doesn't love you. You really are ugly, aren't you? Two eyes! True Arimaspians never have two eyes."

"We get to torture you in that mine. It'll be fun," another guard added.

"And we caught another white griffin," Curly added. "I almost believe that first one when he said he was the only one."

Xander screamed, "No! You can't take them! They're my friends!" Connor hushed him, speaking to his mind to be quiet so the Arimaspians couldn't find them.

The guards looked around, bewildered. "Who said that? Where is he?"

"I don't know. Hearing voices with nobody there is crazy. You think we've been in this weird desert for too long?"

"Naw, it was just a noise. Probably nothing," Curly replied. "Come on, turn this iron crate around and head back."

\*\*\*

After they had gone, Astral landed, "Okay, I just lost my grandcub to Titus's minions for the second time! Now, what?" He stamped the ground angrily.

"We get to Kent as quickly as possible. Digger, can you transport yourself, Xander, me and Astral to Kent?"

"What about me?" Cranny asked, frantic. "I lost my friend, Jaden! If you all are going somewhere fast, what about me?"

"We can drop you off at the garden, Cranny," Xander said. "Connor, Digger can get us to Kent quickly. He's able to travel by teleportation. But Astral must be touching him. I think you can transport yourself, right?"

"Yes, I can."

"Cranny, hop in here. It won't take long to get you where you live. Your roots won't be off the ground for too long at all."

# Chapter 16

Prince Tayson watched his men practice, reminding them to be wary of all sides and not to let anything distract them from what was going on. In the last few days, some Arimaspian soldiers who had been tossed out of their kingdom for being disloyal to their king had come, asking to join forces with them. The prince allowed them if they practiced with his men teaching them the tricks and ways to defeat their former king. They were willing to do so. Tayson trusted them beyond a doubt, though others questioned why. One of his men even reminded him that they had heard King Titus usually killed anyone who spoke out or wouldn't follow his lead. Overall, Prince Tayson was happy with how all of them worked together.

A distant roar like nothing he'd ever heard before drifted up from the village, followed by a loud shriek. The men stopped battling, wondering if they should go investigate, but Tayson held up a hand. He saw their dragon flying overhead, which was unusual. He knew something was off.

"It is a sign of the times." Tayson heard the voice, and turned around to see no one was there. Connor whispered in his ear, "Crow Judge Connor is speaking to you. Stay here. The metal beast will come to you."

Tayson felt his blood pressure drop as the hair on the back of his neck rose on end. In the distance, Walfred, the wizard of Kent, hurried toward him. By the wizard's determined stride, Tayson knew something dreadful was about to happen. The dragon circled, turning in spirals. Dirt, pebbles and leaves rose as if under a spell. The soldiers scattered to make room for the large beast.

"The metal beast will come to me?" Tayson whispered, his hand on his sword handle. "Manitor is not a metal beast. What is it that the villagers are so frightened of? And why is the Crow Judge speaking to me?"

"You, Sire, are part of the play," announced the wizard. He struck the ground with the oak wood tip of his staff. The crystal encased within the diamond spiral of wood glittered. "I came to warn you. I've seen the vehicle in my dreams. It is bewitched. No one, not even a wizard, can free it."

"What should I do?" asked Tayson.

The wizard shrugged. "It escaped from the Arimaspians. Give it back to them. Let King Titus deal with the evil thing." He licked his lips. "One more thing: It got help from a white griffin and a traveler from another world. Don't trust them, either."

"Silence, cruel wizard!" Manitor bellowed. "You know not what you are dealing with!"

\*\*\*

Connor directed Xander and Milo to the gate as it rumbled opened. The sound of their arrival alarmed Tayson. He chose two of his men to accompany him and went to see what was going on. He was further startled to see a metal monster of the likes he'd never envisioned – it had a long metal arm, that ended with a ladle resembling a backward hand. The arm was connected to a hut with a person inside. He didn't know if it was human or not. Manitor came with them, which further divided the crowd, because few of them had ever seen the mighty dragon up close. A tall beige griffin with graying whiskers and feathers walked nobly beside the machine, unafraid. They walked up to the prince; the griffin stretched out his right foreleg and bowed.

"Xander, get out and bow. That's Prince Tayson," Astral whispered. Xander looked at him with a blank expression. He hadn't expected the villagers to be frightened of Digger; His ears were still ringing from their screams. "Oh, Prince– royalty. Yeah, okay." Xander hopped out, put one arm in front of him and one behind him and bowed.

"Greetings, Prince Tayson. I'm Healer Astral of the griffin and minotaur village," the griffin said in greeting.

"Yes, I remember you. You're Geoffrey's grandsire and served as one of the healers in battle. We were going to send for you again, because we've had word Titus plans to attack us soon. We have to prepare and gather all healers, medics and others, humans and griffins, to assist us."

"I am at your service, Sire." Astral stood and bowed only his head this time. "I would like to introduce you to Xander, the Indigo Traveler, from the world called Nampa."

"Hi, Prince." Xander held up a hand and waved, not sure how to act. "I've never met a prince before." He smiled, worried he would misbehave.

Prince Tayson turned his head slightly, smiling, too, amazed that this kid was to be the savior of Curá. He was scrawny and strange looking and his clothes were odd: trousers made of fabric that looked stiff and uncomfortable, so unlike his own natural cotton shirt and trousers. The boy's shirt looked strange, too, with round things on them and slots – not laces.

"What are you?" he asked, looking down the bridge of his slim nose.

"I'm human. You're human, too, right?" Xander moved one foot to the side, feeling like he was being analyzed and found to be inferior. He cleared his throat with a loud cough. Prince Tayson's eyes opened like two large saucers – this boy had no manners!

His thoughts were picked up by Xander. "Sorry, ah, Sire – I'm not used to your customs." Xander put his hands in back of him and looked up apologetically. "It's just I don't deserve to be looked down upon. I know I've only been in your world for four or five days, but I have something to offer you. At least your pet dragon thinks so, and so does Connor, the Crow Judge."

"Manitor is not a pet!" Tayson exclaimed. "He's been the guardian of my kingdom since before I came into existence!"

Manitor roared. "Prince Tayson, it isn't your place to correct or even yell at the Indigo Traveler! Yes, he is inexperienced in battle and with the social customs of this land. He is a guest and is to be my charge until I am ready to give him over to you!" The dragon lowered his voice to a loud rumble. "You will treat him with respect and as an equal. He isn't that much younger than you, by my means of telling age."

Tayson bowed his head. "Okay." He turned to meet the regal dragon' many-faceted eyes. "I'm sorry, Manitor."

"Do not apologize to me, young one, but to your guest," the dragon said firmly. "Otherwise, your father will be alerted!"

"No, Manitor, don't tell Father!" he looked at traveler, "I'm sorry I judged you harshly and spoke so unbecoming of my place. I'm only nineteen years old. And you?"

Xander smiled. "I'm thirteen. That's okay, Prince." He held out his fist with the knuckles out. Prince Tayson gave him a puzzled look, "You knuckle bump shake."

"What?"

"In my world when two guys have made peace, they put their knuckles together." Xander demonstrated by knuckle bumping himself.

Prince Tayson looked at his men with bewilderment. "Sire, I get it," the one closest to him chimed. "Like this." He knuckled bumped the new kid. "Try it, Tayson. It doesn't hurt."

Tayson put his head to one side, "I guess I could." He folded his hand and stuck it out to meet Xander's knuckles.

"Yeah, we're cool now."

"Cool? No, this afternoon orb is actually quite hot."

Xander smiled, trying to suppress a giggle. "That means we are okay. It's slang on my world."

"Oh, slang. Like a phrase that the adults don't approve of?"

"Something like that."

"Okay, so what's this metal monster? It scared the villagers and my guards."

"This is Digger, or Milo. He's a friend of mine who was accidentally turned into a backhoe."

"I see. My wizard said he escaped from the mining camps. He wants me to return it to King Titus."

"No, no way! I was directed to save him so he can be changed back to a human boy. I'm the one who saved him. Geoffrey helped us."

"My Geoffrey? My white griffin?" Prince Tayson stood up straight.

"The very same. But he isn't your griffin anymore! He belongs to himself," Xander snarled, resenting idea that the prince owned Geoffrey. "He and Princess Jaden have been recaptured by the king's soldiers."

"Oh– well, we will save them– eventually. I understand Manitor wants a word with you." The prince turned to his men, "We need to get back to the training area."

Connor became visible so the prince could see him, "Prince Tayson, remember your concerns. If something happens to the young princess, King Titus will be lost to this world. It is your concern. We also need the white griffin, since he is one of the keys to bringing peace to the land."

"Don't think I don't know it!" Tayson snarled. "But I have more important things to attend to!" he called over his shoulder. He continued off, leading his men away, though a few stayed behind to listen to the Crow Judge and dragon.

"And your father will be alerted to your attitude," Manitor reminded him.

"We will get them," Connor stated firmly.

Manitor turned to Xander. "Meanwhile, Indigo One, we need to have our meeting."

Xander's head swam. All around him the villagers were chattering. Prince Tayson was giving him a harsh look as if he wanted to kill him. Gradually, he felt something pulling on his heart strings, pulling him back to the Reflection Pond, reminding him to look for a scroll. Yet he sensed this dragon beckoning to him to follow had the scroll. He saw images of blue skies, and a creature that looked like Geoffrey, only without four lion paws. It had a head like an eagle, talons, and black and white feathers. It called to him, *Come, we have a gift. We have what you most need. The Arimaspians are heading this way, drilling their way into our mountain, trying to find a way to us. The king's son is frightened for his safety. We need you.*

*Not yet,* Xander answered. He was unsure why this creature had called to him, and was further confused as to why he felt a pull to go back to the Reflection Pond. Closing his eyes, he centered himself, exhaled, and allowed his thoughts, confusion and outside turmoil fly. He asked his inner knowing to show him what he really needed to know.

Unconsciously, he breathed in again. A blade with red streaks came into view. He saw a hand reach for it and pull away. The voice said it was hot – it needed two more seasoned blades to protect it. The sword came into view once more, with a scroll over the middle blade. Xander felt himself swoon as he opened his eyes, and realized he had forgotten to exhale. Prince Tayson's men gathered around him to hold him up.

Astral started to run forward, but was pulled back by a large minotaur dressed in a beige tunic with open front and laces hanging loose. "Hang on, Healer, old man! I have this one!" the minotaur said. He bowed his head and ran forward with all the force he could, butting Xander in the stomach with a large smack. The teen started breathing again.

"What hit me?" he asked, after recovering his breath. "That really hurt!" The soldiers backed away.

"It was me, Indigo One," the minotaur said, bowing. "I'm Donnair, Kent court's minstrel and scribe. I heard that my best friend, Geoffrey, was been kidnapped by that truant king. I want to volunteer to help you free him."

Connor looked him and down. "Donnair, you sure grew over the last two years. It seems you're ready for battle. The last time I observed you and your two friends, you weren't interested in fighting, but in writing, playing music and peace."

"Your honorable Crow Judge, I will fight for my friend as long as this Indigo Traveler is at my side. He is the savior."

"I'm just a thirteen-year-old kid from a World called Nampa," Xander objected.

"Come on, everyone back away; give us room to breathe." Connor spread his wings, pushing the crowd back. "Come, gang, we need to form an action plan." He leaned forward and led Astral, Manitor, Xander, Digger and Donnair away from the crowd. The villagers went back to their daily chores, shopping and tending to their booths.

As they walked, Xander described his visions and feelings to Astral, who nodded with interest. Manitor also nodded, very interested. "We will attend to all these demands one at a time. But first, you, Astral, Connor and I need to go somewhere no one will bother us. We need to show you the legend. Legends are truths, even though they happened long ago. Experience the events for yourself, my lad."

"Experience what for myself?"

"You'll see," Manitor responded with a wink. "First we'll go up to my cave. Get on my back, Xander. Digger, are you coming with us?"

Xander touched Digger to sense his response. More than anything, Milo wanted to be free from the metal prison he'd been in for so long. Yet he could also sense there was a deeper reason why he had to stay in it for a little longer. He really didn't want to go up to the cave – he wanted to go after the little giant girl with the deformed second eye. His heart went out to her because he felt so deformed himself.

"He says he can't go, or doesn't want to," Xander told Manitor. "He's concerned about Jaden – he wants to go get her."

"Ah," Connor said. Closing his black jewel eyes, he sent out part of his spirit to get an insight into what was happening to the child and Geoffrey. Instead, a being he'd never met came into his vision, waving a finger at him. *Tut-tut-tut. You aren't allowed to see this, honorable Crow Judge. This is closed to you, but open to the Indigo Traveler. I sense he won't be here for quite a while. Seabon is with the enemy king. He knows me. You shall see the true image later when the masks are taken off. Look to the maze under the one-eyed king's castle. It needs more than you could know. Where is your mighty Albagoth when the kingdom of Kent falls? He who looks within will find only emptiness. He who looks without will see the sky falling down. It is all imaginary – spiritual bliss is an illusion!*

Connor's eyes flew open. "I don't think so!" he spluttered. Manitor, Xander and Astral stopped talking and looked at him. He cleared his throat, stretching his neck up as high as he could. "There's something not right about that mountain. Through my seeing, Jaden and Geoffrey are no longer there. There's a maze deep below the Arimaspian castle that houses a demon of some sort. A wizard who is not who he claims to be is in charge. I recognized him. He's the one King Tonyar trusts here: the wizard Walfred."

Manitor paused, gathering his wits, looking away from the group. "I've warned Tonyar over the years. He trusted him because his father trusted this wizard's kin and owed a debt to them. I can't protect them from everything." He closed his eyes in thought. "Digger, you choose someone to go ahead of us to the mountain or where it is best. The minotaur would be a good choice. Meanwhile, Indigo Traveler, you come with Astral and me to my cave for the scrolls and more preparations. In time, you will be trained to fight."

# Chapter 17

Xander expected the inside of Manitor's cave to be cold and damp; instead it was rather warm. They walked along pathways, of which were there were many, each leading to a different room. Xander wondered why one dragon needed so many rooms. In there were jewels and gold embedded in the walls, which made him wonder if there was a main pile of treasure the old dragon guarded, as the myth said. The cave was lit by a light that the Earth teen had never seen before, although he had heard of lights like this.

"The lights you see were designed by a traveler named Telsa. The lights give off warmth, too, to heat the cave for me. My reptilian blood cannot get too cold."

He sighed, a sound like a sad wind blowing. "Telsa came here in his youth because he was searching for a better light source than electricity. He wanted a safer, more effective science. We showed him. He traveled on a journey like yours, Indigo Warrior, only he had already accepted himself. He died broken, because your world refuses to accept true geniuses who really have a gift to share. They allowed another who pretended to care about the well-being of the populace to discredit him. Arise, my Indigo Warrior! Do not allow others to put you down for what the seeing shows you. Follow it. If others don't share the same vision, pursue it anyway, knowing Albagoth is within you and it will work out." They padded on down the hallway. The semi-darkness made Xander's senses keener, yet he wondered aloud, "Where are we going?"

"To the treasure store, where I will dig for the scrolls to share with you. The blade is there, too, somewhere. Over yon exit, where the day orb shines at end, you, Astral, and Connor wait for me." They looked down the path to see the waning day orb the afternoon light. The three companions headed toward it while the old dragon went on to find the scrolls and sword.

From the ledge, they could hear Manitor digging through the pile. It sounded like he was breaking dishes and trinkets. Xander hoped nothing too valuable was lost. This day, though long, had been exciting. At home his day would've been boring.

Manitor joined them with the scratching, rustling sound of a large reptile dragging its tail through gravel. "I found the scroll and the blade used to cut out the hearts of my ancestors," he announced. He sat down, curling his tail around himself. "Come here, Indigo Teen, I want to give this to you. You will experience the story firsthand. As you touch these, tell me what you sense from them."

Xander approached, remembering the seeings he'd had before. He took the scroll in one hand and the blade in another. They felt hot and cold. From the blade, he sensed a deep love, compassion and longing to save two different heirs to two very different kingdoms. The scroll held the history of these two kingdoms; an agreement and loyalty to one another and to the dragons who pledged compassion. He related his sensations to the dragon his companions.

"Yes, that's very true." Manitor held out a massive clawed paw. He breathed fire over his empty palm, chanting a spell under his breath. When the fire subsided, a golden sheath covered with jewels lay in his palm.

Xander let out an awed breath, reaching for it, "Careful, it's still hot," Manitor cautioned.

Carefully, Xander took the sheath, handling it like a baby animal. He examined it from all sides. "It's beautiful," he sighed. He slid the blade carefully into the sheath. He noticed there was a place for a belt to be put in it, but he realized he didn't have a belt.

"Don't worry about a belt. After this blade is connected to the two smaller blades and the hilt, you will be given a larger sheath for it. Right now, read the scroll. Go off by yourself where you can concentrate."

The teen, nodded and walked off to the far end of the ledge. Astral, Connor and the dragon watched. When he was out of hearing range, they spoke softly, planning what to do. Each shared their worries about the days ahead, and how to accomplish their goal. Connor assured them it would work out because the Creator shared their concerns and goals. Yet he remembered hearing doubters say the Creator was always on both sides in a conflict. They wondered whether this time there was only one side, because King Titus of the Arimaspians didn't believe in a Creator.

Xander sat on a boulder, unrolled the scrolls and began reading. They outlined the agreement of two different kingdoms made with the dragons of Kent.

*The Kent Dragons, being of two hearts and one mind, have lived about the said kingdom since before the Crow Court was in place. They have abided without prejudice and are guardians to the kings and queens of this valley. Anyone who comes in need of a heart to save an ailing child, not of this valley or kingdom, shall agree to live in peace with the kings and queens of Kent. If a disagreement arises between you two, seek the honorable way, requesting a hearing of said dragon or his ancestors so no harm is done. If you or a descendant many eons removed disregards this, you will create a dishonor of said heart given in good faith, and Albagoth, who works in conjunction with all dragons, will cause disruption within your own heart, mind and soul. The traveler with the indigo colors will wield the life force blade. It will bring a remembrance of the pain and anguish the ancestors experienced and the love the Kent Dragons had. Peace will reign supreme once more.*

Xander paused to consider: The sword would cause remembrance of the pain and anguish of the ancestors. How would that help or make the wayward king turn around? What else could he do? Would he have to stab the king to get him to renounce his evil ways? What had happened to make him go astray, anyway? Those answers, he realized, might not be his to know. He remembered his dad saying that sometimes trying to understand another prevents us from seeing a way to accept them for what they are. Maybe the acts of this evil king were good. Maybe everyone needs to go outside their comfort zone. That made him think of Geoffrey. The white griffin had said he needed to fight even though he knew it was not what he was born to do. White griffins were a symbol of peace.

"Well?" Manitor's deep, resonating voice echoed over the ledge bouncing off the distant trees and boulders down below.

Xander roused from his thoughts. "Well, what? The scroll? I don't understand how the sword can help. I don't want to hurt anyone . . . ."

"Thousands died in the span of years before King Titus started the war. And more died after the official start of it. Many more are missing. We need to bring an end to this. He needs to experience what his ancestors felt before they went to my dragon ancestors for another heart."

"I don't see how that will help him," Xander said stubbornly, looking out from the ledge to the valley.

Connor and Astral came over, hearing his response. "You will understand when you experience the events that led up to this day," Connor told him. "Come, Indigo One, it's time to go back to the Reflection Pond. Climb on Astral and we will fly. Manitor, are you coming with us?"

The dragon wagged his head left to right. "No, I will stay here and monitor the Kent Kingdom. Titus is bound to start the war soon. My gut tells me to expect an attack within two or three days. We must be ready."

"Yes, training or not." Connor said in a clipped tone. "Xander, get on Astral. We need to go."

# Chapter 18

King Titus sat in his son's room, crying, remembering the day the gryphons came to get his son, Kontar. Titus missed his firstborn; it had been three years since they took him.

The gryphons were like the social services of Curá, when need be. Kontar had been distressed about leaving his home, but was excited to ride on the bird-like lion creature.

Titus wondered how big he'd grown and how he'd changed. *Someday soon, I will get you back, Kontar. Not someday. I will get you back soon,* he thought to himself. *I hope those you are with are well and getting along. What are they teaching you? I hope it is not faith in that false Creator this world worships so!*

"Your Highness, excuse me," a meek voice interrupted.

Titus frowned. "Who are you and how did you get in?"

"I am Wizard Walfred from Kingdom of Kent. I bear no ill will to you. I've been helping the blacksmith to provide weapons to your soldiers and guards. When the metal creature escaped your mines, and came to Kent, I convinced Tayson to return it to you. It's on its way to the treasure mountain with a minotaur."

King Titus stroked his beard, his large beige eye slightly closed as he considered what he heard. He really couldn't see the use of the metal machine since it had nearly made him break his neck two days ago. His rump still ached from falling. But his thoughts of Kontar lingered, too.

"Wizard, can't you see I still mourn the loss of my son?"

"Yes, I noticed. Need I remind you that the mountain you mine is in the gryphon's territory? You could easily steal your son back."

"Do you want to get me in more trouble with the Crow Judge?"

The wizard's lips twitched in a smirk. "Why do you care what the Crow Judge says or thinks? He's just a bird. He has no real power. It is what we make of ourselves that matters. You want riches and land. I am a wizard of amazing abilities. I can help you win this war." He stepped closer to the king. "King Tonyar is an ignorant fool who puts more faith in his arrogant son than in himself. You need to strike without him being aware you're coming. "

The wizard bowed lazily, looking up at the one-eyed king. "You're wise, my lord. You have noble intentions and want to do away with this phony peace. Together we can create Curá in your image and strike down the false Albagoth. After we conquer every territory here, we can destroy the Crow Judge Realm! We'll create our own rules. You'll be the god of this world."

King Titus considered the wizard's words. The plan appealed to him, yet something didn't feel right. He shook his head, "You have a point. We will venture to the gryphon's mountain and take my son back. But how can we go to the land of the Crow Judge if it isn't real? How can we conquer a mythical place?" He paused, fixing his eye on the wizard. "Unless you have a knowledge of its reality? Am I wrong in my conclusions? Is the Crow Judge acting by the judgments of the court instead of his own decisions?"

Titus shook his head. "My own wizard, Seabon, says he has been to the land of the Crow Court. He described in detail what it looks like, even giving me elaborate depictions of the structures and beings who dwell there. Which of you is telling me the truth?"

"I have met Seabon," Walfred admitted, standing up. "He has come to Kent to mediate treaties." The wizard looked away, not wanting the king to know what really was going on in his thoughts. "Yes, I have met him in passing, but he is not in your favor. Surely you know he has formed an alliance with Kent and with the Crow Judge and will give away your secrets. I, for one, will not."

Seabon, who had sensed something underhanded happening in the castle, paused at the door to listen. The multicolored fluorite stone wrapped in the golden wood of his staff pulsed with Seabon's outrage and anger. The Kent wizard was trespassing on the Arimaspian lands and ignoring his own authority, he thought indignantly.

Seabon silenced his mind and breathed out his concerns, focusing on Connor and Albagoth for advice. One must guide him in what to say. *Knowledge comes when all is quiet,* he had learned. But his mind would not stay calm. As more of Walfred's words drifted through the open door, he couldn't with strain himself any longer. Seabon barged into the room.

"Sire! How can you listen to this weasel? He's trespassing on our boundaries! He's filling your mind with lies! He won't stand by your side once you agree to his terms! How can you even consider following his counsel?"

"Wizard Seabon," demanded the king, "Is it not true that we have the advantage? After all, we have the prized white griffin that is supposed to bring peace to the land. With him and my cursed daughter imprisoned in the maze, guarded by the guerrilla rabbits, there's no way for Kent to win. Peace will go the way of the mythical pledge that my ancestors were supposed to have agreed to before any of us were born." Titus laughed, shaking his head. "Indeed, it is farfetched to say this Wizard from Kent is on our side, yet someone has been helping my men obtain quality swords, maces and battle axes our own blacksmiths couldn't make. He has a power and foreknowledge I haven't seen from you."

The king paced in front of his wizard, glaring at him. "Tell me, Seabon, weren't you heard talking with the Crow Judge not fourteen days ago? One of my sentries passed your door and heard you speaking at length. I've felt for some time that you are not fully with me on my plans to expand my territory. You speak often of forfeiting the fight. You keep telling me that my own heart will fail if I don't stop." Titus laughed again, shaking his head. "It's all a myth, dear Seabon. It won't happen any more than that blasted dragon will come down from his perch and protect King Tonyar and his weak-kneed prince! I will prevail! And this wizard, here, who is *trespassing,* is offering to help me win." He glanced at Walfred. "And if he doesn't, I will feed him to the guerrilla rabbits." He narrowed his eye until it was a mere slit like a line marking boundary not to be crossed.

Walfred bowed slightly. "I won't fail you, your Highness," he said calmly, as if Seabon wasn't even there.

# Chapter 19

Across the meadow, Digger and Donnair walked together, observing the Arimaspians forces gathering, heading in the opposite direction. Donnair feared they were heading to Kent to strike, but he noticed that no one seemed to be leading them.

"How are we going to break into the castle and get Geoffrey and Jaden?" Donnair whispered. Digger tooted softly and waved his crooked arm, though the minotaur didn't understand. The minotaur grumbled to himself, then smiled and slapped the machine good naturally, "I wish you could talk so I could understand you." An electric sensation traveled up the side of the yellow vehicle into his hand and up his arm.

Milo felt the familiar sensation and sighed. "Finally, I'm able to speak rather than clicking, tooting and honking!"

Donnair jumped back. "What happened?"

"You wished it, and I made it so. I'm gifted with the ability to grant things, though it might not be what the one really wants. Sometimes it happens to me instead of the other person." His voice sounded like a reviving engine.

"I wanted you to talk," Donnair said after a moment. "What do you make of those soldiers marching? Where are they heading?"

"Don't know, though it looks scary. That crow said something about a surprise attack. I'm guessing it that king hasn't decided what he's doing. When I was around him, he seemed distracted by thoughts of his son."

"How do you know?" Donnair glanced over at the soldiers disappearing over the hillside, unaware of them.

Digger didn't answer him. "Stop looking at the soldiers, Donnair!" he urged. "They might notice us. Hey, do you know where we're going?"

"No, I thought you did." The minotaur flexed his ears, flopping them forward and back. "Can't you go places, open wormholes or something like that?" he asked. "I'll climb inside you, and wish to go the castle of the Arimaspians." He climbed behind the wheel, and they vanished with the speed of light.

They materialized deep underground, surrounded by a hundred oversized guerrilla rabbits. The leader wore two crossed bandoliers around him, and a bandana around his right ear to the top of the left. He had a scar that went from one ear to the corner of his mouth.

"Uh – erm," stammered Donnair as he faced the tall, muscular rabbit. "I see you don't work out much, eh?"

***

Xander walked back and forth in front of the Reflection Pond. Astral stretched out, lowering his front legs, yawning, with his hind end up in the air, stretching like Xander's cat, Clarence. "Stop pacing, sit down by the water, relax your mind and let go of your concerns. What is there to be afraid of?"

"That image isn't me. He has gray sideburns and creases beside his mouth! He looks like he's at least 30 years old!" Xander replied.

"You're frightened to see yourself older than you are. It's normal for those who aren't used to it."

"What does he know about my life that I don't?"

"The image is your higher self, Indigo One," Astral said gently. "Allow him to teach you and guide you. Still your mind, allow the questions and concerns to float to the forefront so he will know what you need." Astral lay down, resting his head on his crossed forepaws, and closed his eyes. In two seconds Xander heard soft snoring.

"Great," he muttered half out loud. "Now what? The great healer falls asleep!"

"He's an old griffin. The last few weeks have been difficult for him. He isn't used to journeying back and forth. You're a being a pain, too!"

Xander looked around, startled. "Who said that?"

"I did! Look in the water, my younger self." Xander obeyed. The reflection was the same as the one that had greeted him when

Geoffrey took him into the water, but it didn't look quite as old or gray as he remembered. "You're frightened of getting older. What makes it so scary for you?"

"I'm not frightened of getting older. I just can't believe I'll ever look as old as you do. It's like looking at somebody else, only you have my face. It's weird."

The reflection smiled, though it looked more like a smirk to Xander. He scowled back. "You think you're so smart. What makes you think you know more about me than I do?"

Connor, overhearing, shook his head, "My young traveler, let go of your anger. Quiet your emotions and look into the reflection without judgment. What do you need to know most?"

"I need to know what I'm doing here! There's supposed to be a battle, but nothing is happening. I want to know how to get Butch off my back in my home world and why I have to be telepathic. How can I use these gifts for good?"

The face in the water rippled. "You already have the answers for most of those questions, younger self. You have the wisdom within you, but you refuse to see it. So, here I am, showing you. I'm the image of the old soul within you that you're still denying. And I wasn't smirking at you either, younger self. I was merely considering how short-sighted you are. Right now, all you see is what is happening to you at school, how your parents don't understand you and how your teachers are against you. Do you even realize that the girl you dream about is also interested in you?"

Xander shook his head, puzzled because what he heard wasn't what he'd expected. He glanced at Connor and then closed his eyes, deciding to do as the crow told him. He expected to see just a watery image like a reflection in a mirror. Instead, he felt a living, breathing entity with a vibration, emotion and knowledge.

"How do you know so much about me?"

"It's a puzzlement for everyone who visits this pond. I can't give away the hows and whys, because then it would lose the mystery. You already visited the library of your past, but the Reflection Pond deals with your present, too. You need to find the history of the blades and the scroll."

Although there was no breeze, the face dissolved and reappeared. The water was moving in the pond. That meant there had to be an inlet somewhere. Maybe it was underground. Xander remembered when Geoffrey had accidentally fallen into the pond with him. He'd sensed a vast store of knowledge. Maybe the faces he and others saw were just a way for people to communicate. With his gift, maybe he could get more information directly from the pond. He cocked his head to one side, considering what to do. He had to find the scroll and the blades, but his older self was right: He needed to know more of their history in order to know what to do with them.

The face spoke again. "Two dragons gave up hearts to keep two royal heirs alive. One of the youngsters was heir to the Arimaspian throne, the other was heir to the throne of Kent. The price of their lives was a pact of peace. Today's Arimaspian king wants nothing to do with the legacy or the agreement. For peace to come back to the land, we need to remind him of how it was before the agreement. He must remember. His heart will fail him with one touch of the blade that was used to cut out the dragons' hearts. The dragon is central, but he can do nothing until you have made the king's heart stop. You, my young Indigo Warrior, are the promised one who can heal the wound."

Xander leaned back on his heels, wary of this revelation. "I want nothing to do with causing death. I only want my griffin back. All I want is a way to get to Arimaspia to free Geoffrey and Princess Jaden. Will you help?"

"No, that is not my purpose." The reflection glanced over at Connor. "Unless the Creator or the Crow Judge require me to be of help?"

Connor tilted his head to one side as if considering, then shook his head slowly.

Without thinking, Xander took a deep breath and jumped into the Reflection Pond. He surfaced near the other side to take another breath. Treading water while he considered his options, he looked back at the black bird and the sleeping healer. Connor looked like he was smiling.

Xander plunged under the water once more. A small bubble appeared, flashing with green light. The green turned to gold, and the light moved deeper. Xander decided to follow.

They swam through a narrow channel. Xander felt a touch of fear as he passed jagged rocks, coral reefs and sudden drop offs.

Multicolored fish swam around him. Some veered away from him, as if frightened. He thought to them that they were safe. One long, silver-blue and black fish with whiskers came up and blew bubbles in his face. He pushed it away.

The golden bubble led down and down, deeper and deeper. Xander began to wonder when he could surface for air. The bubble turned bright orange, as if to warn him that it was dangerous to surface. Yet he couldn't hold his breath any longer. He began to gasp and choke.

The bubble rushed back, growing in size as it came, until it was bigger than the Earth boy. It was so big that it swallowed him whole. Once inside, Xander took deep breaths of the welcome air. He relaxed, feeling safe, as if he were in his own private exploration capsule.

He was delighted by the sight of many types of fish and sea creatures that he'd never seen before, all swimming by and ignoring him as if it was normal to see a human inside a bubble. The bubble floated smoothly, covering distance way than faster Xander could have.

"Where does this come out?" he asked out loud. Then he realized he didn't have to speak. The bubble showed him visions of many things. At last it carried him through what felt like a worm hole, to a place he didn't recognize. They popped out, landing on the sandy beach.

# Chapter 20

Xander was surprised to see many others, from one-eyed giants to humans, griffins, gryphons, minotaurs, plant people, and other life forms he'd never seen before. They were gathered around playing, eating together and relaxing. The men wore tunics over knee high trousers and sandals; the women wore dresses with aprons and sandals. The boys' outfits reminded him of pictures he'd seen of nineteen-twenties swimming suits, like skirts with knee high shorts under them. He wondered where he was.

The bubble opened and Xander climbed out, feeling a bit out of place because his own tattered jeans were very dirty. In the distance, two dragons sat on large hills, calmly watching the activities. A large black bird flew down and perched between them. Xander realized that must be a Crow Judge, but it wasn't Connor. His heart told him the world was at peace, yet he also felt tension. He saw the two kings, (he guessed they were the kings, because they were dressed in much finer clothes than anyone else), standing off to one side. They seemed to be arguing.

"Get closer, my lad."

Xander jumped. A man in a blue robe stood beside him. "Who are you?" Xander demanded.

"I'm Seabon, wizard of the twentieth realm. None of them can see us."

Xander looked around, taking in everything. He noticed vendors setting up nearby, selling items that reminded him of festivals back home. He thought this must be some sort of a celebration. "Is this a special day?"

The wizard nodded. "It's a day set aside for peace. Connor asked me to accompany you, though I didn't ride the bubble with you. The wormhole from the Reflection Pond took us through a time zone." He gestured to the world around them. "We're back before the dragon legend began. Observe the two kings. What do you see?"

"I see tension between them. Though the two princes are playing together well."

The one-eyed prince, taller than his same-aged human counterpart, ran after him and tackled him. They laughed together, tumbling on the ground. Suddenly the taller boy bent over, clutching his chest and gasping. The two observers walked closer to see.

A woman with long gray hair tied back in a ponytail, and a wooden staff carved with strange symbols, hurried toward the two boys. Xander could not hear what she said to them. She straightened, and Xander heard flapping above them like a large flock of birds were gathering. He looked up, "Hey, isn't that Manitor, the dragon?"

"No, that's one of his ancestors. The woman coming toward us is the wizard for the Kingdom of Arimaspians. She's one of this present king's most valuable advisors."

As the old sage moved toward them, she lifted her finger and pointed, muttering something Xander couldn't make out. It sent chills up and down his spine.

"She must be powerful, what is she saying?"

"Use your ability to see through her, Alexander," Seabon advised, inching away from him. "But keep your eyes on the two princes, especially the taller one."

Seabon continued to move away until he disappeared. Xander didn't notice. He focused on seeing within the old lady.

He could see her concern for the young prince's health, her worry about the failing heart within him. She had felt her own heart falter when she touched him. She looked up as a shadow darkened the celebration. Xander saw a huge dragon approaching. He guessed its wings would cover thirty block or more. Some of the women screamed and children ran to cower by their mothers.

The old woman gathered the young Arimaspian prince in her arms. She sent the human prince back to his people. He didn't want to leave his friend.

The dragon's powerful wings stirred up the sand, and a whirlwind blocked Xander's view. When it cleared, the dragon stood facing him, his large multifaceted, multicolored eyes whirling as if they were drilling a hole through him.

"Indigo Traveler, you are here to observe," the dragon's voice boomed, "to understand. You're a ghost to those who are in the moment. Come, follow me to the Sage and the ailing prince"

"I don't understand. What's wrong with the prince? I sensed he was being admonished for running around with a human. But what's wrong? Why are you here?"

"I was summoned by the King of Kent on behalf of the ailing prince. An agreement must be forged between the two kingdoms." the dragon, swayed his head to look down at the human traveler. "When you get closer, observe the prince. Use your empathy to feel what is ailing him. Do not ask for it to be spelled out for you."

"At least tell me what they're celebrating. And why are they afraid of you, Manitor?"

"My name is Grandor. They are celebrating the Season of rebirth. Today the villagers in all the kingdoms will be planting their crops. A truce is called so all can come together, play under the warmth of the Day Orb and thank Albagoth for this wonderful time. It is said the Creator of All comes down to walk among us during this time."

"Then why can't we see him? If he or she is so real, wouldn't we see?"

"No, Xander." The dragon wagged his large head from side to side. "Albagoth is a Spirit. The way to recognize a spirit is to sense or feel it deep within oneself. Only when one is properly in tune with one's inner self will one be aware of the spirit's presence. The great wizards and sages of this age are very in tune. When you finish your journey, you, too, will be aware; even when you go back to your own world."

The dragon sighed. "We need to come together to honor the Creator more often, but the Arimaspian King is not following the ways that have been handed down."

They walked in silence. Xander observed the crowd slowly coming back to the beach. The adults were cautious and the children were curious. The human king approached, bowing to the guardian of his kingdom.

"Royal Grandor," the King of Kent addressed him, bowing. "The enemy's son is ailing. They want you to look at him. I beg you not to grant their request without consulting us. Consider the best needs of all the nations of Curá." The king's tone was sharp, on edge. Xander sensed panic and frustration.

Grandor lowered his massive head, returning the king's bow. "Your majesty, put your worries to rest. I have been loyal to your kingdom since long before recorded history. My ancestors watched and protected you. We train our young dragonets to do the same. I came to hear and see for myself. I will have an audience with the Arimaspians and ask the Creator to be present, too. We will decide the best avenue for healing that will not threaten our long-standing agreement."

"Thank you," the king replied, sounding less than pleased. He bowed again and left.

Xander marveled at the respect this king showed the dragon. He remembered Prince Tayson's treatment of Manitor. He guessed Tayson either wasn't taught or felt Manitor didn't deserve respect, taking the dragon's presence for granted.

They neared the tent where the ailing one-eyed prince lay. The king and queen sat to one side of their son and their sage sat on the other, preparing herbal treatments for him. Xander noticed the young boy was having difficulty breathing. His face was turning blue and pale. Xander thought he might have asthma.

"Don't think," the dragon advised. "Turn your mind off. Journey inward to your soul's knowledge to find out. If you need to, approach and touch the prince's hand. He may feel you, but he'll think it was the wind. Send him hope, healing and openness to seeing the Creator of All in this moment." At the cot side, the dragon bowed his head, *Creator of All, I answer to your greater wisdom at this moment. Show me what must be done.*

A large crow appeared by his side. "I was sent to watch and observe," he announced to everyone. "The Creator is considering forming a Crow Court to handle affairs on Curá. I'm called Nestor," he added.

Xander approached the cot, reached out his right hand, and let his thoughts drain away. The prince seemed to calm down and his breathing became less labored. He opened his eye, turning to look right at Xander, but the large blue eye was glazed, like it wasn't focusing on anything. Xander closed his eyes, stilled his own breathing pattern and tried to see into the ailing prince. He felt his own heart hurt, skip a beat then go still as a great shearing pain to shot through his left arm. *No,* he shouted inwardly, *I am not the one with the broken heart!* His heart started beating again and he knew this prince needed a new heart.

"Grandor, his heart is failing him. Can't you do something?"

"What would you have me do?" the dragon asked, looking at the Arimaspian king.

"Share one with our son," the queen pleaded. "He is our Kontar, our only son, honorable dragon. We know you do not share your hearts willingly. But if he dies, Arimaspia will be lost."

Grandor glanced at Nestor thoughtfully. A sly look brightened his eyes. "Hmm, so you are asking me to share one of my hearts with you, eh? Do you think it is a free gift?"

The queen looked at the king, and back to the dragon. "What could anyone pay you? You have no use for jewels, gold and crops. Albagoth has given you all that you need or want. Please, give this gift freely, honorable dragon."

"Ah, yes, you're right. I have no need for what you Arimaspians and humans desire as wealth. What I prized is peace within the nations of Curá. This is what the Creator of All also wants, and that is my price. The new Crow Judge here, Nestor, will record the peace treaty. You and your ambassadors and the ambassadors and king of Kent must come to an agreement on a lasting truce, a treaty that will be binding on all future generations. Once you have agreed to the terms set down, I will gladly give your son one of my hearts.

"And if the treaty is broken, then what?" The Arimaspian king stood up tall, head held high. He narrowed his large blue eye until it was a mere slit, and stared at the enormous reptile.

Grandor bowed his head, wishing he could cluck his tongue. He wished he could incinerate the arrogant king, but knew Albagoth wouldn't approve.

The dragon reared up on his haunches and spread his wings. "Know this, your majesties. It is the condition of the treaty. If a future heir to the throne decides this treaty to be folly, and starts war once more in this land, then his only son will be taken from him. A pure white griffin will be born, and a traveler from another world with the aura of pure Indigo will come to wield the three-pronged sword. The middle blade will be the one used to cut out

172

my heart and will be sealed with the dragon's breath of the living ancestor. When it pierces the heart of the offender, his own heart will stop."

The king and queen sucked in their breath in unison, and the king of Kent, standing nearby, turned pale.

"We have to agree to those terms, Davon," the queen whispered. "If not, our son will die." The king closed his eye, bowing his head.

"I don't want to give up my quest for more land. Kent Kingdom has more than their share! We can't have that! We are a larger nation that towers over the puny humans! Our lands are meager compared to theirs."

Xander saw the Kent king's hands clench in anger as he heard his enemy's words, but he kept silent.

"It isn't the size of the lands that measure how noble a king is. It is the size of their heart and their ability to bless their people with good will and to help their neighboring countries," Nestor scolded. "The Creator of All wants peace in this world. That spirit of love and soul are within each living person, both animals and plant life. Now, where do you stand?"

"Father," the young prince said haltingly, "please submit. Prince Mason and I are friends. We don't want this war to continue. We will do much better in peacetime helping each other and our own people. Please, Father, agree to the dragon's demands."

A shimmering wave of air, like a heat wave on a summer day, blurred the scene. When it cleared, Xander was standing at the cave above Kent Kingdom. The sages of both kingdoms were present, as was Grandor the dragon, the king and queen of Arimaspia and the king and queen of Kent. They signed the treaty.

Grandor lay on the ground. The prince lay on a flat boulder nearby. Sage Saybon held up a long blade, reciting a prayer and incantation for the ceremony to be blessed and honored through the centuries to come. Then the sage thrust the knife into Grandor's chest and cut out his spare heart. Grandor shuddered. The other sage opened the prince's chest, removed the damaged one and inserted the dragon's heart.

Another shimmering wave brought a different scene. Xander saw a new land, a different Crow Judge, and a young prince of Kent who was very ill. A sage told his father and mother that the boy needed a new heart. The king agreed to ask the dragon, a descendent of Grandor, for the favor. Xander saw the same procedure take place, using the same blade that had been used on Grandor and the Arimaspian prince. Although it seemed to be many years later, he knew that this was the second half of the treaty, sealing Kent and Arimaspia in a pact of peace.

Xander felt himself floating. The bubble reappeared, and he stepped inside. He fell asleep pondering what he'd seen.

He awoke as the bubble popped out of the aquaduct onto green land. He felt wind tickling his face as he stepped out. Nearby, he saw a tall hill topped by a castle many times taller than any he'd ever seen before. It was made of bricks with gold edging and jeweled designs that seemed to large red eyes on each stone. A flag with the eye symbol flew over the main tower.

"This must be the Arimaspian home," he said aloud. "Now what? I guess I walk up that hill and find a way to break in and free Jaden and Geoffrey."

# Chapter 21

Donnair sat in the corner of the labyrinth strumming his lyre and singing a sad tune he'd just written. The last place he wanted to be was here. Over in the next cell, he could hear the Guerrilla Rabbits marching, and their leader, Rabbito, dividing them up to make sure all the cells were guarded. For some reason, Rabbito was preparing for a raid. He was a bunny that wasn't content with hopping around in a meadow, digging holes and munching grass. He wanted action, and if there was no action, he would stir it up.

"Hey, minotaur, why are you so unhappy? Can't you sing a marching or fighting tune?" taunted a guerrilla rabbit as he rounded the corner. "We're preparing encase your friends come to break you out!"

"No one will come to break us out. No one knows we're here," said the minstrel sadly.

"I could always release the deformed girl the king's soldiers brought in a few days or so ago. She'd be a tasty snack for you!"

Donnair puckered up his bull lips and shuddered at the thought.

"What's wrong? You don't like female Arimaspian children? You must be a picky eater, hmm? I bet you'd love that griffin. He's pure white; sure, would be special to eat him! After all, if you do, that means the prophecy can't come true and the war will go on forever until the Kingdom of Kent is conquered. If any humans remain, they'll be the slaves of the King Titus and his son." The rabbit lowered his voice. "That is, once he gets him back."

Donnair turned his head upward, wishing he had a connection to Albagoth in order to change the circumstances. Then he lowered it to stare into the eyes of the mean rabbit. "The white griffin is my friend. I refuse to eat him. I came here to free him. Now, where is he? And where is the princess?"

The guard bunny laughed and shook his head. "You really think I'm that dumb? The king ordered you to be put here. Your orders are to fight, terrorize and eat anyone who comes into this maze." He paused, wiggling his nose in a rabbit's version of a grin. "After you tire of playing with them, of course." He stuck his head in Donnair's face. "You're an ugly creature! You're half human and half bull! Surely, you've had human before, right? I have it on a good authority a boy from a different world maybe coming. If he does, kill him. Got that?"

Donnair laughed. "I'm a singer, poet and storyteller. I only eat vegetables. No meat shall pass these fat lips!" He sucked them in as he imagined them sealed and padlocked.

The brown and white splotched bunny lifted his nose in the air with a huff. "I eat plenty of meat and it don't hurt none! And we rabbits are supposed to be vegetable eaters. Rabbito says meat helps us be more vicious and on guard." His long ears twitched toward the passageway. "I better go; I hear the leader calling. Better see what's wrong now!"

The minotaur was glad he was alone, though the silence, which was usually comforting, was deafening to him. He didn't want that evil rabbit back, though. He put his lyre down and stood, wishing he knew what to do next. He walked a little way, curious about the winding passages before him. His nightmares always showed him in a labyrinth, so he was living his worst fears. The clip-clop of his hooves echoed through the hallway. He didn't find anything wrong, yet it was creepy. The pathway was circular, twisting and turning so that his head almost started spinning. He knew there had to be a way out, but he couldn't find it. He remembered hearing old stories about labyrinths that sometimes-changed directions. He jumped as a sparkle light went off to his right. He looked again, turning fully to see, but it was gone.

"I wish Connor or someone was here to help me," he muttered under his breath. "I wonder what happened to Milo or Digger or whatever that machine goes by. I gotta find my way out of here."

In the corner, the very far corner of the maze, a spider, wearing a bridle with reins, clung to the wall. Its tiny rider clucked his tongue, listening to the minotaur. "I can help him, Gretchen," he told the spider, "but it wouldn't be right. The traveler will be coming. We need to get back to our own world." The little man shook the reins. "Come, Gretchen. We'll mark the way for him."

He took out a pouch, reached inside and pulled out a pinch of gold dust. He blew it into the air and reached for more as the spider made its way out of the labyrinth, leaving a faint, glittering trail along the passageway behind them.

\*\*\*

Xander reached the top of the hill, wondering how to get in. The ground at his feet shimmered faintly with gold. He followed the golden path, hoping it would lead him to an entrance.

As he walked, he saw a sparkle light off to his right, where a little man was riding a large spider. Xander peered down at them. The little man wore a tunic and had a tiny ankh around his neck. His spider had a tattoo on its forehead in the shape of a triangle. They disappeared so quickly he almost thought he'd imagined them. He bent down, looking even closer. Where they had been, a shiny blade poked out from under a bush.

Xander pushed the branches aside. The sparkle of light he had seen was the day orb reflecting off the tips of two curved blades. Leather wrapped all but the tips. Xander picked up the bundle and opened it carefully. Inside he found a fancy hilt and a scroll. "'The Alchemist Blacksmith of Kingdom of Kent shall make one blade of three,'" Xander read aloud. "That must mean these go with the dragon's blood blade I already have."

He put them in his belt loop, tying them with the loose leather thong, and followed the path that wound around the castle. He hoped there would be in entrance nearby. Eventually, he saw a doorway with a bull's eye painted above it. He thought he saw the little man and his spider hanging there in midair. He sensed the man smiling at him.

He walked closer. The little man and spider really were there, suspended by a silk thread. "Who are you?" Xander asked. "Why are you helping me?"

"We're here by mistake, Indigo Traveler. But as long as we're here, I want to help you. We're supposed to be in the World called Nampa to alert another Indigo Child of his own quest. I'm a Murdoc. I'm called Terence and my noble steed is Gretchen." The spider waved two front legs at Xander. "You better go in and find your friends," the little man continued. "We're off now, to get a map of our dimension portals back on our home world."

They disappeared again, and Xander shook his head. He was sure he hadn't imagined them this time, but he had no idea what the little man had been talking about. Were there other Indigos back home? If so, he hoped he could meet them. He wondered what they looked like and if he went to school with any of them.

He brought his thoughts back to rescuing his friends. The door in front of him was small, which puzzled him. The Arimaspians were a race of giants. In his world, they would be called Cyclops. This doorway was far too small for them. The door looked like it was made of oak. It was rounded on top and the handle was made of iron, with a large loop hand grip and a place to press down with your thumb. The moment he touched it, though, the handle disintegrated. Puzzled, he tried knocking on it to see who would answer.

*** 

Inside the labyrinth, Donnair sensed some kind of movement outside the castle. "There has to be a doorway somewhere," he muttered out loud. His voice echoed, startling him. He heard knocking again, but couldn't see a door. He held his breath and listened to hear which wall it was coming from.

"Hello? Won't someone let me in?" The voice was so faint it could have been a cockroach.

Cautiously, Donnair walked to the wall. He heard the voice again.

"Jaden? Geoffrey? Are you in there? Somebody open the door for me."

The minotaur smiled. "You're a friend of Geoffrey!" he told the wall. "There's no door here. But if you see one, maybe it's magical. I wonder what kind of magic we need to get it to open."

Terence and Gretchen spun down from the ceiling in front of Donnair. "Must we do all this ourselves?" grumbled the little man. "What kind of a minotaur can't perform magic?"

Donnair's jaw dropped. "Um, sir." He paused to consider. "I think – I mean – my people aren't magical. My people are farmers and my mom and sisters work with the healer. I, myself, am a minstrel, and a sad one at that. But if you can help open the door for this traveler, I'll be eternally grateful."

Terence reached into the satchel attached to his waist, and pulled out a small bag and a stick. They grew as soon as air hit them. The Murdoc sprinkled silver and orange dust towards the wall, muttering strange words at the same time. He waved his staff and the wall changed into a small oak wood door. Another wave of the staff opened the door.

"No need to thank me. Just you two be sure to stop the war. The Arimaspian soldiers are receiving their marching orders to invade the Kent Kingdom. Do what you need to do quickly. Now, I really must be going before my superiors chew on my backside!" Terence and Gretchen vanished again.

Xander quickly crawled through the door. Donnair hugged him, forgetting how much bigger he was than the teen.

"I'm so happy to see you!"

They jumped as the doorway disappeared with a 'pop,' leaving the same brick wall that had been there before.

"Now what do we do?" Xander half expected the little man and large spider to return, but they didn't.

"You're Donnair, right? I think we met briefly. Where are we?" Xander asked as they walked along the path.

"Yes, and you're Alexander, the Indigo One." The minotaur perked his ears. "We're in a maze or labyrinth. It's guarded by these big angry rabbits. They get in and out of somehow. They expect me to eat whoever is thrown in. I'm supposed to be mean ugly and scare everyone off."

Xander thought he sounded despondent. "That's the least of our troubles, Donnair. Geoffrey said you have a good heart. You're a poet, so you should know that words have power. Maybe we can use them to find a way out. For now, though, let's be quiet so we can use our other senses to find what we need."

"Okay, you're the one with the insight, I've been told."

The labyrinth reeked of dust and mildew, and they could hear unseen things scampering around in the darkness. They knew whatever it was had gotten in through some small hole or doorway; they just had to find it.

\*\*\*

In the cells above them, Jaden and Geoffrey sat with their heads together, trying to think of a way out. "Milo is here," Geoffrey said. "Maybe he can help us."

"Milo is a digger," Jaden agreed. "But he's guarded, too." She thought of what the guards had said. "Do you think they'll really take him back to the mines?"

Geoffrey shook his head. "I think it was an empty threat. He won't work for them."

"Xander will come and save us," Jaden said with certainty.

Geoffrey was quite despondent as he stared out through the bars. He wished Milo was in the same cell with them so they could plan. He was a firm believer that three heads were better than one. He put his front paws up on the window sill high in the wall. The day orb was at its highest point in the sky, telling him it was noon.

They heard footsteps in the cobblestone hallway. Geoffrey put an arm around Jaden. Her large green eye blinked with fear. The footsteps began to slow, and then stopped abruptly outside the cell. A roundish face with a gold eye in the center appeared at the window in the cell door.

Jaden jumped up and ran to the door. "Seabon! You came! Are you going to get us out?"

Geoffrey looked at the man. He was tall, and dressed in flowing blue and silver robes. He held a wizard's staff. His odd, half-human face lost its welcoming smile.

"I'm sorry, Princess, I can't. But I will do what I can. I pledged myself to Connor. I will help the Indigo Traveler and the metal machine, too. I've done what I can to make sure your father's plans fail, but he's working with the wizard of Kent now. Walfred is working to overthrow his own king. All I can do is to study my books and scrolls."

"You will get us out!" Jaden demanded. "You aren't old, Seabon! You know the right spells! I command you to get us out. Xander and that bull-human are trapped in the maze downstairs! You must free all of us!"

"Ahem!"

Seabon looked down to see a rabbit tall enough to come to his waist standing beside him. The rabbit had ammunition belts strapped across his chest and an eye patch. He also had a machine gun pointing at them.

"What are you doing down here, Wizard? I've been directed to watch your every move. You try anything and I will blast you across the hall!"

Seabon smiled as he lowered his staff, pointing the jewel at the burly, angry rabbit, "Pund ungunish!" he muttered, blasting the threatening rabbit clear across the hallway. It hit the wall with loud 'smack!" and slid down, dropping the machine gun. Spare bullets scattered like marbles, pinging and rolling everywhere.

"Quickly," the wizard urged. He searched the rabbit's pockets for a key. "No one is coming now." He unlocked the cell door and Jaden and Geoffrey hurried out. "Now to free the metal monster. C'mon!"

They found Digger in a room by himself chained to a wall. Seabon walked around to see what the chain was attached to so he could free him.

"I'm so happy you came," Milo greeted them. "I was worried you all forgot about me!" He tried to lift his crooked hand shovel, but couldn't because the chains held him down.

Seabon held out his hand to feel the bond, sensing whether there was also a spell binding him in place. Closing his eyes, he asked to be shown what needed to be done. The words began to roll across his inner vision. The old wizard opened his one good eye, uttered the words he was given, and the chains disintegrated as if they were made from ash.

"Thank you, Mr. Wizard," Milo said with his engine voice. "Now, can you give me back my human body?"

"No, I'm sorry, Milo. Albagoth guided me that your metal body has a few more tasks to do. After they have been completed I will be shown how to change you back."

"Then we need to find Donnair," Milo said. He raced ahead of the others, even though he didn't know where they were going.

Seabon raised his hand for them to wait. He cocked his head to listen beyond the walls and under the cobblestones.

\*\*\*

Far below, Xander and Donnair wandered through the labyrinth. Donnair's hooves clopped like heels, echoing through the maze. Xander wondered how they'd ever find a way out. He stilled his thoughts, sending out his extrasensory perception to show him what to do. Instead, he picked up on the minotaur's worries.

"You're afraid of being found by the wrong people, Donnair? I saw images of the bunnies you mentioned. I vaguely remember seeing them a few days ago when Geoffrey and I were captured and taken to the mine." Xander paused as a thought came to him. "What if we could get to the king and stop him before the war starts?"

The minstrel shook his head sadly. "We won't. What kind of weapon do you have? All I have are my songs and my stories. I can entertain him to death, but I doubt he'd like what I would say."

The teen took out all three blades. "I have these, but they aren't attached to the hilt. I'm supposed to take them to the Alchemist Blacksmith in Kent. But I think I could use the dragon's blood's blade without one. What's the harm?"

His new friend shrugged his shoulders, "I don't know. But Healer Astral, my sire, and my dame always stressed the importance of following directions. Especially when it came to magical tools. I was going to apprentice with a minstrel who would teach me stories and songs that had a magical element, but he disappeared. Don't know what happened to him."

They walked on in silence. Gradually, Xander's senses sharpened. He sensed voices and footsteps above them. Then he heard Milo's engine running. He knew he could get a telepathic message to him if he tried.

*Milo, the minotaur and I are down below. We're trapped in a maze or labyrinth; can you use your shovel to dig down here to get us?*

# Chapter 22

Milo paused, listening to the message. He turned to Seabon. "Wizard, what's underneath this floor?"

"The king put in a labyrinth a month or so ago. I don't know who gave Titus the means to build it. I heard some half-human half-bovine creature was put there. There's no door or entrances as such. They're hidden. Only a very strong magic can get through. I wasn't a party to developing it, though. Why?"

"Xander just sent me an internal message that he and a minotaur are lost down there. He asked me to dig into the floor to get to them."

"A half-bovine and half-human?" Geoffrey exclaimed. "That's my friend, Donnair! We must free them!"

Seabon nodded, understanding. "Something's blocking my magic in here. I can't transport them out."

"Well, then we start digging," rumbled Milo. He did his best to sink his crooked back hand down into the hard cobblestones, but he couldn't penetrate the floor. He sighed, sounding like a motor struggling to turn over only to sputter out. Geoffrey urged him to try again.

"We may need a powerful chemical to eat through the rock," Seabon suggested. "Not that we have any. Titus uses explosives in the mines sometimes, but we couldn't use those even if we had them. Too dangerous."

Geoffrey scratched his head with one talon. As a white griffin, he thought, he should have some magical abilities that would help. Then he thought of something someone had said about Milo and his beak opened in an eagle's version of a grin. "Everybody put a hand on Milo."

"I don't see how that will help," grumbled Seabon, but they all did it anyway.

Geoffrey placed a paw on the cab of the backhoe. "I wish we could go to Xander and Donnair." He felt a pop and they suddenly found themselves standing in front of Donnair and Xander.

Geoffrey laughed at the surprise on his friends' faces. "We came as quickly as we could."

"So, what do we do now?"

"We leave!" Jaden exclaimed. "We gotta get out of here before my Pappa knows we escaped. I had a vision of him sending some of his best men to Kent to start the war again. And others are going to the gryphons to get my brother. We need to hurry."

Seabon spoke up from behind them. "I found a door built into the wall over here. It leads to a stairway, but I think it would be better to use magic to get us out of here. My staff seems to be working again."

He held it out, drawing a circle around them with the jeweled end while muttering an incantation. As he completed the circle, smoke rose around them. They heard the guerrilla rabbits yelling and stampeding down the hidden stairwell. Just as the rabbits reached the door, the group vanished.

Connor was waiting for them in a nearby tree. Xander laughed, happy to see him. "Sometimes your Crow Judge senses come in really handy. I'm glad you knew where we'd appear."

The gang stretched, taking in deep breaths of the fresh air and loving the heat of the day orb on their skin. The heat warmed Milo's metal body and he made a happy, revving sound.

Connor watched a moment. "Sorry, but there's not much time. We need to fly. Milo, take Xander, Jaden and Donnair to the alchemist blacksmith in Kent. Prince Tayson will be meeting us there. Battle is starting sooner than we expected."

"What about me?" Seabon asked.

Already in flight, Connor called over his shoulder, "Make room, for Seabon, too."

Geoffrey looked at his friends who were busy trying to cram inside the backhoe's small cab. "Not everyone will fit," he observed.

"No duh, Geoffrey!" Xander exclaimed. His words echoed back to him and he heard the anger.

"Someone can ride on my back," Geoffrey suggested. "Xander, Seabon, or Jaden. Don't mean to offend you Donnair, but you're too heavy."

"No offense, old friend. I can squeeze inside Milo and take Jaden."

"I think it's better to put Xander in there since he has to carry the sword," the old wizard suggested.

Xander untied the two smaller blades from his belt loops and wrapped them carefully in the leather with the larger dragon's blood blade. He pushed the bundle into the cab and climbed in after it. "Let's not waste any more time!"

# Chapter 23

Alchemist Tarrier was at his forge, spinning his tongs in the hot fire to make sure the horseshoe would be perfectly round. He took it out and blew on it, scattering sparks. He was generally pleased with his work. A black and gray striped cat lay curled in a ball on the stool behind him, lazily wagging its tail, very content to be in the shade of the awning. Out of the corner of his eye, the old blacksmith saw a blur of colors swirling.

"That magic metal monster is coming in, Master," the cat said.

'Yes, Lynx, I see it." Tarrier went back to his work.

Milo came into full view, the day orb's late afternoon light bouncing off his windshield. Xander and Donnair climbed out, happy to be in one piece.

"Hey, there. Quite the travel machine," Tarrier called. "How'd you get it made? Sure, it took a lot of gold and jewels to commission it."

"No, actually, it was made by accident," Xander answered, walking up to the burly man. Tarrier scratched his thick beard, watching the teen approach, sizing him up. Xander took the blades from his pack and unwrapped them as he walked toward the blacksmith. "So, you be the Indigo One," said Tarrier. "You have fine blades for me to appraise?" His baritone voice boomed, sounding like he had a built-in megaphone.

"I have three blades that need a hilt." Xander started to say more as he handed them over, but was interrupted by a crowd of villagers yelling.

Tarrier put down the horseshoe he was working on. Lynx stood, arched his back and stretched. Finished, the cat shook himself, splattering drool everywhere. He giggled as his owner shot an evil look his way. "The Arimaspians have finally started a raid," Lynx stated blandly, jumping up onto the counter. "We'd better get these blades in a hilt and in a hurry."

"Aye, they're fine blades," Tarrier started. "One is the legendary dragon's blood blade. You'd better be careful when wielding this so you don't stab yourself. And these two smaller, curved ones are to be treated with poison, I take it," he summarized, scratching his chin again.

"One needs acid and the other a deadly element. Put the shorter blades on either side so the curves meet across the longer one," Lynx advised.

"You blasted feline, stop telling me how to do my business. The ole dragon gave me thorough instructions already, as did Connor." As he said that, Connor and Astral landed. "Speak of the judge himself." Tarrier smiled broadly, showing teeth with some gaps and some made of gold and silver.

"The enemy is nigh," Connor told them. "They're coming in the gates, stomping on any villagers in their way and grabbing produce without paying. Can you hurry?"

"I can only do what I can, Your Honor. As it stands now, I have to find the right hilt and jeweled shield."

"It doesn't have to have jewels," Xander objected. "I'm not a girl."

"The finest jewels set in the shield, my boy, are the power stones you will need to ensure you have confidence," the alchemist explained.

Tarrier rummaged through his big bin of parts, leather and gold, steel and wood. He knew he needed something solid to fit the blades into. Xander and the others grew uneasy. They glanced back to see what was happening, still hearing the villagers yelling and women screaming.

"I'll go alert Prince Tayson and his men," Connor said. "Someone will be down here soon." He took flight, not waiting for anyone to respond.

"You Nervous Nellies better go see what you can do," Tarrier told them. "Take that machine with you, too. Whatever is trapped inside is distracting me from my thoughts. Lynx, go with them. You're not much good for anything!"

"Like you ever give me compliments, eh? I find my own food, Old Man." The cat jumped down, flicking his tail. "Come with me." He walked proudly away, his tail straight up in the air, showing his behind. He thought of something and turned his head. "Where's that wizard from the other kingdom?"

"He's right here. He came with me," Geoffrey stated, catching up with Lynx.

"What makes you so special that you can talk and act like you do with that blacksmith?" Xander questioned.

"When I was a kitten, Tarrier found me under a broken-down, half-burned cart. He took me home, healed my burns and nursed me back to health. He used his knowledge of alchemy to open up my speech and language center, so now I speak his tongue, reason like the humans and also speak feline when I have to. I've been able to travel in dimensions. I can even cast spells. After all, we felines are magical creatures that few people really appreciate. We've been around for ages, so we're like brothers, or friends who know each other so well that we rib each other. He calls me worthless, but I know he means the opposite."

"Words have power, my mom always told me," Xander said, frowning, "I'm bullied back home, and the taunts echo in my mind over and over. Every time I hear them, I feel bad all over again. Listening to you and your owner talk and tease each other reminds me of what I hear in the hallways in my school. It sounds hurtful,"

"Aye, words have power indeed, Young Traveler. Tarrier is not my owner; he's my friend. The bullies you speak of...." Lynx closed his eyes to get a better view of what he heard. "Hmm, yes, some taunts directed to you are meant to be hurtful. But the words that you hear from your friends-- they call it teasing. Next time you hear them, pause to look deeper inside each person to see how the words are meant. I can't say more without being present. Felines aren't allowed at your school, isn't that right?"

"Yes, it is," Xander agreed. They heard what sounded like a stampede of a thousand head of cattle. They turned to see soldiers on horseback with Prince Tayson in the lead.

"Get out of the way!" the Prince shouted. As he ran by Xander and the others, he looked over his shoulder. "Gerald, when you get up here, grab the foreign kid and take him with us! Geoffrey, we need your magic now!"

"I ain't ready, your Highness!" Geoffrey yelled back. "Neither is Xander!"

"No time for protests! Come along, now! No time for explanations."

One of the soldiers reached down and grabbed Xander by the collar of his shirt, yanking him up. Xander felt like he was going to be choked.

"Get help, Lynx!" Geoffrey called, taking flight.

"Won't do that, Master White Griffin. You are where you need to be. I'll tell Tarrier what happened, though. And I'll call that Wizard Seabon. You all need assistance."

# Chapter 24

King Titus moved stealthily through the desert, hoping no one would see him. He approached the mountain of the gryphons. He noticed one or two were flying around the large, barren mountain, which was covered with a few trees and bushes similar to sage brush. The wizard of Kent, Walfred, trailed behind, looking around warily.

"Sire, there is a way into the cavern and stairs that lead up. We must get your son before the battle gets going too strong. We don't want to miss Prince Tayson's last breath." His laugh was mean. "Remember, if anyone gets in our way, that little traveler from the other world will also die. "He imagined rubbing his hands together since he couldn't do it. One hand held his staff and the other was reaching out to sense the cave.

A bronze-colored gryphon swooped down, calling to them. "Halt, King Titus, where do you think you're going?"

"I'm just out for a morning stroll." He smiled, his blue eye glistening, though the mountain's shadow hid it from the gryphon.

"You're mighty far from your homeland to be strolling. Even with your long legs, you couldn't get here that fast. You've been traveling for a while, haven't you? That isn't your wizard behind you, either."

"I follow him willingly, gryphon. He's in the right to want war. Conflict is good for the human condition."

Titus's neck hair rose along with his ire. "I'm not human, you imbecile! I'm an Arimaspian!" The king removed his whip and coiled it in his hand, ready for use.

"Sorry, your Highness," said Walfred. "Still, conflict is good for the soul. We need to hurry. I sense the armies are gaining back in Kent."

"I'm not leaving until I have my son back! Move, gryphon! Let us through!" Titus swung his whip at the guard. The gryphon repositioned himself and grabbed the whip with his talon. He turned and flew as fast as he could to raise the alarm.

Other gryphons responded. Many had donned their armor and carried weapons in their talons. From the top of the mountain, Titus and the wizard could hear a little boy calling down. "Papa? Papa! I'm here!"

Hearing his son's voice, King Titus was both excited and angry. He was excited to hear his son again, but he was angry that the gryphons were stronger than he had been led to believe, angry that his whip had been taken from his hands. Fuming, Titus jumped up and down, shouting, "Bring my whip back, you miserable birds!" He looked more like a spoiled rotten child than a ruler of a country.

"Sire, may I remind you that you are taller than those flying lions?" observed the wizard. "All you have to do is reach up and grab them out of the sky

"Oh, yeah." Titus stopped, thought a moment, and broke into a run.

One of the gryphons came back to taunt him. "Hey, Arimaspian, you may be able to catch us, but we can still fly higher than you can reach!"

"Don't taunt him, Rico! We don't know what he can do. Be careful of the wizard, too!" another called from above. Rico looked down to see that Walfred was pointing his staff at him, preparing to zap him.

"I have my own special magic!" Rico called back. He jutted all four of his talons and paws outward. "Tabber ah zinc ar quin eat ya!" he screamed. Lightning came out of his front claws at the same time as the zap came from the end of the wizard's staff. Rico's lightning formed a large creature with head, terrifying teeth and horrendous claws. It grew huge, and roared, wrapping its jaws around the other lightning bolt and devouring it. Instead of fighting back, Walfred stared dumbfounded.

Titus stopped running. He reached up as far as he could to get the blasted gryphon, but he couldn't reach the creature. Each time the king landed on the ground, the mountain shook, small pieces of it fell down, hitting both the gryphons and King Titus.

"Papa, stop! The mountain will collapse!" Kontar called out. The leader of the gryphons came up, hushing him and urging him to climb on his back.

A larger piece of rock hit Walfred, bringing him out of his shock. He shook his head, considering what to do. He had dropped his staff. He bent down to pick it up, ducking as two gryphons came flying on opposite paths. Intent on striking the wizard in the head, they collided with each other instead. Walfred stood up, gathering his thoughts as he mentally shuffled through all his spells. He had to have one that would work.

"Vivia la lotion contra obstleclas snake or rake!"

The whip came alive, and brought itself up, stretching until it could wrap around the leg of the gryphon carrying it. The pain made the gryphon yell and drop it. The whip twisted like a figure eight and back again. Kontar, on the back of the leading gryphon, reached out, instinctively knowing it was his father's whip, but couldn't quite get it.

"Don't touch that!" Valor, the leader of the gryphons, warned him. "It isn't what you think it is."

"It's my father's whip, Valor. It's safe." Kontar smiled as he spoke. "I've always wanted to touch it."

"It isn't safe, Kantor. It's been enchanted."

King Titus saw them overhead and took a running jump, flaring his arms and hands doing his best to catch the gigantic bird, but missing. He kept trying until he was able to touch Valor's claw. The whip landed with a thud, falling lifeless at his feet. The king picked it up and began threading it through his fingers again as he watched the direction the gryphon took with his son.

"Sire, don't strike!" Wizard Walfred warned, though the king seldom listened to anyone.

"I know what I'm doing, wizard! You are proving yourself worthless! If you have tricks up your sleeve that will work, you'd better start pulling them out. I want my son back!"

"Yes, Sire, right away." Wizard Walfred turned around, cursing the position he was in. He wanted to get the prince back for King Titus, but it wasn't working the way he wanted. Somehow, he had to find a way to do it without the cursed abominations bothering them.

More gryphons came to the call of Valor and the guards. One began following the wizard, observing what he was doing.

"Alert the Crow Judge!" Valor's mate called from above. "He must know the prince's safety is at stake!"

"Shut your beak trap!" Titus roared as he aimed his whip at the gryphon carrying his son. It sizzled through the air, striking Valor's tail, sending him into a spin. Kontar screamed.

"Papa! What have you done? Valor is my friend and protector!"

"The only protector you need is *me*, Kontar! Don't hold on! Jump! I'll catch you!"

Kontar didn't intend to jump, but Valor was having difficulty getting his balance back. The more he flapped his wings and tried to straighten out, the more he lost it. Kontar fell, tumbling down, spinning, and calling to his guardian for help. Inwardly, the gryphon leader asked Albagoth to assist him.

*Don't worry, Valor. Allow the boy to be with his father for now. It is almost over. Be watchful of the wizard. He is a wily one not true to anyone,* came the answer from the Creator.

The gryphon looked around. He couldn't see the boy until he saw Titus with his arms extended, waiting to catch his son. The gryphon let out a veer and the others turned their heads to listen. Several of them dived from the cliff to help their leader. They were too late. Titus caught his son, turned and ran.

# Chapter 25

Xander twisted around to look at the soldier who was carrying him. "Hey, I gotta go back and get my sword! The blacksmith has it. I can't go into battle without it!"

"No time, Indigo Traveler," the knight replied. "We have our orders. The blacksmith will get the sword to you. He's an alchemist and can transport objects from one place to another easily enough. We need to hurry. There's word the enemy is threatening the villagers."

*Patience, little one.* The words came into Xander's mind as if someone else was talking to him from afar.

*Who are you?* he asked.

*I'm the one you want to meet face to face. I'm the one who also dwells deep with you. I'm in all things and in all creation, regardless of the world a creature or being lives in. I'm called by many names, Xander, especially in your world. Don't worry about the exact name.*

The knight's cold gauntlets on Xander's bare arms brought him out of the private inner conversation.

"Up ahead," the knight said, pointing. "Smoke." He looked at Xander. "I thought you were asleep. How could you could sleep with the thunder of the horse's hooves all around us?"

"I wasn't asleep; just musing inwardly," Xander replied. He straightened up in the saddle, to get a better view. As he did, he thought he saw tall plant creatures fighting off the one-eyed monsters. They reminded him of Cranny. "What are those vine creatures?"

"Those are elder Criatias from the lesser desert area of Senilona. I've never seen them this far from their garden village. Something's really got them riled. I hope they're on our side."

Xander thought of his friend, Milo, and turned around; Milo was rolling behind as fast as he could. Xander heard wings flapping, and looked up to see Geoffrey flying overhead. He smiled. Connor and Astral joined Geoffrey. All my friends are here to help me, Xander thought, smiling.

Connor swooped down. "Be watchful. There may be a trap up ahead. We need to lure these enemy soldiers away from town. I'll fly ahead and get the Criatias to move out, too."

Xander sighed. He looked up at the sky, wishing he could be on Geoffrey. He felt squished between the knight and the small horn on the saddle. The galloping of the horse was giving him a headache. He wasn't used to the way it moved. He closed his eyes, trying to center himself, digging deep within his being to ask what to do up once they got the battle.

Sensing two flying animals approaching, he opened his eyes, worried about an attack from the enemy, but it was his friends, Astral and Geoffrey. They flew down low until they were even with Xander, Astral to the right and Geoffrey on the left.

Astral spoke aloud. "Let Xander ride on Geoffrey. They need to be at the center of the field. King Titus isn't there, but over with the gryphons. I'm sending Digger and Jaden there. Donnair can stay with us."

"King Tonyar told me to obey your directions, Healer," said the knight as he let Xander down. "But what use is a singing minotaur to the battle?"

"He has some magic tricks up his sleeve. He's learned to sing spells that may be quite useful to us." He turned his attention to the white griffin. "Geoffrey, you know how to get to your cousin's mountain, right?"

"Yes, Grandsire. I know. Don't worry, we'll make it fast and be back for kippers." He bowed, flying in place.

"You have your orders. Be careful, and remember to access the information you learned at the Records Library." Astral waved them off.

"Yes, Grandsire." Geoffrey turned to fly off with Xander. "I will. I'll be careful with all in my charge."

As they flew past the fighting, Xander and Geoffrey saw the Criatias using their spikes as weapons. The taller ones would position the smaller plant beings behind the Arimaspian soldiers and trick them to stepping backward until they didn't just trip over the smaller ones, but landed on top of them so the spike-like needles were embedded into their behinds and backs. Some of the elder plants had long, slender limbs they could stretch out and wrap around the one-eyed giants. Soon, though, King Titus's men had all of them on the run.

# Chapter 26

Xander, Geoffrey, Milo and Jaden watched the two sides clashing from the sidelines. The noise from the battlefield was both awesome and frightening. The clang of the swords, bang of the catapults and shouting of the soldiers reverberated inside their heads, making their teeth to chatter as if they were chilled to the bone.

"This isn't where we're supposed to be," Xander said to Geoffrey. "We're supposed to be where that misguided king is."

"We'll get there, don't worry. I sensed a disturbance here. Something is happening that shouldn't be." Geoffrey looked around, wondering where the wizard of Kent was. He spotted Wizard Seabon and called to him. Seabon looked around, but Geoffrey couldn't hear what he said.

"He doesn't hear you," Milo roared. The friends were all talking at once.

"Quiet! We aren't supposed to be here!" Jaden shouted over the uproar. "Astral said to go somewhere else. We're not part of this battle. My papa is trying to steal my brother back. We've got to get to them first. This battle frightens me," she added, crowding next to Xander for protection.

The Indigo Traveler sucked his lips in, and narrowed his eyes, thinking. He remembered what he needed to do. Closing his eyes fully, he centered himself. He imagined turning off the around him. *Okay, Albagoth, you answered me once. I ask again: show me where I am, or where I'm supposed to be. Astral directed us to somewhere else and we landed here by mistake. But Digger felt guided here, and so did Geoffrey.*

*Wait for it,* came the response. A blurry object that looked like a white orb with a long slender green stem came to Xander's inner sight. As the object grew nearer he saw it was a pure white rose with a long green stem. He cocked his head, struggling to understand the meaning. The moment it came into full view, the gray and black striped cat showed itself, grinning, and grabbed the object between its teeth.

*This is for you, Master Traveler. It's a two-edged sword. You've no time to train to use it. Just know my friend and master, Tarrier, says to be careful of the two smaller blades. One has been treated with acid that will burn you to a crisp in an instant if it touches your ski. The other was treated with a poison that will rot you from the inside out. It needs a special sheath, but there's no time. King Titus has a weakness that he cannot strengthen. Be careful where you go.*

The cat's thoughts faded out in midsentence as Xander's focus shifted to a wizard of medium height and unnaturally yellow eyes snarling at him. *You will not harm King Titus with your toy! You're no match for me!* The wizard paused. *This is your seeing, so why am I threatening you in it?*

*So that I'll be warned you're coming to prevent me from my task,* Xander replied. *I have news for you, though. Albagoth is on all sides of this battle. Though she wants what is best for Curá, and that is peace. Your heart tells me that you really don't care if Titus survives this. You only want the riches and plunder. You think King Tonyar gave you a raw deal when his ancestors signed the peace agreement. You seek to bring Kent down. The dragon and Crow Judges work closely with the Creator. You want a share of that, don't you?*

Wizard Walfred frowned, looking hurt and bewildered. *How did you know?*

*I saw it. I was there. I saw it and felt the hurt. Though it was the dragon's legacy to protect the Kingdom of Kent, because when Curá was brand new, the Kingdom of Kent helped nurture the flying lizards and saved them from a plague. It's all there. I felt it when I touched the mighty Grandor. He shared much with me. You owe them much more, Walfred. You owe them.*

The wizard turned away.

Geoffrey nudged Xander and whispered in his ear. "This is a fine time to fall asleep. Look, Seabon is coming this way and that wizard of Kent who's helping Titus is over with the enemy. You'd better be watching and prepared to act."

"Can't act yet, Geoff," Xander whispered back, opening his eyes. Glancing over at his friends, he explained, "We aren't in the right place. Why did we end up here? There has to be a reason. My seeing tells me that there's a weakness; we have to watch for it."

"Not here," Jaden whispered back, her second eye, bright blue, open wide. "We need to meet the wizard coming to us and leave directly afterward."

The battle raged on, though it felt like the slow-motion button had been pushed, as the threesome and the metal machine focused on meeting the wizard. Xander wondered when the cat would come with the sword. His mind was still. He felt a strange peace.

Wizard Seabon raised his staff, waving it, stilling the battle and pushing the giants aside if they tried to get in his way. He focused solely on the misfit foursome coming his way. The closer they approached to each other, the more anticipation he felt, curiosity mixed with fear. He knew that only Jaden felt happy to see him and believed he would help them.

Xander noticed a dark cloud in the distance, coming in at a fast pace. He alternated watching it and watching the wizard. They reached him at the same time. Seabon's arms flew out, palms upward. His staff tumbled to the ground and he stumbled backwards as the gray cloud settled in his arms, taking the form of the feline from the alchemist blacksmith's tent.

"Nice catch, Wizard Seabon. So, glad I can still control you." Lynx smiled. He turned to Xander and snapped his claws, "Drat! I hate not having opposing thumbs! Got to speak to someone about that." Instead, he clapped his two front paws together, bringing forth a cloud of white, orange, and red. He held out his front legs, paws upright. A brilliantly jeweled scabbard appeared. "Your sword, Master Indigo Traveler. Beware of things that are not what they appear to be."

Xander took it, thanking the feline. Lynx smiled, gave a bow and disappeared. "What is it with that cat? How can he just pop in and out like that?"

"He's a werecat, Xander," Seabon explained. "He's very annoying, but useful." He bent down and picked up his staff. "Walk with me." Xander exchanged a look with his friends, and they all followed the wizard.

The sky cleared as they walked away from the fighting. Trees and mountains came into view, and Xander noticed more Criatias moving in their direction. He had never seen so many walking plants. The taller ones in front appeared angry.

Jaden pointed and shouted, "Look! Cranny!"

Cranny rushed forward, though the elder near him tried to pull him back. He wiggled out, saying they were friends, and hurried toward them as fast as his roots could swerve.

"How've you all been?" he asked gleefully. He hugged each of them, careful not to poke them with his needles.

"Fine," Xander replied for all. "Hey, what's happening?"

"The Arimaspians have harvested about ten of our garden members who were out looking for me. They put them to work in the mines and denied them water and food. They threw them out when they withered and almost died. We're on the warpath. We've joined the fight. Some of the one-eyed monsters have come to our garden to harvest us, too. We don't normally leave. But we have to. We want peace, too. We don't want to be a part of this at all."

"I see." Xander sighed.

"Don't worry. We'll get this solved before anyone else gets hurt," Wizard Seabon comforted.

Cranny waved his limbs with excitement. "I'm not worried. I'm excited that my elders are venturing out, exploring this wonderful world we live in. They'll see that there's nothing to be afraid of." Cranny bounced up and down as he spoke. A tall Criata, with brown in some of his limbs, approached them.

His mouth twisted in a grimace as he came up behind the young offshoot. "Cranium! Don't talk to strangers! They have no stake in preserving our garden! The evil that has fallen on our fellow members is all your fault!"

Cranny quaked, but stood his ground. "Elder, this is the Indigo Traveler. He is the savior of Curá. He will right the wrong that has occurred. I didn't force the others to leave on my behalf."

"How dare you shirk responsibility for your part in this! You brought all this on us! And you," he snarled, turning on Xander, "Go back to your world!"

Xander sucked his lips in, unhappy about how his friend was being treated. "Sir, you want Cranny to be sorry and admit guilt for doing something dangerous, but he was safe as he traveled. He met the princess here and later us. We were protecting him." He closed his eyes, remembering Cranny's request a few weeks back to read him. He reached out, touched one of the young offshoots limbs, and asked for permission to see inside him.

Xander opened his eyes, smiling. "Cranny, you asked for what I see in you. I see you are a curious young Criata. The colors around you are pink, gold, green and brown. You have a deep connection to Curá and to those around you, and seek to bring peace to all, like an ambassador of sorts. You, Mr. Elder, you mean well for Cranny and the other young offshoots, but you need to allow them to explore. Take this as a new beginning."

The old elder's mouth flew open. He sputtered, shaking his limbs and his whole body, not knowing what to say. "Who are you to talk to me like that?"

"He's the Indigo Traveler," Seabon said calmly. "And you'd better hurry. We have to go. The warpath waits for no one." He waved his free hand in a half circle. "Come on. We need to leave."

They traveled into the mountains. The scenery changed from sparse trees to woods, with sage brush and more insects. The wind blew, too, whistling in their ears. Xander moved around to Seabon's side.

"You wanted to tell us something? I got the feeling back in the battlefield you wanted to warn us about something."

The wizard wagged his head. "Nay. I wanted to accompany you." He paused, looking the Indigo Traveler in the eyes. "Yes," he said in a lower voice. "I wanted to warn you about the battle. You aren't prepared or trained. The time is drawing close. We need to hurry."

Xander sensed there were some other issues that Seabon wasn't mentioning. He looked closer at him, remembering him from the journey back in time. Something was vastly different between this Seabon and the other one.

"Do you remember appearing with me when I went back in time to see Grandor and the ailing prince of Arimaspia?"

The wizard shrugged. "No, I don't. Though at one point I felt like part of me left. I don't know where it went. I had a vision of a beach somewhere. Crow Judge Connor came to me, bringing back the other part of me with a touch of his wing."

"But you knew who I was. We haven't met before, except in the vision."

"I've seen you in many visions and through my scrying glass. I've been expecting you since before King Titus started the wars. Nothing is as it appears to be. Consider this, my lad. You think you are unable to wield that sword. You think you will be the one harmed, because you have no training. But you know more than you think. Remember, my lad. Remember who you were long before you walked in the World Called Nampa. Remember . . ."

Xander felt giddy, as if his head was suddenly filled with fog and smoke; smoke and mirrors. He glimpsed again the young prince from Kent receiving a heart from Grandor. He looked deeply into the boy's eyes, eyes that looked much older than his nine years. Xander knew that was because he was so sick, just like the Arimaspian prince a hundred years before. They merged, becoming one, and Xander knew he had to change Titus's heart. *Peace must be kept. Keep this dragon's blood knife safe, Fallor. Keep it safe until I come again. It's mine this time. No one shall know. Be sure to put the other two blades with it. The ones my father gave me. The Alchemist will remember.* Suddenly Xander understood: The young prince's thoughts were his directions to the dragon, Fallor. The prince had expected to be reborn knowing he'd lived before.

Xander felt like he was on a roller coaster with the wind rushing against his face. He opened his eyes to find he was on Geoffrey's back. "What's happening?" he demanded. "Weren't we in the war zone, walking with Seabon?"

"Geoffrey looked at him strangely. "No, we weren't. We left Prince Tayson about two hours ago. We're almost to Gryphon Mountain where King Titus is holding off my cousins and trying to take back his son. I sense, though, that he's already taken the boy. Milo and Jaden are probably there already."

They flew on in silence. The only sounds were Geoffrey's wings and the wind rushing past them. Xander pondered his dream; *the seeing* Connor and others here in this world called it. If he was the former prince of Kent who had received the dragon's heart, then who was King Titus? Did he carry the leftover hurts of his ancestor who had received the other dragon's heart?

*Things aren't what they seem. What is that supposed to mean?*

"Glad you're awake, kiddo. You were beginning to feel like dead weight. You were muttering in your sleep about the wizard's battle and the Kent prince from days gone by. You're afraid of facing Titus, aren't you?"

Xander nodded. "He's so much bigger than us. He could step on me before I even reach him. How am I supposed to stick this blade in his heart?"

"Not his heart, Xander. Put it in his shoulder. I can get you close enough. My armor is thicker than it looks. He can't reach us if we fly close to his eye. He's very farsighted, so the closer we are to him, the blurrier we'll be."

Xander thought that made sense. He bent over the griffin's neck and looked at the battlefield below. A group of soldiers were pushing catapults. Some were dragging maces and others were riding in a wagon drawn by an animal that looked like a cross between a horse and a rhino, with a long elegant blond mane and two horns, one above its nose and the other on its forehead.

He remembered the soldiers who had pulled the wagons with the cages when they'd been captured. Xander's back hurt just considering the effort it would take to pull a wagon like that. These wagons didn't have cages, though they were covered. He wondered what was under the coverings.

"We're getting close to my cousin's village," Geoffrey observed as they saw gryphons flying towards them. One was carrying something in his talons.

"Geoffrey, long time," the gryphon greeted him. "Who is this?"

"This is Xander Veh, the Indigo Traveler."

"Yes, yes. I see the colors. They're very bright," the green-eyed gryphon observed. "I'm Marcas."

"Where are you off to?" asked Geoffrey.

"Gotta take the garbage away. King Titus got away with Kontar. Kent's wizard helped him, but he got away before we could stop him. I don't like it. Valor said the wizard is up to something. He isn't on Titus's side or on Kent's side, either."

"Is the Crow Judge there?"

"No, I heard he's with Prince Tayson at the main battle site. Grand Uncle Astral is there, too. Got to fly. See you when I get back." Marcas banked to his left away from them, heading to the Reflection Pond.

The mountain loomed ahead. Xander's heart began to speed up as he waited for the meeting. "Hey, in the dream, that cat gave me my sword. If what I experienced wasn't real, that means I don't have my sword yet."

"But you will. Feline, that's his animal type. He'll be meeting us when we land. I'm in mind speak connection with him. He's an odd lot, that one. . ."

"Yeah, he was in a fire and the alchemist blacksmith rescued him, and nursed him back to health with herbs and healing magic."

"How did you know?" asked Geoffrey, peering over his shoulder.

"I saw and heard in the dream."

Geoffrey set his wings back. "Brace yourself, we're going down." He pointed his head and front legs forward and his back ones out like an arrow. Xander wished he had goggles to keep the wind from drying out his eyes. He closed them, imagining the sound of fighter airplanes soaring down. Geoffrey extended his back legs and lowered them as he prepared to land.

The whole gryphon clan gathered around to greet them, both excited to see them and anxious to catch up on the news. Xander felt suffocated by all the gryphons that looked so different than Geoff and his clan. He ducked out of the way, looking for a quiet place to relax.

The day orb's light reflected off of a silver metal object, or so he thought. He squinted his eyes to look closer, and realized that the cat, Lynx, was sitting in the shade of tree. He walked over.

Lynx lazily flipped the tip of his tail, smiling in that strange way that made Xander's skin crawl. The nearer the teen came, the straighter Lynx sat up. When he got closer, Lynx pulled out an elaborate, jeweled scabbard.

"I saw that in a dream while Geoff and I were flying here!" Xander exclaimed.

"No dream, Master Traveler. It was a seeing. Tarrier and I assisted you in seeing it so you would know what to be watching for. We are for the side the Creator has shown us to support. Peace will reign again here. Be wary of Wizard Walfred of Kent. He no longer serves his king, offering his services to others. Mostly, he serves himself. He wants to see both sides fall."

"What about Wizard Seabon?"

Lynx smoothed his whiskers with one paw before he answered. "Seabon made a promise to the Crow Judge. He is of pure heart and intention. He will be here presently to assist in any way he can."

They heard a motor and looked up to see Milo, Jaden walking on one side and Donnair on the other.

"It is about time you showed up!" Donnair greeted him. "Where's your partner?"

"He's over with his cousins." Xander motioned behind him. Donnair and Jaden followed the arm wave.

"In that seeing, I saw the Criatias moving toward the main battlefield," Xander told Lynx. "Is that real? Cranny was among them.

Lynx nodded, "Yep, they're coming. They're angry about their members being captured. Connor is moving some over here. Cranny, the young one, will be among those."

"Don't look for Titus here. He took off toward Arimaspia with his son. We have to meet him halfway. Some of Kent's men are heading that way." Lynx stood and shook himself. "You'll make it first, though. Don't worry about the training. It will all come back to you when you touch the sword hilt." He stood on his hind legs. "I need to be off." He brought his paws together. "This will be easier once Tarrier gives us werecats opposable thumbs. Lucky humans!" He clapped his paws and was gone.

The threesome wondered what do. Xander took the sword out of the scabbard. The minute he saw the long blade, striped with the dragon's blood, and the other blades positioned on either side of it, curved inward, he felt a charge of electricity run up his arm and explode inside his forehead. He saw a vision of a young prince wearing the Kent colors of blue and gold training with a master swordsman. Xander moved with each movement of the prince, unaware that he was doing it. He could sense the power and the precision in each step, knowing it was the correct way.

Geoffrey peeled himself away from the clan when he noticed Xander was in what looked like a trance. He hurried towards them. "What's going on? Who's he fighting?"

Jaden smiled, clapping her hands. Her second eye opened, twinkling, "He's being trained by a memory. Isn't it wonderful?"

"No. I worry he's under a spell. What did that alchemist blacksmith do that sword?"

"No worries," Connor soothed. "Your charge is fine. He's preparing. This won't take long. He has it down. When he comes out of this, we have to go. King Titus has his son and that wizard Walfred is nowhere to be found. The Criatias have divided up. We need to leave. Milo, can you navigate without knowing exactly where you're being directed to?"

"I think so. Mostly, I'm making it where they say to be. What's the destination?"

*** 

*Xander wasn't himself. He felt like he had leapt into the body of a prince named Micah. His swordmaster was a cruel man who had no patience with failure.*

*"Pick up those feet! Mind the placement of your thrusts! Now turn! Your opponent is behind you!"*

*Young Micah turned, holding the sword with two hands, imagining the opponent behind him. It was difficult without seeing the battlefield for real. He saw something glittering like a star off to his right and looked away. A sharp slap on his back sent him sprawling to the ground face first with his arms and legs out spread eagle. His trainer laughed cruelly. Micah felt angry, hurt and humiliated.*

*"Never let a pretty shimmer draw your attention away from your task!"*

*"When will I get to practice with a real opponent?" Prince Micah complained, pulling himself up.*

*"When I see you are ready. Which is soon. As soon as . . ."*

"Xander, Xander, Connor says tomorrow or sooner. We need to go. My grandsire is waiting for us," Geoffrey barked. Xander stuck the sword in the ground and shook his head to clear it.

"Are you ready?" Jaden asked hopefully.

"Ah, I think so." He rubbed his eyes. "That hilt has been in someone else's hand. Prince Micah."

Everyone gasped. The trees even stilled their quivering limbs. "What's wrong?"

"Prince Micah was the second prince to receive a heart," Donnair explained. "The dragon, Fallor, gave Micah his second heart when the boy was ten years old."

# Chapter 27

Xander and his friends woke up early. Over breakfast, Connor filled them in on all that had happened, up to the point that Titus got his son back. The day was still early; the day orb was barely rising in the east. They wondered what would be in store for each of them.

"Do you know where we're going, Milo?" Xander asked as he went to the nearby creek to wash his hands and face, the digging machine rolling beside him.

"No, not really. The Crow Judge said to have you or someone else wish to be where the Arimaspian king and his son are. He felt the wizard would be near. But we have to steer away from the mines."

"That won't be a problem." Xander stood and adjusted the scabbard around his shoulders onto his back. The belt attached to it was a bit too big for him. "We need to get the others and go before it gets too late."

"It's not that late, Xander. The day orb isn't even the sixth hour of light." Geoffrey glanced around, frowning. He looked back at Xander. "Did you see those wagons the Arimaspian soldiers were leading?"

"Yeah. What kind of animal was that pulling them?"

"They're called arhinorse, but that's not important. What do you think's under those tarps?"

Xander shrugged. "It could be weapons. We've heard there's a blacksmith in Kent working with the enemy king to make illegal weapons. He says he's just working for anyone who wants them."

Across the camp, Valor and his mate were calling others to come gather around. "C'mon," Geoffrey said. "My uncle is gathering us in."

As they walked to the center of the gathering, Milo, Jaden and Donnair joined them. "Aren't we supposed to leave soon?" Donnair asked. "I have a bad feeling about this delay."

"We'll leave soon enough," Xander assured him.

Valor looked at them and the others gathered round. Connor appeared, nodded, and whispered something in the old gryphon's ear. Valor looked at him, nodding too, and whispered back.

Valor gave the crowd the last known location of the renegade king, his son and the wizard, based on reports from the guards that were following them. He added that wagons carrying unknown cargo were spotted going many different directions to fool anyone who might be looking for them.

"One says the wagons contain weapons. Another says they contain the gold, silver and jewels. I have a hunch King Titus may have hidden his son in one of those wagons," Connor advised. "The Crow Court will be gathering as soon as the battle is near over. Until I'm called, I will oversee the metal machine, Indigo Traveler, Princess Jaden and Donnair, getting them safely to where Titus is."

"What changed? Weren't we supposed to go alone?" Xander called out.

"I won't be seen, Indigo One. I will journey unseen to anyone but those, like Jaden, who have a natural instinct to see me."

Jaden cheered and clapped her hands, expecting others to join her. As she looked around, she slowly stopped and tried to hide from them.

"It's okay, Jaden, I wanted to cheer, too," Xander whispered, giving her a smile.

The meeting was over in fifteen minutes. Connor gave them last minute directions. "Don't be concerned. I've directed Tayson to be there, too, so he can assist you with the confrontation. He's flying over with one of the larger gryphons. Milo, you know what to say, right?"

"We wish to go where King Titus is," Milo's engine gurgled.

Connor nodded. "Get in, all who can," Connor directed, one wing motioning for them to go.

"I can't fit in there," Geoffrey complained, rising on his back legs.

"Maybe I can get on Geoff's back, and he can perch on top of Milo," suggested Xander.

Jaden and Donnair hopped into the Milo's cab. With Xander on his back, Geoffrey flew to the top, changed his front paws to talons, and held on. They counted down from 10, all mentally holding the thought of going to where Titus was.

*** 

Prince Tayson flew on the back of the gryphon Marcas, wondering why the change of plans. One moment he had been with his men and the Criatias, fighting off the invaders from Arimaspia; the next minute the Crow Judge said he needed to be somewhere else to back up that darned Indigo Traveler. Connor had brought the prince extra shields and swords, but he was still unhappy. He never liked change. Yet his father had told him that the Crow Judge was the head of the judiciary for all Curá.

He was glad they had been able to beat back most of the enemy that had attacked their gates, and that they'd arrested the blacksmith who was aiding the enemy. Tayson had wanted to talk to his wizard about the needs of the wounded, and had looked high and low for him, but no one had seen him. He was glad a healer from the minotaur and griffin village would be coming to help.

"Relax, Your Highness," Marcas called back. "I can tell you're nervous by the way you're sitting on my back. There's nothing to worry about."

"How can I relax when the wind is in my eyes and I don't know where we're going or why? I don't like being jerked around like this."

"Sorry, Sire. I can't do anything about the turbulence, but we're nearing the landmarks. Connor told me to watch for that metal monster and the traveler from another world. Close your eyes imagine you're on a flying horse."

"A flying gryphon is bad enough, thank you," Prince Tayson grumbled. Maybe the gryphon was right, he thought. He tried closing his eyes and leaning forward, like he would with his horse. He exhaled, relaxed and let himself enjoy the ride.

"They've cornered King Titus and the Wizard Walfred," Marcas called over his shoulder. "Brace yourself, Sire, we're coming in for a landing. Wizard Seabon is there, too. He must have flown in with Healer Astral."

"I can't see that clearly from this height," Tayson told him. "Your eagle eyes give you sharper vision. If that truly is my wayward wizard, he'll be dismissed from the court as soon as we land."

"Sire, if I may speak freely, I doubt he will much care."

They landed and joined the others in the shade of a tall shrub. The shrub, with long limbs and a thick body, opened its eyes and bowed. "It's an honor to have you under my shade, Prince Tayson."

Tayson gulped, "Um, yeah, um, it's an honor to be under your shade. Do you have a name?"

"I'm called Gaylord. I'm the oldest Criatia still be able to walk, though my roots are old. I'm here to guide and protect our young offshoot, Cranny. He's the one who urged us to follow the Kingdom of Kent into this war. We protest the Arimaspian king since he has left many of our members either with root rot or dying of thirst. His men even squashed the insects they tried to eat."

Cranny, Jaden, Xander, and Geoffrey were standing off to the side chatting when Cranny heard his name. He pulled up his long, thin roots and made his way over. The others followed.

"I heard my name, Elder Gaylord. Have I done something wrong?"

"No, no, my lad. You've done something right, for once. We fight for peace, like you and your friends want. Meanwhile, I beg you, Prince Tayson, to take notice of where the erring king is. What make you of it?"

Tayson's mind wasn't on what the elder Criatia had to say. He was seething about having to help Xander. He knew he should let it go, seeing as how the traveler was here to help, but wasn't facing the king his own job? Why should he let someone else do it? Tayson crossed his arms, his face crumpled up, eyes near slits as he fumed.

A small needle poke brought him out of his musing, "Um, what?"

"I was asking what you make of the erring king? What're your plans, Sire?"

"Why don't you ask *him*? The precious Indigo Traveler? Isn't he the one in charge?" Tayson retorted, turning his back on everyone.

Xander moved to stand beside the prince. "Sire, I want to work *with* you. You understand battle tactics better than I do. In my world, teens our age don't go to battle. We don't learn how to fight unless we join the military after high school. What I know of battle is only what I learned when I first put my hands on this sword." Xander pulled the sword out of the jeweled scabbard.

Tayson turned to look. The sparkling jewels and glittering steel brought the prince out of his anger. "Isn't that the legendary dragon's blood blade? My ancestor, Prince Micah, received one of the dragon's hearts. May I hold it?"

Xander held out the sword and Tayson took it with an expression of awe. "It was said that the spirit of Prince Micah would return if anyone ever violated the dragons' agreement with the Arimaspian and Kent kingdoms. And when he did return, the dragon's blade would be given to that person to bring the erring ruler back to the correct path."

Xander quieted his mind, centered himself and focused on reading the prince. He saw yellow and gold around him. Anger, a reddish color mixed with black and sick green, faded as a blue came in to replace it. He smiled. "Prince, what do you feel?"

"I feel the power of my ancestor. I sense I have wronged you. I need to welcome you as my ancestor returned to help steer us back to the correct path." Prince Tayson handed the sword back, his head bowed. He dropped to one knee, "It is a pleasure to serve you, Indigo Traveler. What do you want me to do?"

Xander smiled, yet he felt strange with the prince bowing to him. He knelt down and extended his hands. "You are the prince; you bow to no one. Not to me. I'm just a human who really doesn't know what I'm doing. As I said, I don't know battle strategy. We can put our heads together and think of something."

Prince Tayson took the traveler's extended hands and stood. He tried to smile, but felt ashamed.

\*\*\*

Connor, observing from the sky, saw King Titus and the wizard confer. Each wondered what the others who opposed them would do. Titus knew Kontar was safe, traveling back to the kingdom of his birth.

"What are they plotting, Sire?" Wizard Walfred asked.

Titus crossed his bulky arms and glared at the annoying wizard. "How should I know? I haven't a trace of magic within me. Can't you turn yourself into an insect and go spy on them?"

Wizard Walfred's shoulders slumped. "Yes, Sire. I suppose I could. But that Crow Judge could be lurking somewhere near, eavesdropping on us. I don't think it would be safe to be an insect around him."

Walfred's mind spun on many tracks. He wanted to turn and run to somehow get out of this battle. The other wizard might show up with the legendary sword that would negate conflict of any kind, but how would a sword do that? No matter what happened, Walfred might lose everything he had schemed for. The second track was to get the Arimaspian soldiers to hand the riches and jewels over to him so he could flee to another world with them and start a new life. The third track was to convince the Crow Judge he was actually spying on Titus until the king could be brought to justice. He winced at his own stupidity, knowing that Crow Judge would see through his façade and punish him.

"Well, what're they going to do, just stand there and stare at us?" Titus grumbled angrily.

"Sire, if I may say so, we're the ones standing here staring at them." Walfred chewed on his lips, wondering what do. His mind was still spinning, plotting how he could get away from Titus. He hadn't expected the king to accept him so readily. Now he didn't know how to get out of this.

"Sire," he pointed out, "Prince Tayson is bowing to the stranger. That's a sign of weakness. Something is amiss."

"Yes, something *is* amiss, Walfred, and it isn't them!"

Titus turned to the frightened wizard, bringing down his arms, his green eye so filled with anger the wizard felt it was shooting lightning at him. "You were so sure of yourself when you talked me into this. Now we're facing down Prince Tayson himself. You got me trapped. What's our next move? I'm not a trained warrior, Walfred! I rely on the captains of my guard to plan the strategy. My captains and my wizard. Seabon wouldn't be quivering in fear! If I didn't know better, I'd say you're trying to finagle your way out of this fight! You promised me I wouldn't be facing down the traveler and the prince! Now what are you going to do?"

Walfred shrugged, looking away. He slumped down even lower, trying to think what his father would have done.

"I could squash you, Wizard Walfred!" Titus yelled. "I am a giant compared to you, with your puny human body! Magic or not, I can and will squash you if you don't get me out of this!" The king untied his whip from his waist.

"Look, Sire! Isn't that a little Arimaspian girl from your village? They've kidnapped her!" Walfred exclaimed, hoping to distract the king. He began to sneak away, walking on his tiptoes.

King Titus looked closer. He saw the little girl, but couldn't see that well. Suddenly the girl turned and looked right at him. Titus gasped. "You fool! That's no village girl! That's my daughter! I threw her out of the castle and disowned her. What's she doing over there with them?" He remembered Wizard Seabon's words when she was born: *She will be your downfall.* He shivered with fear.

"Sire, don't worry," Walfred soothed from a safe distance, wishing he had his spell for traveling back to the mines memorized. "I'm sure she won't hurt you. She's just a little giantess." Titus didn't hear him. He was already marching toward the enemy.

Walfred quickly ran off to the sidelines, only to be cornered by Seabon. Both wizards raised their staffs, and lightning flashes erupted from both the tips. Seabon forced Walfred back, marching him toward Healer Astral and Connor.

"I didn't mean to take your place beside your king," Waldred said, trying to sound like it had been an innocent mistake. "If you're angry because he preferred me to you, I will go back to my own kingdom."

"I think not, Walfred. You're dismissed from our service." Prince Tayson approached, landing Marcas next to them. "We know you helped the new blacksmith make weapons for the Arimaspians and smuggle them out of our kingdom. We honor loyalty. We don't employ traitors like you."

Walfred hung his head. "Honestly, I didn't mean to hurt anyone."

"No," said Seabon. "You were just out for yourself." He prodded the other wizard with his staff.

"I'd rather serve the crow court," Seabon announced. "Come, Walfred. Let's talk to Judge Connor to see what he has to say about you."

xxxxx

Xander and Prince Tayson both turned to see King Titus coming toward them across the field. His long legs ate the distance quickly.

"My father sees me and is angry," Jaden said, her second eye wide open. "He's worried that I'll hurt him. You have to do something. You know what to do."

"Thanks for the confidence," Xander said, hoping it didn't sound sarcastic. He looked at Tayson. "Okay, so are we ready?" He looked around for Connor. "Where's the Crow Judge? Maybe he can direct us."

"He's up there." Jaden pointed at the Criatia elder's upper branches. Connor flew down, revealing himself. "You don't need direction, Indigo Traveler. Look at the wizard, he's leaving. King Titus is coming this way. What's missing?"

They all looked at the scene, thinking. Jaden's second eye opened, appearing almost normal.

"My brother! He doesn't have my brother! Where is he?" she yelled. She turned and ran toward her father.

"No, Jaden!" "Come back!" "He doesn't want you!" Xander, Geoffrey and Cranny yelled at the same time. Xander wasted no time. He jumped on Geoffrey and urged him to fly after her.

King Titus shivered with fear and dread, but he was determined to keep Jaden away from his enemies. He grabbed her by the hair. "Who let you out of that dungeon? I warned you to never come near me again! And what are you doing with that scum over there?"

"They aren't scum, Father. Where's Kontar? He was taken from the gryphons and you're supposed to have him. Where is he? Is he safe?"

"That's for me to know and you to never find out!"

"King Titus, I call you out! Leave the princess alone! It's me you want! Just hand her over to me."

"Never! I don't know who you think you are, but you have no business here telling us what to do!"

"I'm the Indigo Traveler, Sire," Xander announced, pulling out his sword. "I wield the dragon's blood blade. You have two choices. One is to release your daughter so no harm is done to her. Two, stop mining Curá for gold, silver and jewels. Stop demanding more taxes than your people can afford, and stop demanding Kent turn over land that was freely given to them years ago. I beg you to remember the Dragon's scroll agreement your kingdom and Kent exchanged for the heart that kept your ancestor alive."

"Those are more than two choices, Traveler. Actually, they sound more like demands. What will you do if I don't obey you? Who will back you up?" Titus released Jaden's hair. "I will let my daughter go, but I will not go easy on you and that white beast you ride!" He took out his whip and started snapping it at them.

"Geoff, grab the whip when you can!" shouted Xander.

Geoffrey turned his claws into talons and caught the tip of the whip. As he flew higher, he lost his grip and the whip fell back to the ground. Titus pulled it up, winding it into a large loop as he watched the creature he despised as much as the Crow Judge.

"I'll get you, evil griffin!"

Tayson, watching the action, felt his heart speed up. He remembered that he hadn't given Xander a shield. He rushed to the sack of weapons and shields, took one out and yelled, "Xander! Geoffrey, come back for this shield! It will help fend off the whip!"

Geoffrey turned to look at his rider. "Well?" Xander nodded and the griffin turned back.

"You always were a yellow livered coward!" screamed Titus. "You're the one who ran two years ago, aren't you, griffin? You haven't changed at all. I'll squash you! Just wait!"

"Father, don't hurt Geoffrey," Jaden pleaded. "He's special! He'll bring peace to the land. You've got to listen, Father. You've got to stop this war. If not, your heart will fail."

"My heart is strong, you imbecile," Titus snarled. "You don't know anything! Your stupid deformity hasn't made you a speaker of wisdom but a speaker of misguided myths! That's just a griffin who lacks normal coloring. Now shut your trap, or I'll shut it for you!"

"Father, you're the misguided one. You need a new heart. The one you have is so cold it must have frozen in the ice last winter and never thawed out."

Titus gave a grim smile. "I've always had a frozen heart. I like it that way."

Xander and Geoffrey got the shield and hurried back to King Titus, worried that he would hurt Jaden. "We're back, King Titus. Leave your daughter alone! She's done nothing to harm you. This matter is between you and me. You need to tell your men to stop raiding Kent villagers and demanding their lands!"

"Those lands were given to Kent under false pretenses! My ancestors gave them the lands because the dragons lied to them! They said we made war and stole those lands. No! They were always ours! Myths are nothing but lies. Dragons only have one heart and they would never share with us one-eyed beings anyway, because they hate us."

"Is that right?" Xander called back. "And I suppose you love your own people? I've seen your mines, King Titus. I've seen your villages. You enslave your people and still you overcharge them taxes. You must hate your own people."

"What if I do? They're miserable scum! They work hard so they can give me what I deserve. They hated me long before I hated them. When I was a child, my mother took me to visit their village. They made fun of me because I was dressed like a prince instead of in the miserable rags they wore. They wouldn't even acknowledge me. Me! Their prince! I can never forgive them for that.

Xander's own heart felt heavy as he realized how easily he could feel that way. Though it was reversed at his school. They all dressed in the expensive styles that society encouraged them to wear in order to be hip, but his folks preferred to shop at the less expensive stores and thrift stores since they didn't have the money that the other families had.

The Indigo Warrior considered what to say. He stilled his thoughts, asking to be allowed to see what Titus needed most to hear. He was shown the heart beating deep inside the king. It was huge compared to a human one, yet it was not beating normally. He wasn't a doctor and thought maybe Arimaspian hearts beat differently than human ones, but his seeing also showed him that something was definitely off.

"Your heart hurts you, Titus. You're about to feel the pain your ancestor felt back when Grandor was asked to share his second heart with him. Did you know you look like your ancestor?"

"I've seen portraits of him. But I have no similarities to him at all. My heart is just fine, thank you for asking. But yours won't be well for long." Titus took aim with his whip and slashed it at them. Xander moved the shield in front of him. The whip struck it with a ringing sound, and the force almost knocked the shield out of his hand.

"Go in more, Geoff," Xander urged, "I've got to get close enough to strike him."

Titus sneered at them. "I don't have a sword! How do you expect me to fight fairly when only you have a sword?"

Prince Tayson, riding on Marcas, came near with an extra sword. "Here, Sire! A sword from Kent. Now you can't say we fight unfairly." He tossed the sword to the king.

King Titus caught it and laughed. "How do expect me to fight with this? It's just a toy for someone my size. Wizard!" he roared, "Make this toy into an honorable weapon for me."

The two wizards stood beside Connor on the sidelines. Connor looked at Seabon. The wizard nodded and lowered his staff. "You chose to be his wizard, Walfred. Give the king what he wants." Walfred waved his staff at the sword, which grew in Titus's hand.

"Much better!" Titus took a giant step toward Geoffrey and Xander. The griffin backed away. Their swords met in with a loud clashing of metal. Xander pushed hard enough to make Titus back up and almost stumble over his own feet. He managed to catch himself.

The king stood up, his large blue eye hard with anger, his mind set on bringing this warrior down. "How did you learn to fight? I heard you don't fight this way on your world."

"It came to me naturally as soon as I held this sword, Titus. One strike with this blade and you will remember, too, what is right and what is wrong!"

Geoffrey flew as fast as he could toward the king, Xander was set on hitting the sabre just right to knock it out of the king's hands, and he succeeded. Titus lost it, and fumed as he stood there, hands helplessly hanging by his side, staring at the sabre. Xander saw his chance and thrust the dragon's blood blade into the king's heart.

"Don't touch the other blades, Father, they're poisoned!" Jaden gasped as she watched her father stumble, his hands on the sword.

"And the main blade isn't?" Titus choked. "My heart! My heart aches! It isn't blood or the piercing. I can't function." He fell to his knees, clutching his heart and rubbing his left arm. He collapsed, barely keeping his eye open, though he watched Xander and Geoffrey as long as he could focus. As soon as the teen turned away, Titus pulled the dragon's sword out of his chest. With is dying breath he flung it at Xander, stabbing him in the left shoulder. Xander went down quickly.

# Chapter 28

Xander looked around. The buildings were familiar but very different. He walked with uncertain steps, considering why he felt so light. He looked down and noticed his feet were not touching the ground. He heard a voice asking where he wanted to be. *I want to be with Albagoth,* he responded without thinking. *Swoosh* he found himself in a totally black place as if he was standing at the edge of the universe, looking out at all the stars and galaxies that spread for miles at end.

"Where am I?" he called, not knowing if anyone was near to hear. The stars moved around, blinking on and off as if they were taking turns winking at him. Some changed colors each time they blinked. Gradually the stars begin to move around, forming patterns or pictures. He felt they were putting on a show just for him.

"Enjoying this?"

"Yeah," Xander answered, looking around to see who was talking to him, but he was alone.

"Pay attention to the shapes they form. Are you understanding the connection in all those images, Shawndre?"

Xander watched with awe and curiosity. The first shape was his cat, Clarence. The next two were his parents. "Love and compassion," he said, suddenly understanding the connections. Then he saw Digger and Geoffrey. Finally, there was Butch. "Butch? Why am I seeing him?"

"You need to understand where Butch is at and see how he is helping you to be stronger."

"I'm not stronger, though. I'm putting up with his abuse and his demands for me to turn over whatever I have that he wants. How is that helping me?"

"What have you learned while in Curá?"

"I...." He considered his words carefully, reviewing every detail. He was awed by what he felt. "I learned that I had another life before this one. I learned that bullies are here to teach me something... Something about love, maybe?"

Perhaps he was supposed to stand up for himself. Perhaps he had to put himself in the place of Butch to understand him better. *I wonder if someone was mean to Butch when he was younger because of his clothes?* Butch's parents were totally rich and he got everything he ever asked for. *Why are clothes so important, anyway? Shouldn't we be looking inside a person more than the way he's dressed?*

Xander realized that he might have one thing that Butch never had: the chance to face his fears and doubts and learn who he really was, deep in his soul. *I got what I was searching for. What is Butch looking for?*

The voice seemed to read his mind. "Maybe you're onto something, Shawndre. You need to go home to find out."

Suddenly, he felt a surge of love and confidence. Beside him, an image gradually revealed itself. It had the appearance of both male and female depending on how he looked at it.

"You're Albagoth!" Xander's heart sped up, as if he was meeting his favorite singer.

"Indeed, I am." the Creator smiled. "Now, tell me how the other images are related."

"My family and cat love me. My griffin is my friend and protector. I miss my parents and my cat. Geoffrey is my family, too. May I take him home?"

"Yes, if it is okay with the Crow Court."

Xander felt a sudden sadness. "I killed King Titus. I thought I was supposed to heal his heart, not kill him. How can I live with that?"

Albagoth smiled. "Titus is having his own audience with me in another room."

"How can that be? I saw him die."

"Titus had to die in order to really look at his life. I'm bringing him back so that he can make the changes he knows he needs."

"What about Jaden? What will happen to her and Kontar and Prince Tayson?"

"Peace will come back to the world of Curá as planned. The white griffin has done his job in bringing peace, and so have you."

"How can you be with Titus and me at the same time?"

"I am a big Creator, Shawndre. Part of me is here with you; part of me is with Titus. Another part of me is tending to the needs of other Indigo Children across your world who are lost, confused and afraid to step forward to rebel against the way things are. Rebellion can be done in peaceful forms, my child, so offer love to those who abuse their power. Speak in love, forgive and be grateful, even when bad things happen. See the lessons and move on."

*Forgive what?* Xander thought. *Forgive Butch for his evilness? The way he hurt me? The way he threatens to take things away from me that were never his to begin with?*

"Alexander, you know you are an Indigo Child. You go back with full memory of the events here on Curá and of your past lives, both here and in other lands. Use all to be a better you back in your own world."

"Um, I guess so." He didn't really hear what the Creator said, but turned. "How do I get back? I forgot my body again, I think."

The Creator took a deep breath and exhaled it, pushing the Traveler out of the void. Xander landed on the golden path in the Crow Court village. He gathered himself up and looked around. A young Crow Judge came up to him and extended its wing.

"Hi, I'm Tanner. I understand you're from the World called Nampa? Sebastian and I have just been assigned to go there. Do you need help?"

"No, I don't think so." Xander looked around, feeling confused. His head was buzzing. "Where am I supposed to go?"

"You need to go this way, Shawndre. Judge Connor will be with you shortly to take you back to Curá and then back to your world." He paused, and said gently, "Only one Indigo Child can keep a griffin, Shawndre. It may not be you."

The buzzing was louder, making it hard to think. Xander wondered how the crow knew he wanted to take Geoffrey home with him. Other crows gathered around. "Follow the golden path, Shawndre. Follow it."

Xander looked down, feeling like he had just dropped into a scene from The Wizard of Oz. The smell of the ocean filled his lungs and he saw a lake that looked the Reflection Pond. A boy about six was sitting there dangling his feet in the cool water, humming a tune. Xander recognized the boy as Milo the way he had looked before the unfortunate wish. He glanced at the other side of the pond and saw a taller man with one eye, and he knew that was Titus.

"Hi, Milo. How'd you get here?"

"Connor brought me here to wait for you. We'll go soon. Sit down and put your feet in the water. You need to clear your head. The buzzing you hear is information overload."

Xander sat down beside Milo. The water felt cool on his feet, and the warmth of the day orb relaxed him.

"Now what?" he asked, exhaling. He stared at the pond. He saw his older self-come up out of the moving stream.

"Give yourself a pat on the back, Shawndre. You've done well. Go home, give your cat a good rub down, hug your Mom and Dad. Listen to your inner knowing and turn Butch into a non-enemy," said the older self.

"I was expecting wiser words from you," Xander chided.

"No wiser words than that," Milo told him.

Xander turned to his friend. "What about you? Where have you been? After you were turned into a backhoe, where did you go?"

"I'm not sure. Some little people that called themselves Tarradonnas came to get me and took me to another land. I saw lots of wild things, but I missed my parents. Connor says when we get back to Curá Wizard Seabon will change me back to my human form. Only I've missed most of my childhood. I'll be jumped into my teen years with no preparation for it. What's it like?"

Xander laughed, "Murder! One minute you hate girls and the next you don't know how to live without that one special girl that refuses to look at you. And then these little growths erupt all over your body and face. No matter how much I wash my face they still come!"

"Whiskers?"

"No, pimples; I'm not shaving yet. Though it would be interesting." His words trailed off. The boys laughed.

"Isn't that King Titus over there?" Xander asked. "What's going on?"

"He's talking with his older self. He's been there for a while now."

A black blur flew to a landing beside them and folded its wings. "Ready boys?" Connor asked. "We're back to Curá. This world has a lot of changes in store."

"Who will take Titus back?" Xander asked.

"I will come back for him in time."

*\*\*\**

Xander woke up under a tree, with a minotaur nurse wringing a wet, cool sponge out over his head.

"Astral stitched your wound," she said. "You weren't hurt too bad. The blade wasn't meant to harm you, only to allow you to finish your journey." She helped him sit up and gave him a cup of water and flat bread.

The day orb was down at the sixth hour position. A light breeze blew through the window. Geoffrey, Cranny and Jaden came in. Behind them were Seabon and a teen-age boy who looked familiar.

"Milo?" Xander asked.

The boy nodded.

"You're going home?"

"Yes, I'm going home with you. I can't wait to see my parents!"

Xander's smile fell. "I think they moved away from Nampa. But we can find them." He looked at Connor. "How do we get home?"

"I can take you."

"I can't take Geoffrey with me, can I?"

"No, he belongs here."

"What will happen to King Titus?" Xander asked.

"His heart will be changed. He has learned to forgive and move on. Curá will have peace for now."

*\*\*\**

Two weeks after getting back home, Xander and Milo went to school together. They sat at a table in the library, Xander and Sarah on one side, Milo and Kimber across from them. Butch came up to them, looking angry. Xander wondered whether anything had changed while he was gone.

Butch shook a fist in his face. "I'm glad you're back, freak. You and I have a score to settle. You and that stupid statue. Nobody believes what I saw, but you and I know it really happened. Don't try to say it didn't."

"It really happened," Xander agreed, remembering what Albagoth had told him. "You're not crazy."

Butch took a step backward. "You think you can just agree with me and I'll go away? Do you have any idea how much trouble you got me in with that stupid griffin trick?"

*I didn't get you in trouble,* Xander thought. *You did that yourself.* Instead he said, "You're right. I'm sorry about what happened."

Butch glared at him. "You're *sorry?*"

"Yeah," Xander said, meeting his eyes. "Sometimes we make bad choices and other people get hurt. I'm sorry."

He put his hand on Butch's arm. Instantly, he had an intense vision of Butch's father coming unglued on him for the smoke bombs and bullying. Even worse, he saw Butch's friends laughing at him when he tried to tell them about a statue turning into a griffin. Everyone thought he was crazy. He nearly got kicked off the football team, and lost his position as team captain.

The bell rang, and everyone gathered up their books. "Gotta go." They rushed off to class, leaving Butch staring after them.

As they hurried down the hall, Milo looked at Xander. "You're *sorry?* What was that about?"

"I'm not sorry for what I did. And I don't pity Butch. But I felt what he's feeling inside when I touched his. We can't solve his issues for him, and he can't solve them until he's ready to face them."

After class, they saw Butch leaning against a locker, staring at them.

Xander called out to him, "This is Milo, Butch. Do you remember him from preschool? It turns out a big backhoe kidnapped him and I tracked it down to get him back. He's staying me with until we can find his parents."

For a minute, Butch stood there with his mouth hanging open. Then he snapped it shut. "Big backhoe? No way could that happen, dude. You just want me to repeat that so everyone will be *sure* I'm crazy." He shook his head and walked away.

Sarah and Kimber met them. "A big backhoe? Butch is right. That could never happen."

Xander laughed again. "Truth is sometimes stranger than fiction."

# List of Characters

**Albagoth** (**Al**-buh-goth): The Creator of All Worlds and the one who created the Crow Court.

**Alexander Veh** (Al-ex-**an**-der **Vay**): The Indigo Traveler who is central to the story and is dissatisfied with his life. He seeks to understand why being an Indigo Child is so important. He is usually called Xander.

**Arhinorse** (Are-**ayn**-horse): Part horse and part rhino. They are large beasts that the Arimaspian soldiers use to pull their wagons.

**Arimaspian** (Ar-uh-**mass**-pea-un): Tall, one-eyed giants who live in the country of Arimaspia.

**Astral** (**Ass**-trul): Healer of the griffin and minotaur's village. He's Geoffrey's grandsire.

**Bonnie** (**Bah**-knee): Female minotaur nurse who tends to Xander at the griffin and minotaur village.

**Butch** (**Buch**): The captain of the football team at Xander's high school and school bully.

**Clarence: (Klair**-ense):** The Veh's family orange and white cat who is a guide to Xander.

**Connor** (**Kon**-or): Crow Judge who observes and judges Curá. He also guides and advises Xander and others.

**Criatias** (Kree-**ah**-tea-us): Cactus people that live in the desert. Their village is a called a garden. They move, think and are able to fight when they need to. The young Criatias are taught to be careful of travelers from other worlds because they might get eaten.

**Cranny** (**Kran**-knee): The young Criatia offshoot that wanders off and friends Jaden, Xander, Digger and Donnair. His name is short for Cranium.

**Curá** (Kur **ah**): The world Geoffrey and Connor originate from with the countries of Kent, Arimaspia, villages of the griffins and minotaurs, gryphons and the Criatia Gardens. The desert of Senilona is there, too.

**Curly** (**Kur**-lee): The Arimaspian soldier with a scar on his face who works with a partner to capture travelers to enslave in the mine.

**Davon** (**Day**-von): The very first Crow Judge Albagoth chose to help set up the laws for Curá.

**Donnair** (Don-**air**): Minotaur scribe to the Kingdom of Kent and good friend to Geoffrey.

**Fallor** (**Fal**-or): Dragon who gave second heart to Prince Micah two centuries before the present prince and one century after the prince of Arimaspia received a heart from Grandor.

**Gaylord** (**Gay**-lord): The eldest Criatia

**Geoffrey** (**Jef**-free): A pure white griffin whose birth was prophesied to bring peace to the land. He hates fighting and doesn't want to be a war. For peace to come, he has to assist Xander.

**Grandor** (**Gran**-door): The first dragon who shared his spare heart with the Arimaspian prince who would've died without it. He is the one who made the agreement between Arimaspia and Kent Kingdoms.

**Gretchen** (Greh-chin): Terence's spider who is just as magical as her rider.

**Griffin** (**Grif**-fin): Creatures with the head and wings of eagles but the body and feet of lions. Their front paws can be changed to talons when they need to grip an object.

**Gryphon** (Gry-**fon**): Half eagle, half lion creatures with feathery chests and eagle forelegs and talons. They foster King Titus's son and help fight for the freedom of Kingdom of Kent.

**Jaden** (**Jay**-den): Arimaspian princess who was born with two eyes. The second eye will open when she has an insight or prophecy to share.

**Jephra** (**Jep**-ruh): Male nurse and healer in training who helps care for Xander.

**Kaida** (**Kai**-duh) - Arimaspian prince who was given the first dragon heart.

**Kimber** (**Kim**-ber): A girl Xander befriends on the bus who learns to stand up for herself.

**Kontar** (**Kon**-tar): Oldest son of King Titus who was given to the gryphons to punish the king for going against the dragon's agreement.

**Lynx** (Links): The werecat that lives with Tarrier the Alchemist Blacksmith. He has a stubby tail, ear tufts and fur that makes his cheeks stick out. His paws are large, like he's wearing snow shoes. He's a magical being. What he wants most is to have opposable thumbs.

**Manitor** (**Man**-i-tore): The present dragon who guards Kingdom of Kent.

**Marcas** (**Mar**-kus): Gryphon who helps transport Prince Tayson to the meeting of King Titus and Xander.

**Maxil** (**Max**-il): leader of griffin and minotaur village and Geoffrey's sire.

**Micah** (**Mi**-kuh): Prince of Kent who received a heart from a second dragon a century after the Arimaspian prince.

**Milo** (**Mi**-low): Xander's childhood playmate who vanished. Xander finds him in Curá trapped inside a backhoe.

**Samantha** (Sah-**man**-thah): Female minotaur nurse assigned to help Xander.

**Rabbito (Rab-**it-oh**):** Leader of the Guerrilla Dust Bunny Commandos.

**Rico** (Ree-koh): A gryphon who has special magic he uses to fight King Titus in battle.

**Sarah (Sar-**uh): A goth girl that Xander has a crush on. She likes to hang out with him and stands up to the school bully.

**Seabon (See-**bon): Wizard of Arimaspia whom Connor approaches to assist him in bringing peace to the world.

**Shawndre (Shawn-dray):** Xander's secret name or soul name that his spirit self and Albagoth call him.

**Tanner (Tan-**ner): A young crow student training to be a judge. He will be the first crow paired to work with a griffin to travel to another world.

**Tarrier (Tair-**ee-er): Alchemist blacksmith in Kingdom of Kent who forges, treats and merges the three blades of the dragon's blood sword.

**Tayson (Tay-**son): Prince of Kent. He's jealous of Xander and wants to be the one to save his land and world. Yet he is fair and decides to work with him.

**Terence (Tair-**ense): A little man with a round belly. He's magical and helps Xander get into the labyrinth and break out Donnair, Digger, Geoffrey and Jaden.

**Titus (Tie-**tus): King of the Arimaspians. He feels he is entitled to be the leader of all of Curá and starts a war.

**Tonyar (Tahn-**yar): King of Kent, Prince Tayson's father.

**Valor (Val-**or): Leader of the gryphons

**Walfred (Wall-**fred): Wizard of Kent Kingdom.

**Wisewoman (Weyes-**woo-man): Female crow on Xander's world who likes Connor.

**Xander** (**Zan**-der): Alexander's nickname

## Excerpt from

# Indigo Travelers and the Keys to the Shadowlands

Titus found himself in a dark forest. The trees grew together so densely, no light could filter through the canopy. It was grey, black and off white, but had no natural light. For a few moments, Titus stood completely still, not daring to breath. Finally, he took a cautious step forward and then another. Soon, he was roaming through the dense woods. He felt lost, afraid and not sure of how he got here. Voices could be heard in the distance. Some whispered, but they were overshadowed by a few shouting voices. His heart pounded in his chest. He felt alone, yet knew something was there, watching him, waiting for him to make a move.

A creature made of sticks and stones wobbled out from amongst the trees. The creature's eyes grew wide when it saw Titus, then it cowered on the ground trying to cover his body in fear.

"Names are names. Just labels that can't hurt me. Words are empty and meaningless," it said. "I can hurt you worse."

"Your words are brave, yet you cover your body as if you fear me."

"Aye, I am afraid of giants like you. You erupt at a moment's notice–your temper–your rage. You hurt people with that whip you wear around your waist and send them to a dark place."

"Dark place? You mean a place like this?"

"No, dark places within them, belittling them, telling them they are useless, don't measure up to your expectations and are no good. From then on, all they do or see is reinforced. It is the dark place that you are experiencing now. You, you, you see, see what you have done."

Rustling steps echoed from deep within the forest in the distance, like leaves being displaced as something came through. Titus' whipped his head around, listening and trying to see what was approaching him.

"No, no, I can't bare this! Take me away!" he screamed. "I'm sorry for the pain I've caused others. I can't ever be happy again. Sticks and Stones, Sticks and Stones, they heard and break my bones. But the words are replayed over and over and over. My mother and father could never see me for what I was or wanted to be. The village kids hated me for being the prince. Take me away!"

"No, I can't take you away. But I can lead you to another place where you see more. Do you dare continue?"

"I–I–I can't."

Heavy footsteps drew near. The creature roared, jolting both the sticks and stones creature and King Titus.

"What is that?"

"It is the one that stalks the shadows. It is a dragon. He thrives on fear, sadness and tears."

Titus gulped. His heart began beating so fast, hard and loud, he was sure all in this strange land could hear it. He thought it was amplified a hundred times, and all were tuned in to him, echoing through the trees, shrubs and off the mountains. It was so loud, he thought for a moment it couldn't be his heart beat. "What's that?" he said, his voice shaky with fear.

"It's your knees," said the Creature. "Come, let's leave this place. I will show you the path you need to follow. No one can find you here. Only the promised one can enter." The stick man began walking on his trunk-like legs, the boulders wobbling as he strutted.

"I want forgiveness, but I can't forgive myself," Titus said, followed him, nervously scanning the dark forest. "What are you called?" he asked the strange stick and stone man.

"I'm called Mandy. Mandy the Pansy I was called. Names will not hurt you like sticks and stones, they say. Yet they echo deep within the crevices of the subconscious. Names, Titus. Horrible names. I am a nature goliath named Mandy. No more shall they speak."

"No more shall who speak?"

"The trees I am made from. And those who you hurt for calling you pansy, fancy pants and those who would not honor your standing as emperor and successor to your father. You showed them through brute force. Deep inside, who are you are most afraid of?"

The roar of something in the distant sent a shiver up and down Titus' body. The land shook each time it put a foot down.

# About Merri Halma

Writing is a way for Merri Halma to express herself and is an outlet for her active mind.

She lives in Idaho with her husband, son, and two feisty cats, Clarence and Demon Lynx.

# Contact Me

https://www.facebook.com/authormerrihalma/

https://www.facebook.com/DreamingLizardPress/

https://www.facebook.com/IndigoTravelerbook?fref=ts

https://www.facebook.com/Clarence-from-Indigo-Traveler-Series-926226174154752/

www.spiriualmusings.business

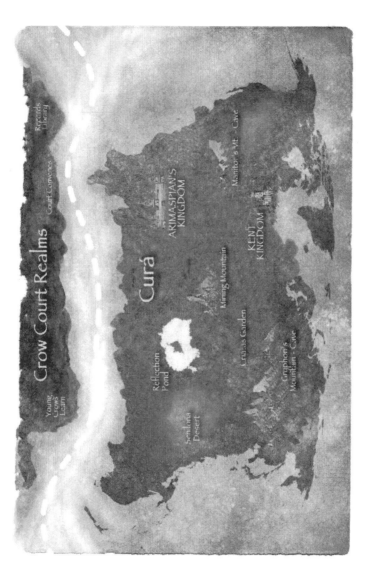

92574075R00148

Made in the USA
Columbia, SC
30 March 2018